The Knave of Hearts

The Knave of Hearts

a novel by

P. J. Hatton

The Knave of Hearts

Copyright © 2020 P. J. Hatton

All rights reserved

ISBN-13: 979-8-6666-5077-6

This novel is entirely a work of fiction. All the places, characters, situations and events, portrayed in this novel are a product of the author's imagination.

Any similarity to real persons, living, or dead, is coincidental and not intended by the author.

To my lovely wife, Daphnee, who has put up with me all these many years. She is, indeed, my very own Anabelle.

Prologue

It was an age of knights, chivalry, valour and heroism. Of courtliness, loyalty, bravery and nobility. One of handsome princes, pretty princesses and beautiful damsels in distress, in need of rescue. It was an age of courageous constabulary only wanting to uphold the law, and honourable governors thinking they were doing their very best, yet failing, miserably.

But it was also a time of tyrannical kings, lawless highwaymen, evil sheriffs, brutal war and raging pestilence and disease.

Somewhere in between all of that, was a different sort of man. A true and moral sort of man, a most appealing, very friendly person, a gallant rogue of high character and empathy. An honest champion of the common man, a protector for the poor, the oppressed and the downtrodden.

In an age of unjust laws and despotic, unfeeling lawmakers, those found breaking the rules were not necessarily always criminals. In some cases, proper justice might only be found at the hands of great hero, an advocate for the populace, who actually cared for others and what was happening in the world. A true believer, one who understood right from wrong, good from bad, light from dark. A gracious champion, one able to discern fair and just laws, from oppressive and unnecessary edicts. A man who would be there, in all ways and situations, to fight for the true rights of the people, regardless of the consequences.

In a small part of an even smaller country, contrary to the local leader's firm beliefs, this man did exist. He was decent and dependable. He was ever present and ever watching.

To the constabulary he was a criminal, to the rich a royal nuisance, but to the poor he was a godsend. Still, to select others, he was an endearing rogue. He was hated, he was despised, he was liked, and he was loved.

But one thing was certain, he was an absolute necessity in this time of turmoil and insecurity, of persecution and unrest. In this time of great need.

He was the swashbuckling Knave of Hearts, a man by the name of Sebastian Corazon.

And this is his story.

Chapter 1 - Damsel in Distress

A filtered, yellow light gleamed brightly off the golden wheat of a wide-open meadow, a vast field illuminated by the sun, revealing it from on high, out of a beautiful, clear blue sky. Although the intense radiance provided a very welcoming effect on the overall landscape, the thick woodland, surrounding the large, wide pasture's perimeter, lent a rather sinister edge to an otherwise very tranquil scene. Lofty, deep green trees with dark foreboding looks, stood tall like titanic, guardian sentinels, presenting a most menacing border to what might have first appeared as a very friendly clearing.

A small, extremely beat-up passenger carriage and two horse wound its way through this thick, buttery toned grassland, on a dry dirt track. A continuous sprinkling of fine grey dust rose from its rapidly rotating wheels, as it progressed, rather energetically, along the beaten drive.

Inside the black coach's somewhat rustic accommodations, sat a young girl, no more than two and twenty, bravely glancing through the open window, her arm resting gently on the worn, dark wood of the sill. Her head swayed gently back and forth, with the movement the carriage, as it leapt and bounded over the uneven surface of the seldom used road. The intense rays of the late afternoon sun had already heated the inside of the meager conveyance to stifling, the muggy heat warming its lone occupant to perspiring. Extracted by this extreme warmth, were a series of salty liquid rivulets, steadily erupting from her skin's pores. These flows accumulated between her slim shoulder blades, before dribbling down her back and wetting her already, dangerously tight corset.

Thankfully, as a result of the vehicle's anxious, and rather speedy, movement, a brisk wind blew through the small window. This welcome breeze tossed about her abundant and unrestrained, reddish auburn hair, providing the woman with at least some measure of relief. The timely coolness counteracting the worst of the heat. Still, the passenger squirmed awkwardly on the shabby leather bench, unsettled and uncomfortable, a growing feeling of foreboding rising in her rapidly heaving chest.

The occupant was dressed smartly but appeared in no way one of the privileged class. Her lithe body was clothed in a dress of crimson velvet, lined with ivory lace, that had clearly seen better days, the material excessively worn and threadbare. The thick material of the garment did nothing to combat the carriages continually rising temperature, in fact only helped in worsening the female passenger's plight. This prompted her to push her head that much further out of the rambling conveyance, catching whatever relief the rapidly flowing airstream could provide.

The young woman's face was thin but extremely pretty, her skin pink, but delightfully pale, with a large pouty mouth, encircled with dark, cherry red lips. She had marvelous eyes, cat's eyes, as they were a bright green, like that of a jewel toned emerald. And they were large, highlighted smartly with heavy dark liner around the edges. A fine scattering of light brown freckles graced her button nose and her aquiline chin jutted out nicely, but, as her father always said, perhaps just a tad too far.

Her body was slim, and her small breasts extended just briefly above the tight corset of her dress, revealing a thin waist above the wide flare of the gown's skirt. Her legs were unseen, but prudence would dictate they clearly reflected the same grace as her slender, almost petite form. Overall, her appearance was extremely agreeable, despite the constant perspiration running down her face from under her hairline and the large patches of dark wetness, now appearing like blood, steadily ballooning under her arms.

"Hurry up, driver!" she called, rather desperately, up to the liveried man on top of the coach. "Faster, we need to go much faster!"

"We are going as quick as we can, Marm!" the heavily sweating coachman replied, "Mark my words, we will lose the wheels, if we travel any quicker."

"Just go as fast as you can then," was her rather curt reply. "I do not like the feel of this place." saying this as she glanced forebodingly into the darkness of the approaching treeline.

"Nor do I, Marm, nor do I. They say..." but the prim and proper, uniformed man did not finish his thought. A heavily drawn arrow, suddenly penetrating his frail chest, instantly forced his uppity voice to quit. With a hoarse, guttural moan and a wash of red, splattering heavily upon the front of his sweat soaked waistcoat, he dropped his head.

The unfortunate driver's hands immediately fell limp from the reigns of the team, his body slumping even lower on the cracked leather bench. Gradually tilting sideways, until gravity took over and completely toppled him from the now runaway carriage. There was a rather gruesome thump as his dead carcass dropped under the rear wheels and the coach jumped, forcing the vehicles only other remaining passenger to bang her head on the hard roof of the coach's interior.

"Ouch!" the girl stated rather obviously, reaching up to feel the top of her head, a tiny drop of crimson coming off in her hand. Unknowingly, she casually wiped it off on her gown, the colour of the stain, melding quickly with that of the dress.

By now, without a driver to control them, the horses had slowed their pace, eventually drawing the carriage to a gradual halt, just shy of the towering dark green pines at the edge of the valley. Once more, the girl peaked out of the opening, looking cautiously around the seemingly abandoned clearing, sensing, rather than knowing, that something was up. Someone, or something nasty, with a foul purpose was out there. Her driver had just been murdered, and if she was not careful, she would be next. Or perhaps, subjected to something even worse.

Before she had even completed a full sweep of the area, a sudden noise made her start. On reflex, she rapidly pulled her face back into the cabin, out of harm's way. It was a splendid choice, as another arrow directly impacted against the vehicle's door frame, the blow splintering the wood, stinging her face and hands.

Within moments, her stationary coach was surrounded by a motley band of very sorry looking thieves, eager to retrieve their presumed reward. The rough, incredibly nasty sounding voice of the leader shattered the heated quiet of the late afternoon.

"Come on out here, missy!" he was snarling, his voice taunting, "We know yer in there, girly. It'll be better if ye come out on yer own." he stalled, looking at the ground, shifting the dry dirt with his boot, "Come on out now, befores we 'ave to come in a get ye."

The young woman was clearly frightened and temporarily sunk down on the seat, as if to hide. Obviously, she was completely on her own with nowhere else to go. Her only male companion lay dead on the trail, half a mile back in the open field and night was rapidly approaching.

With little choice, fostering her courage, she gave a startled reply, her soft voice quivering, "Okay. I heard you. I'm coming."

Rising off the seat and opening the door, the girl stepped bravely into the last of the days' dying sunlight, alighting down from the battered carriage, her head held high.

Not standing on ceremony, she was immediately grasped by two ugly men who had come up behind her. Detecting their rather foul manly odour, she struggled, but only very briefly. Because their sweaty hands were like a blacksmiths' clamps on her arms, she quickly relaxed, realizing the futility of her actions and her most awkward, inescapable predicament. Breathing through her mouth, the young woman let the thugs lead her away from the coach, toward a grizzled, rather obese man who was evidently the leader of the gang.

He was truly an ugly fellow, one you would not want to meet in any situation, let alone by yourself and unaccompanied in a field. The bandit's clothing was tattered and sweat stained and his pot belly burst from his tunic, covered only in a light sheath of white material, now beige from all the accumulated dirt. The soil on his mud-soaked boots and calves, now all dried and crusty, was cracked and crumbling, dropping off his leggings with every movement. The man had evidently been living off the land and had not cleaned himself in some time. The rank stench coming off his body was unbearable, prompting the girl to turn her face away as she approached the fiend.

"Well, well," he sneered, "aren't ye a cute little one." looking at her first, then back briefly at the coach. "Would've thought ye'd be an old damsel with lots of dough. Looks like we've lucked out 'ere boys." roughly rubbing his grubby fingers across her cheek and leaving a streak of grime, "Dis one's definitely a keeper!"

As he rotated on his stubby legs to address his gang, in pure defiance, the young woman spat in his face.

With spittle dribbling down his chin, he sharply turned back, less shocked than anything, a wicked smile braking out on his coarsely chiselled features, "My, my, aren't ye a feisty one."

Glancing greedily up and down her body, he walked around her, all the while slowly wiping the wet saliva from his face with the back of his hand. She stared back at him with boldness, wanting it all to end soon.

The goon warned the girl, "Ye'll live to regret dat one, me pet."

When she provided no response, he just grinned, temporarily ignoring her.

"Check it out, boys." he said, gesticulating wildly towards the abandoned carriage, "I want everything in it, tear it to the ground if necessary. Then burn it. But keep de 'orses."

After handing out his instructions, he turned back to the woman. "Ye, my dearie, will stay right 'ere with me," and taking hold of the girl in red's shoulders, he forced her heavily to the ground.

Not ready for the sudden assault, she dropped unwittingly to the ground. The dust puffing up around both of them as her seat hit the hard floor of the valley, while her attacker, once again briefly looked over at his men and their pilfering.

The earth was rough, the sharp gravel digging rather painfully into the soft flesh of her palms. But she sat there smiling to herself, knowing there was absolutely nothing for the brigands to find in that old coach. The only prize they might find, if any, was herself.

After he was sure his men were well occupied, the group leader eventually returned his attentions back to his young captive, now covered with dust, as well as soaking with sweat. He immediately noticed the remnants of her cheeky smile.

"M' dear, ye 'ave little to laugh about. Yer alone in the middle of nowhere with four big men, just waiting to 'ave their way with you." pausing slightly, before asking, "Do ye think yer up to the challenge?" and then he ginned devilishly, revealing two missing teeth, all the others brown with grime and age.

"I assume you'll be first, will you?" she asked, crossing her arms in defiance.

"Well, obviously me love. Why do ye think I sent de others to check out yer lovely carriage, over yonder?" his grotesque smile widened, as he bent down closer to her.

At this almost intimate distance, the horrid man's body smelt even more pungent, but now on top of that, was his awful breath. It stank of onions, garlic and something else; perhaps horse dung. The young woman cringed outwardly at the horrid smell.

"No sloppy seconds for moi," he said, gesturing to himself by putting his thumb against his chest and standing up tall. "Come on, love," reaching down, grabbing her arm, "let's 'ave that dress off, shall we?"

Rather violently, he lifted the girl back to her feet. Strangely, she made no attempt to stop him as he forcefully tore the old red dress from her shoulders. It didn't take much, with the man's eagerness, the somewhat threadbare gown split rather easily along its seams. Dropping to the ground, the remains of the soiled garment left the young woman clad in only her shift and pantaloons. They too were soiled and sweaty, which was a very odd look for a lady, but normally the garments never saw the light of day. Her lightly covered breasts were left poking smartly over the top of a white, whalebone corset that had survived the attack and remained firmly attached around her slim waist.

Bodily, he heaved her over toward a fallen log at the edge of the wood. It was the shattered remains of a very large tree, knocked over by a recent windstorm. The top of its barked surface lay about a meter off the ground and he roughly slung her over it, face down between branches. Chuckling wickedly, as he viewed her most agreeable backside, his next obvious intention would be to have his way with her. The brigand licked his lips with delight, the course spittle dripping off his fat, stubbly chin.

"Well, me love, I 'ope ye like it from behind." saying this with a look of glee on his face.

Pushing her forward hard against the wood with one hand, he dropped his own soiled leggings with the other, exposing himself. As he was reaching up, about to rip down the helpless woman's drawers, a large hunting knife suddenly appeared in between his eyes, imbedding itself deep into his cranium. The horrid man collapsed heavily on top of the frightened girl; a blank stare frozen on his tortured face.

The young woman screamed and, turning her back to the tree, pushed the weight of his fat body away. Like the poor footman before him, he too toppled to the ground, quite dead.

Lifting her hands to see him fall, she realized the attack had been so sudden and so quiet, the three remaining thieves had not even noticed the passing of their leader. The group of them calmly persisting in ransacking the empty coach.

Quickly moving around to the forest side of the fallen log and turning in all directions, the girl looked in vain for her saviour, seeing only green and more green. Then suddenly, arising in the clearing, there was such a beastly shout, that set all the nesting birds a flight and into the developing sunset.

Obviously, the girl's feminine shrieks had been expected, not attracting the slightest attention from the other criminals; just their boss having his way with the spoils. At this strange new sound, however, the three lingering thieves abruptly turned towards the call, the girl and the forest behind. Not understanding, each urgently attempting to decipher the source of the most unnatural exclamation. Knowing something was amiss, they moved forward in a pack, away from the carriage toward the frightened young woman. Only then did they notice their fallen comrade, his hose still around his ankles, the snowy white flesh of his naked bottom stuck high in the air.

"What de...?" one of them said, before an arrow pierced his own heart, dropping him like a stone, not even realizing his life had ended. Two down, two to go. Pulling their swords, the remaining pair scanned wildly at the forest's edge, looking for their unknown assailant.

They were still searching in vain, when the third outlaw found an arrow, equally imbedded in his chest, dropping straight to the dirt like his brethren, blood gurgling from a punctured lung. He lay there wheezing for a moment, before passing away with a great, moaning sigh. A large puddle began to develop beneath his rigid body, his rapidly draining blood staining the dry wheat with a ruddy brown patina.

The fourth bandit yelled in fear, dropping immediately to the ground for protection, before hurriedly crawling back toward the only real cover available in the clearing; the old coach. If not for the fact that she was disrobed, watching the thug crawl frantically across the yellowed grass, a curl of dust rising in his wake, the girl might have burst out laughing.

Oddly, the last remaining thief somewhat foolishly chose to stop and look back at his friend's demise. As he did so, another arrow, expertly strung, flew high through the air in a wide arc from somewhere amongst the trees. The lone remaining brigand spotted it and mesmerized by its flight, rather stupidly watched it reach the peak of its graceful curve. Then, too late, realized it was aimed right at him. At the last moment, he tried in vain to escape, desperately thrashing in the dirt, away from the wood.

The bandit got one arm up and about a meter away from his position, when the incoming arrow pierced his right thigh, pinning him solidly to the ground. Screaming in agony as the shaft penetrated his leg, he tried frantically to free himself. It was no use, the arrow had obviously been weighted and was so deeply imbedded in the hard soil, he was stuck fast. Tugging futilely, he continued to whimper, as a second projectile flew just as true, this time impaling his flailing chest to the solid ground. He expired just as the girl turned to see her liberator, walking out through the small shrubberies on the edge of the extensive treeline.

Her saviour was a rugged, upright man, dressed in a deep green tunic. Displayed quite boldly, stretched tightly across his muscular chest, was scarlet coloured shirt, his very large muscular arms exposed and well defined, obviously perfect for drawing a bow. On top of his head was a cap of sorts, the same deep red colour as his shirt. To complete his outfit was brown hose, surrounding each of his strong legs, plus a pair of tough, black leather boots enclosing his feet.

For weapons, the man had a leather satchel hung across his body from one shoulder and he carried a longbow, with a quiver of arrows slung over his wide back. A short sword swung back and forth in a scabbard on his left thigh and an empty sheath hung from the other side of his leather belt, the dagger missing.

The new arrival wore a friendly expression on his wide face and walked toward the young damsel in distress with the agility of a fox. The dark hair under his cap blowing in the light wind and his bright blue eyes sparkling in the dying sunlight.

"M' Lady, it appears I have arrived just in time." he said, bowing reverently to the young girl, who was very ineffectually trying to hide herself, leaning against the bark of the fallen tree, arms crossed over her body.

She was speechless, completely dumbfounded at the appearance of the knave, unbelieving of her luck and very thankful for the man's courage and skill at the bow. But also embarrassed beyond belief and completely unaware of what to expect from this heavily weathered, but certainly handsome rogue. Was she going to receive any better treatment from him than the others he had just killed?

Without a moment's hesitation, the lone warrior bounded swiftly over the fallen log, as if it didn't exist. Bending down, he retrieved the remnants of the girl's torn red dress, shaking it out briefly before reaching over the log and dropping it gently over the uncomfortable woman's shoulders. Then, equally as quick, he attempted to withdraw his knife from the head of the deceased bandit. But it was stuck fast and having some trouble, had to place the toe of his boot on the dead man's face just to obtain the requisite leverage to pull it loose. With a loud crunch of broken bone, it came smartly away, a small trace of blood and grey matter still evident on the blade. Wiping it clean on the corpse's tunic, he turned once more to the frightened lady, who had covered herself as best she could with her mutilated garment.

"How are you, M' Lady? I trust these arrogant fools didn't hurt you?" his tone was even, genuine and displayed true concern.

"No. Sire, they did not. All though, as you can see from the appalling state of my attire, they did try." she hesitated, looking again at his striking features, "It appears I am safe once again," nodding at him, "and it's all thanks to you."

The girl was breathless, still uneasy, "Where on earth did you come from?"

"I came from my home, over there in the wood, M' Lady." he smiled broadly at her. "For this is where I choose to live."

"You reside here in the forest and not the village?" she asked incredulously.

"Indeed, M' Lady," flashing his pearly white teeth, "I find it wonderfully relaxing and real to be one with the environment. Also, it is the only way to successfully retain... my privacy."

"Well, who am I to tell you otherwise, as it obviously worked in my favour today." she stated, wiping some loose hair out of her eyes, all the while holding the damaged dress material against her chest, "Can I ask your name, good Sire?" her tone showing genuine interest, now believing the man to be harmless.

"Please, just call me..., Corazon." he stared at her, his eyes sparkling.

"Well, Sire..., Corazon, I am much obliged for your very timely help." looking back at him with equally bright and interested eyes.

Politely, but still rather abruptly, the knave broke the look. Almost as if to ignore the nervous young woman, he now occupied himself with an additional scout around the clearing, just to be certain there were no other dangerous, residual distractions.

When her rescuer said no more, feeling she had to fill the uncomfortable silence, the girl added, "Unfortunately, I do not have anything to pay you for your troubles, good Sire. I mean..., Corazon. As you can see, I am a poor merchant's daughter..."

Rotating to reacquire her eyes, he cut her off sharply, "Forgive me, but I beg to differ, M' Lady." he stated simply, grinning, his gaze remaining steadily on the woman's pretty face.

"Excuse me?"

"M' Lady, you are the second daughter of the Duke of Eastborough." pausing briefly, "Recently run away from your family's estate. And with the aid of your chamber servant, I would guess. You are, or shall I say were, dressed in her clothes, were you not?" pointing to her destroyed outfit.

"Now, just a minute, Si..." the girl's face showed open shock.

Once more the knave cut her off, even more sharply than before. "M' Lady, next time you chose to run away in your maid's clothes, you should remember to remove your fancy whalebone corset first."

Pointing to her middle, with the blade of his knife, "No lady I know, but the very wealthy, own corsets of that design." he continued, unceasingly, "In addition, the carriage in which you chose to ride in here, on your adventure this very hot afternoon, may be old and scruffy but it clearly came from within your father's custody, as his coat of arms is still visible on the faded paintwork." for a second time, the knave politely gestured with his knife.

Disbelieving, the girl turned, and in the last light of the setting sun, noticed for the first time, the remnants of the family crest etched into, and clearly visible on, the tattered black door.

Enjoying himself, the knave concluded, "Finally," pointing to the two animals still tied to the coach, casually grazing on the heath, "your horses, M' Lady are of prime stock. While it appears you certainly did your best in managing to dig up the oldest carriage you could find on your father's property, unfortunately, you could not find any old or decrepit horses to match." at this point, Corazon was almost laughing, "These particular stallions are magnificent. Like no other. These lively brutes are undoubtably the reason your father is so angry and has listed you missing."

Incredulous, the girl looked at the man who had just saved her and slouched down, finally relenting to his most excellent, deductive arguments. Apparently, she had been found out by one of the best.

"I must hand it to you, Sire Corazon, you are indeed thorough." the girl's face reddened, as her secret had been exposed, and her voice went quiet, "And you are also correct..., on all fronts. I *am* the daughter of the Duke. Lady Anabelle Bolton. But my friends...," she stopped herself, "but you can call me, Bella."

The knave said nothing as he returned to her side of the fallen tree.

Anabelle paused, watching the man as he approached, admiring him. Then her voice changed now slightly annoyed, looking back at the abandoned carriage, "Imagine that, the devil cares more for his horses, than his youngest daughter."

"Clearly, the gentleman's taste is waning." Corazon hiding a complement, finally coming close to her.

The knave's praise evidently pleased the girl for she responded with thanks. "Your kind words are appreciated, good Sire." smiling at him a little flirtatiously.

When nothing more was forthcoming, she sighed very loudly, believing she had to explain herself, "I just wanted to get away for a while, out from underneath all the scrutiny of the court. Go out on an adventure for once. Sometimes, you just need to be by yourself, you know?"

"Indeed, I do, M' Lady, I know exactly what you mean." the knave responded, seriously appreciating everything she had said, "Thus, the prime reason for my rather unique choice of very unassuming residence," swiping his arm towards the forest and returning the smile. "But quick, the light is failing, and darkness will soon be upon us."

Finally, returning his dagger to its sheath, and holding out his hand, he motioned to assist her. Still a trifle unsure, she stood up tall, holding the ragged gown around herself with one hand and tentatively taking his with the other. Corazon led Bella around the end of the fallen tree and back over to the abandoned carriage, the fine pair of horses still munching on the dry grass.

Then he produced another cheeky grin saying, "And, as the local predators love to feed at night, they will be seeking sustenance quite soon. And you, M' Lady, Anabelle, do look very tasty."

"Sire, you presume too much!" dropping her arm in astonishment and tearing away from his light grip. Anabelle gave him a shocked expression of the *how dare you sort*. Complements were one thing, she thought, but this brute of a man had crossed the line with that outburst.

Ignoring her outraged appearance, he looked back down at the four corpses, moving his arm in a sweeping gesture. "Don't worry, M' Lady, I will keep you safe." kicking the nearest carcass, "Instead, of your fine flesh, the beasts will surely feast on this lot tonight.

Corazon held out his arm once again to help her into the old coach, saying, "Let us, therefore, adjourn to my humble abode, where we can speak more of your Ladyship's particular… taste for adventure."

Not yet completely over his racy comments, Bella stopped, refusing to take the offered arm. Where was this man going to take me? Will I be safe? What have I got myself into?

Then, taking a deep breath, she calmed down a bit, reasoning, where else was she to go? Anyway, his rudeness aside, for some reason, she had a good feeling about this man, and they always say, first impressions are always the best. And the truest.

"M' Lady?" he asked, arm still extended.

Finally, Bella relented, taking the offered hand and climbing aboard the shabby conveyance, a smile returning to her ruddy cheeks. But never once releasing her very tight hold on the ragged remains of her dress.

After assisting the slightly awestruck and embarrassed lady through the creaking door, with the faded Bolton family crest, and back onto the ancient coach seat, Corazon climbed up onto the vacant driver's bench. Then, rapidly taking the reins, he promptly led them all, the horses and the old rickety carriage, into the ever-darkening forest.

Chapter 2 – The Knave's Lair

The night darkened quickly and as the coach wound its way along the cart track through the forest, the light slowly disappeared. The knave drove the team of horses like he owned them, promptly bringing them into a small clearing at the end of a turnoff, just short of the main road. The junction he used was not very obvious and initially, the large vehicle had a tough time negotiating the turn. As a result, several small wood boughs broke off as the carriage passed through the entrance. It was clearly a passage that had previously only been used for a single horse and rider. The clearing at the end of the trail, barely held the coach and two horse and appeared completely deserted. In the fading light, Bella was able to distinguish the presence of a sheer rock wall, close by.

Thankfully, it did not take long to make it that far, the glade's location only about two miles into the wood against the edge of the surrounding mountains. It looked to Bella to be nothing but a dead end, making her wonder what the knave was playing at, and once more reawakening her uncertainty. But as Corazon brought the team to a halt, he jumped down, indicating through the window for her to do so as well, revealing that they had apparently reached their destination.

"Welcome to my humble home," he invited, holding her lightly by the waist as she descended from the carriage doorway still clutching her ragged clothes.

"What home? We are in an empty clearing in the middle of woods. I can barely see?" Bella was getting upset, not to mention scared.

"You see, M' Lady, but do not perceive. Behold." he stated proudly, pointing to a dark part of the hillside, behind a tall pile of boulders.

Evidently, the knave's habitat was not a tree house, as Bella had originally believed. Instead, it was a cave amongst the rocks, penetrating deeply into the granite core of the steep mountainside. A veritable black hole, cleverly disguised and protected by a surrounding crag of stones. Had someone not already known it was there, they would have journeyed past it, never even noticing the hidden abode.

"The horses will be fine here overnight, M' Lady," he offered tying the beast's reigns to a nearby tree branch. "The night animals never venture this close to the rocks," and smiling again added, "and anyway those ravenous brutes will have plenty to eat out there in the field anyway."

Bella gave him a fearful expression, not appreciating his casual levity of the situation at all.

Corazon looked slightly critically at Bella, his eyes shining in the rising moonlight, "I apologise for my brevity, M' Lady. Please, don't be afraid, you are in very good hands. Safe hands. You have my assurance that no harm will befall you. Come."

He invited her by pulling lightly at her hand, before stepping around the natural barrier and disappearing inside. Looking briefly around the glade and realizing there was not much of an alternative, Bella followed, but still with slight trepidation. Not sure what to expect, but also not willing to remain outside in the cold and emerging night. Pausing, she patted both of the horses lovingly before quickly following the knave inside.

For a plain stone cave carved out of a mountain side, it was surprisingly well appointed. The dwelling was quite spacious inside, with several 'rooms' separated by man-made, roughened timber barriers. There was a set of rustic wood furniture, chairs, tables and even a bed, with wool blankets and pillows. Off to one side, in the main front room was a fireplace, with a roaring blaze dancing in the hearth, vented to the outside through a crudely drilled chimney. The flickering flames provided a dim, orange glow of light, both illuminating the space and making it appear very cozy.

The grand place even had its own supply of running water. A mountain creek, passing over the top of the hill, had been cleverly tapped and a portion redirected through a second vent opening in the ceiling. It fell lazily into a shallow collection pool, carved in the floor of a separate room, at the back of the cavern. From there, it eventually overflowed and passed out of the cave, through another underground opening, carrying on its way. First into a small creek, then onto the main river a few miles distant. Conveniently, the pool also supplied drinking water that was constantly refreshed by the cascading waterfall.

"Quite an impressive little place you have here," Bella offered, "I see it even has running water. Fascinating! Now, I can see why you like the place."

"Yes, it does have its advantages." the knave nodded, smiling brightly, "I obtained this cave from an old bear that no longer had any use for it. After cleaning it up, adding these dividers and making some other adjustments, it has become quite homey."

He chuckled, inviting her in, at the same time motioning to the cascading waterfall, "I am particularly proud of the water feature, definitely a highlight. It also doubles as a shower for morning clean-up. I can even turn the water off if necessary, using the diverter I installed up top. But I've found the sound of its constant fall rather enjoyable and relaxing. And the great thing about leaving it running, is that the continual flow quickly refreshes the reception basin after each cleaning. Rather effective, if I do say so myself."

Finally, motioning with a large open hand to his sitting room, he added, "Come on in and take a seat. We can chat in the parlor."

The parlor turned out to be the second room inside the large space, that housed two comfy chairs with straw filled cushions and the main fireplace. A small side table was located next to each chair and two rustic ottomans provided a place to elevate one's feet. Corazon continued speaking as they walked inside, "It's not Eastborough Hall, M' Lady, but I trust it will suffice for now."

"It is more than sufficient, good Sire. It'll just be nice to put my feet up for a few moments rest,"

Bella approached the nearest couch and dropped down into the comfortable seat, slightly dislodging her hastily repaired dress. The knave joined her on the other chair, slowly lowering himself down, before removing his boots and placing his feet upon the footrest.

The two sat in silence for a minute, enjoying the blaze of the fire, which warmed their faces and bodies with its welcome, therapeutic heat.

"M' Lady forgive my saying it, but it looks like you're going to need a new outfit, if we're to get you home tomorrow." it was a casual observation, stated very matter of fact.

"You want to take me back home? What happened to talking about my taste for adventure?" Bella was shocked and dismayed, after finally having felt more secure and thinking she had found herself an understanding advocate.

"Well, my dear we can talk of that as well, because I am very interested in your various reasons and motivations for initiating your escape. But there is no doubt that your family is worried about you." he ended with, "And, therefore, there is no doubt, you must go back"

"My Father just wants his darn horses back." Bella pouted.

"Perhaps. But what about your mother?" Corazon asked, raising a bushy eyebrow.

Considering this, Bella's eyes dropped towards the floor, "You're right, of course. She must be sick with worry." the young woman hesitated, thinking deeply, "But can I at least stay here, tonight?"

"M' Lady, there is no way we could travel that far this evening anyway, with all of the hungry wildlife walking the wood. So, yes, you may stay." then to soften the mood, he asked, "Tell me, M' Lady, why did you run away?"

"I will agree to tell you, Corazon, but only under one condition." Bella smiling at the older man.

"And what condition is that?" he asked, honestly curious.

"That you call me Bella, like I asked." she chuckled, finally feeling comfortable, safe.

"Ah! That might be a little hard, M' Lady," Corazon stated, offering his own version of a laugh, "considering your extremely scrupulous pedigree, but I will try my best...," he stopped, before adding, "Bella. Please, tell me why you left home?"

"Mostly because of my Father, I suppose. Because, he can be such a trying man. He thinks I should be a typical lady of the house, seen and not heard. His other beautiful daughter, only to be lined up for an eventual arranged marriage and then, ultimately, a grandchild bearing machine." she looked toward the fire, contemplating the flickering flames, "Sometimes, his beliefs are just so old fashioned, I just can't stand it, you know?"

"While I know nothing of being a rich man's daughter, although I'm quite sure there are highs and lows to it all, I certainly can sympathize with you."

Saying this, he studied the girl again from top to bottom with his observant eyes, the wood of the fire crackling in the background, "Furthermore, I completely understand your feelings on the matter, as if they were my very own."

"That's nice to hear, Corazon. For once, it's good to have someone showing a bit of empathy for me and my position."

"Yes, M' Lady. Life is already difficult enough, without one having to play one role, when one only wishes to play another."

"Well said, Corazon, and please, call me Bella."

"Bella, it is."

"Have you ever had a time in your life when you wished you were someone else?"

"All the time, Bella, all the time."

"This home for instance, and its location." this time Anabelle looked right into the knave eyes, "You have no doubt chosen it because you too are running away from something."

"Yes, but I would say rather more like..., hiding from something." without stopping or elaborating, he deflected back, "but we were talking about you and your own reasons for escape. Is there anything specific other than your role at home, and its potential match made future, that you disliked?"

"Well, one thing, I suppose it's the way my parents treat our staff. Susan, our maid and Simon, our butler. They are such nice agreeable people, but my Mother and Father still insist on ordering them around like there're slaves. No care in the world for how they might feel or what they might want, only thinking of themselves. As if their money and family lineage make them better humans. I do not like, nor do I appreciate, that attitude at all. I always make it a point to be courteous to Simon and I'm best friends with Susan." Bella sounded pleased with herself.

"Thus, your easy access to her wardrobe?" he teased.

"Indeed, Sire!"

The two of them laughed together, enjoying the moment.

Speaking of clothes, throughout their dialogue, the one thing that remained on Bella's mind was what the knave had said regarding her need for a new dress. She could not possibly return home tomorrow in the scraps of Susan's gown.

So, she inquired, "Corazon, considering that very topic. Earlier this evening you stated that I would need new clothes for tomorrow. Can I ask how we might go about that?"

"Bella, I have been around a few years and rescued my share of damsels in distress. Many of whom come here, in a similar state to what you are now." smiling even wider, "I have, therefore, taken the liberty of acquiring certain items during my daily exploits that may be of some service to you."

Gesturing to a very old, knotted wood, sea chest across the room, "Please feel free to browse through the chest in yonder corner. You might be able to find something you like in there."

Bella's eyebrows contracted sharply as she looked at the chest and getting up, walked over, still attempting to keep her damaged garment from falling off her body. When she opened the box, she was surpized to find an assortment of women's gowns, all in very good condition, some of them very rich and very expensive looking.

"Where did you get these, Corazon?" rifling through the selections in the wonderful wardrobe, "I take it these are not yours?"

"No, Bella, they are not. But come to think of it, I did quite enjoy trying on the yellow and chiffon frock you are holding in your hand just now." teasing her again.

Bella dropped the garment back into the wood chest in disgust, "Sire?"

"Relax, M' Lady," he said, laughing heartily, "I jest." Bella's shoulders drooped a little as she calmed herself.

"So, they really belong to you then?" she asked incredulous.

"Well, let's just say, they belong to me..., now." and he made a flashy swipe of his arm at the storage chest, "I happened to acquire all of them during the course of my daily enterprise."

When she stared at him with a questioning look, he hesitated before continuing, "My daily work is complicated, M' Lady. But yes, these items did indeed, belong to various rich womenfolk, who just happened to be accompanying persons of questionable repute. And unfortunately for them, those same persons and I happened to have had a.... disagreement." he paused, "As such, those particular ladies no longer have any use for them." Corazon produced a wicked smile. "Consider them, if you wish, spoils of war, M' Lady."

Making a face, Bella shrugged her shoulders, not really understanding. Looking back into the garment filled box, after a bit of searching, did manage to find something she liked. It was a floral pink gown, with a bright white bodice. It was fairly frilly, a little more so than she would have liked, but it happened to rather closely match some of the dresses she owned back at the manor house. Bella felt, if she was going back there, she might as well look the part.

"A very good choice, Bella. That particular selection suits you very well." the knave admired the gown appreciatively. "You will be pleased to note, there are also replacement undergarments in there for you as well."

As she spun the dress in front of her, Bella remembered about her sweat stained clothes and dust encrusted body. Upon careful consideration, a rather wildish thought came to her, "Corazon, would you mind if I ask you a favour?"

"By all means. You appear to be enjoying yourself, who am I to spoil your fun."

"Would you mind terribly, if I borrowed your shower? I wouldn't dare try this beautiful frock on, in the state I'm in."

"All too right, M' Lady. I must admit, as far as your attire goes, the day has not been very kind to you. I don't doubt you could use, as they say, a little freshening-up." Corazon was smiling cheekily again, "Please go right ahead. I was going to recommend you wait until the morrow, but tonight is a fine time as any. Just watch it though, the water will be fairly chilly at this time of day."

Making to leave the room, she nodded, giving him a look that requested privacy.

In order to placate her, he added, "and don't worry about me, Bella," he chuckled, "I would only interrupt you if I heard a horrible scream or some such thing."

Deliberately turning his head away from her, he continued, "I will remain here in front of the fire. Take all the time you need. Soap is also available there for your convenience."

An amused expression remained set on his chiselled features, as he looked appreciatively into the roaring flames. The shadows of his handsome face highlighted selectively by the flickering orange glow.

Corazon sat there, hands comfortably laced behind his head, contemplating this fascinating girl, who was truly a most interesting find, when the brief quiet was shattered by a stifled scream from the back corner of the cave.

"Ah!" mostly to himself, "Bella must have just stepped beneath the waters," the knave smiled, "I told her it would be cold."

Out loud he asked, "Is everything alright back there?" by now snickering gleefully with delight.

"Uh, I think so.... Yes!" came Bella's somewhat quiet, very wet, soaked reply, "Just a little cold is all. But I'm good, just had to get used to it."

He could tell from her response that she was shivering under the flow, "Just remember to wash well, M' Lady. It's best that we present you all clean for your parents when you go home tomorrow!"

"Don't remind me."

It was the only thing he received in return. So, closing his eyes, he slid back in the comfy chair and listened to the soothing crackle of the blazing fire, enjoying the soothing heat.

Chapter 3 – Returning Home

The following day was cool, the bright, hot sun having difficulty breeching the thickness of the forest canopy overhead.

As the couple emerged, into the dim light, both of them had pleasant, wide-awake expressions of persons very well rested. For both Corazon and Bella had slept extremely well, she on his comfortable bed and he in the not as comfortable chair by the fire. Corazon had no issues giving up his bed, as in his present line of work, he had gotten quite adept at sleeping almost anywhere.

It was only inevitable that after her wash, he had left Bella well alone. Not due to protocol or prudence but because, despite her cold shower which had clearly refreshed her, Bella had returned to the sitting room very sleepy. Comfortably dressed, in her brand-new undergarment, her only request was where she might bed down for the night. Initially, as a lark, Corazon had thought of telling her "outside", but then considering all that she had been through, decided the young woman had had enough teasing for one day.

After retiring into the provided bedroom, she settled off to sleep soon after, all the while Corazon continued staring into the roaring flames of the fire, considering their next day's adventures. Eventually, he too nodded off, a pleasant expression on his wearisome face.

***

$\mathscr{S}$tarting early, with a light breakfast of bread and cheese, the pair listened to the morning birdsong, the light-hearted chirping raising their spirits. For each had a reason to be slightly saddened that day, Bella returning home to face the music, and Corazon, losing his new companion by sending her there.

As the pair left the cave behind, and they entered the forest again, the two of them enjoyed the breeze and smells of the fresh morning air. Eventually, finding their way back to the clearing, they returned to the carriage, to find not only the conveyance safe but the horses well rested. The sides of the dark coach cabin glistened with a light veneer of dew, as Corazon courteously opened the door, offering his hand. Bella climbed, rather reluctantly, into the rear seat of the coach.

With an edge of hesitancy in her voice, she half-heartedly asked, "Do we really have to go?"

"I'm afraid so, M' Lady." was Corazon's simple reply as he watched her climb inside.

She stopped suddenly, before committing herself, "Well then, may I ride up front with you?"

"I'm afraid we can't have you arriving on the driver's bench, M' Lady." the knave replied, matter of fact, "What would your father say?"

"Oh, go on then," Bella smiled, "I'll sit in here and be happier for it," jesting playfully and chuckling as she said it. She rather liked this knave who had rescued her and was already feeling quite comfortable in his presence.

Thinking back, and briefly remembering her experience, perhaps travelling the countryside on her own had not been such a good idea after all. Remembering, Anabelle shivered at the thought of what that putrid bandit might have done to her. How close he had been to her, how she had felt his strength as he physically ripped the clothes from her body, the smell of his rancid breath as he pawed at her flesh. The horrors that had been so closely awaiting her, without this brave man's interference. What Corazon had done for her yesterday had really been something quite fantastic, as if it was destined. A critical favour that might never be repaid.

Assisting her inside, the knave noticed, not only the reflective look on her pretty face, but once again how absolutely gorgeous the young Bolton girl looked in the pink and white ball gown she had selected. The snowy toned bodice enhancing her slight figure, the rose-coloured skirt looking very regal in the gathering light. Corazon also observed almost immediately, that Bella had however, retained one thing from her previously decimated wardrobe. The girl had preserved and wore rather proudly, her expensive whalebone corset. This critical accessory aided extremely well in conserving her very feminine hourglass shape, that no other material a seamstress might provide, could ever produce. He felt his gaze linger slightly longer than necessary, or what might have been permitted by protocol, as he helped her comfortably into the carriage.

With a quick sigh he closed the door, stepping back and walking a perimeter, just to be sure all was in order before they set out. Climbing up-top and settling against the low backrest, he took a deep refreshing breath, filling his lungs with the clean mountain air. Reaching down and grabbing the reigns of the pair of horse, he received a welcome bray and shake from the team, who were now ready and willing to get on their way.

"So, M' lady...," hesitating, he continued, "apologies, I mean Bella," the knave stated sheepishly from the upper bench, "Are you ready to face the music?"

"As good as I'm ever going to be, I'd wager." Bella responded, clearly still a bit unhappy to be heading home.

"Well then, let's be off!" the carriage wheels screeching loudly, as he gently guided the hoses away from the clearing and out onto the forest pathway.

Once out on the main road, away from the trail and its low hanging branches, Corazon encouraged the horses a bit further. As he suspected, they quickly took themselves to a hard gallop, heading swiftly out of the wood and into the golden light of the open meadow. The bright morning sunshine, now able to reach them, blinded him temporarily, but it was of no concern as the experienced horses easily guided the coach along the available path, unrestrained.

They soon passed by the scene of yesterday's unfortunate incident; the large fallen log clearly still visible along the side of the roadway. As the knave had presumed, however, the bodies of the fallen thieves had all disappeared. A sprinkling of abandoned weapons and a light staining of brown on the grass, the only sign that they were ever there. Not even the fabric of their threadbare clothes remained. Evidently, they had made an excellent nocturnal meal for some appreciative beast, or most likely, beasts.

Unfortunately, the body of the girl's coachman had also disappeared in a similar way, he too servicing as the evening meal for one of the ravenous carnivores of the forest.

Because of this he did not slow, now of the impression that the girl sitting in the coach below him, was too deep in thought to have considered the empty clearing anyway. It was evident the young Bolton woman was clearly troubled and certainly did not wish to be returning home. After all, who could blame her, with a father like that! His eyes now adjusted, Corazon pushed the team a bit further and their speed accelerated, the dust from the rapidly spinning wheels minimized by the presence of the heavy morning dew.

Being well outside the dense forest, and the sky all opened up to reveal a beautifully clear day, he relished in the warmth it offered to his still cold face. The twittering of the birds and whistle of the light wind kept Corazon company the further they rode. The weather was perfect for an open ride, for even with the direct sun, the day's slightly cooler temperatures prevented the potential build-up of unwanted perspiration for both the horses and the driver. His passenger remained quiet, keeping to herself for most of the ride.

It was a few hours, before Corazon thought he could detect the light fragrance of lavender as they crested the final hill above the nearby township of Eastborough. The new day had just started for the villagers and grey twirling smoke could be seen rising from the chimneys of the many little cottages haphazardly strewn about the valley. A cow mooed a loud greeting as they passed a field of meandering livestock, the animals already released for their morning graze.

But it was not the freshly awaking town that called to the travellers but instead, a large, Victorian manor house, looking very stranded within its huge estate, lying well off in the distance. The knave took a left at the next junction in pursuit of that lofty destination, quickly leaving the warm, inviting village behind them.

"We're almost there, M' Lady, you'd best arrange yourself." the knave called down to his charge, over the wind.

"Do we have to?" was her sad reply, "I was rather enjoying the ride."

"I am very pleased that you're enjoying the ride, M' Lady. But unfortunately, as I said, when you asked me before, I'm afraid you have really no choice but to return. I'm sure your mother, and your father, will appreciate knowing that you are safe."

"I suppose, your right." Anabelle acquiesced, then paused, before adding an invitation, "But I must insist that you come in. I will demand it. They must not turn away my saviour."

"I will do as you wish, M' Lady. If that will make you feel any better."

"It will, Corazon. Truly it will."

Neither of them said anymore as they crossed the threshold of the property and onto the wide, treelined gravel roadway that ran up to the main house. The sound of the old coach's wheels on the stone was rather harsh, lending an aura of foreboding, as the very pleasant, morning ride neared its undeniable end.

As they drew into the main reception yard, there was no question that Bolton manor was magnificent. High mullioned windows graced every corner, pointed arches capping their crystalline surfaces, all glittering radiantly in the intense daylight. Numerous pointed, black cast iron spires extended bravely from the slate tile roofline, as if each were attempting to burst the fluffy white clouds in the sky. A pinky beige, interlaced stonework graced the walls of the mansion, its surface smoothly luxurious, no doubt imported from a quarry in some distant Mediterranean land.

The many openings and edges of the manor, were all tastefully surrounded by a bold, snowy white wood trim, kept clean by the bleaching effect of the burning sun. Several arches leading into the courtyard were sizable and ornate, stretching across vast distances, unsupported. The towering, milled columns around the entry and corners of the granite façade were capitalized with scroll shaped volutes in the style of Greek Ionic, giving the affluent abode an even thicker air of decadent opulence.

The immense and ancient, deep brown, cherry wood entry door was stained to perfection with a glossy sheen that glimmered in the morning sunshine, producing an almost iridescent sparkle. Its large knocker appearing to be made of solid gold, as did the entry handle, each no doubt just heavily plated brass. Everything about the home stated affluence and luxury, Corazon guessing the place would even have running water in many of its lavish interior bathrooms. As well as hot water to boot!

The massive construction was truly marvelous in every way and the knave could not help but inspect it fully, appreciating the estate home's abundant beauty as he expertly drew the horse and carriage up to its main entrance. Upon bringing the old coach abruptly to a halt, the door opened, and someone dressed entirely in white came bounding out, running excitedly to see who had arrived.

"Bella, darling is that you?" the question of concern, hung in the still cool, late morning air, obviously voiced by the girl's worried mother.

The Duchess was a mature woman but had managed to retain a slim, shapely body like her daughter. She also harboured an equally pretty face, much older of course, but under the present circumstances made worse, her attractive visage displaying additional lines of recent distress. It was clear, however, where young Bella's good looks came from. Her voice sounded wispy and light, almost like a breath of calm wind.

"Yes, it is I, Mother," Bella answered, not even waiting for the knave, opening the battered door and climbing down from the carriage herself. Corazon stayed the reigns, then jumped down himself, the two of them ending up together in front of the extremely anxious Duchess.

"Oh, darling!" taking her daughter in a big hug, "I am so glad to see that you are alright. We were all so worried." then pushing back, her hands placed lightly on Bella's shoulders, "Where on earth have you been?"

It was a rhetorical question that the young girl answered with only a brief shrug of her shoulders.

Noticing the knave for the first time, Anabelle's mother questioningly eyed the stranger, "and who is this, you have brought with you? Certainly not Johnson!" Madam Bolton's azure blue eyes surveying Corazon's rustic clothing with utter distaste.

"Johnson is dead, Mother." Bella stated simply, looking down.

"Oh, my! That's so awful! He was such a good coachman." her mother replied, not caring in the slightest, looking back towards her daughter but never once taking her eyes off the knave.

"Obviously, he was not good enough." Corazon offered, to the utter disgust of the Duchess, the unimpressed woman presenting him a rather evil stare.

"This man," Bella continued, ignoring her mother's look, and coming to her companion's defence, "Sire Corazon, bravely rescued me from an even worse fate! Dispatching the horrid bandits that killed poor old Johnson. Mother, he is my saviour!"

"What is this nonsense about a saviour?"

They all turned towards the new voice, emanating from a well-dressed, much older man, who had come up unseen from the open, front doorway. Clearly, Bella's father, reasoned Corazon.

The Duke was indeed elderly, perhaps over half a century old. He was also short in stature, the top of his pointy head barely coming up to Corazon's shoulders. He was slim, like his wife, and had on an expensive waist coat and tails. An expertly trimmed, salt and pepper, goatee graced his thin, bony face, but he retained a regal air about him. One that just seethed richness and power.

His voice was harsh and raspy as he asked, no, rather demanded, "And who are you, young man?" he too offering the knave a look of abject revulsion.

"My name is Corazon, Your worship."

And, as if in court, he bowed reverently to the old Duke, impressing both the man and his stuck-up Duchess, the latter left with her thin mouth hanging open.

"I am pleased to inform you that, on the off chance, I happened by your daughter's conveyance as it was put upon by bandits. Regrettably, I was not able to help your driver, but thankfully, was able to save young Lady Bolton here, from a fate worse than death."

"A fate worse than death! Bandits! Poppycock!" then his eyes shifted and no longer looking at Corazon, he asked, "Where are my horses? They're alright are they not?"

And without another word, or as much of a greeting to his lovely daughter, he walked around the front of the coach, and proceeded to vigorously pat the necks of his two, prime stallions.

"How are my babies? That silly girl did not drive you too hard, did she?" and he dropped his sharp forehead against that of the closest horse.

"What did I tell you?" Bella stated quietly, looking directly at Corazon. Then turning to the Duchess, stated loudly, "Mother, this man is a hero, he must be invited in. At least for a cup for tea, before he heads home. I insist."

"Well yes.... Why certainly," sounding completely unconvinced and ignoring Corazon, "come in, come in. My dear child, you must be famished!" then, as if an afterthought, she finally noticed Bella's gown, "Oh, I do so like your dress dear, Grandma made that one for you, didn't she?"

Bella smiled at the knave, and he returned a lopsided grin, "Why yes, Mother, this is one of Grandma's. I got it... last Easter." looking warmly at her mother.

"Well, come along then, leave your Father to his horses." the Duchess quipped, leading the odd couple through the massive door and into the pleasing shade of Eastborough Hall.

Walking inside, they heard the old Duke shout at someone, presumably the stable boy, "Carson! Come and release my babies from this god forsaken contraption."

He continued relentlessly, barking order upon order, and always at the top of his lungs. "Then I want you to take these two safely back the stables. After a vigorous brush down, they are to be fed and watered. After that is done, I want you and David to take this ugly thing out into the back quarter and burn it, you hear me!"

Doubtless, with the last order, he was referring to the rickety old carriage.

"Yes, your worship! Immediately your worship!" was the frightened stable boy's reply, but this was mostly drowned out by their own footsteps echoing loudly in the grand hall of the house.

Chapter 4 – The House, the Story and the Arrest

Eastborough Hall, the Bolton's prime residence was very grand, and as the trio stepped into the towering main foyer, it was never more evident than it could be there, considering its magnificent, colossal entryway.

If not for the gargantuan crystal chandelier hanging down above them, the huge reception area may not even have had a ceiling. The massive access was adorned with all methods of art; tapestries, paintings, and sculpture abounding. Entirely constructed from faultless marble, the floor reverberated the hard sound of their footfalls, particularly the knave's strong boots, as they made their way slowly inside. The walls themselves were painted a bright peach, making the space appear even larger, due to the lightness of the chosen tint. Several Chippendale tables and sideboards were visible, and a large Indian rug further enhanced the beauty of this main vestibule.

Off the chief foyer, were numerous entryways leading deeper into the house, each one like entries to an unknown labyrinth, demonstrating the sheer extent of the building's grandeur. And behind all of that was the grand staircase.

And it certainly was grand, in every sense. Leading forever upwards onto the higher floors, the stairway had a central landing that split into two separate wings, one to either side of the mansion's lofty upper regions. The ornate railings were crafted from dark mahogany wood, with a quantity so vast and workmanship so exquisite, it may literally have taken a small forest to create.

Corazon smiled to himself, figuring his entire mountain home would have fit easily within that one, single vestibule of the Bolton's manor.

The Duchess directed them into a large comfortable sitting room off the main hall, facing out into the courtyard. It too was a very opulent space, complete with numerous comfortable sofas and chairs, all of the fabrics in various shades of golden yellow, the overarching colour scheme of the room. Even the carpets, thick under foot, were of a light dandelion tint. The knave felt slightly uneasy dragging his dirty boots across the soft, obviously expensive surface but then, remembering the recent and rather harsh treatment of stable boy, he rapidly reconsidered.

The tall windows were embellished with lacy edged, butter yellow curtains to match the rest of the room's colour scheme. All were pulled back to reveal the bright sun arching through the clear glazing, providing the space with a comfortable, natural light. But even with the large number of well-lit openings, the sheer size of the chamber promoted many areas of dark shadow, fostering a strange, mysterious air to the home's front reception room.

"Please be seated, while I arrange for some refreshment." the Duchess stated simply, gesturing to one of the many seats in the room, "Now, where is that Susan? She's always missing when you need her." the lady mumbling this as she left the room, in anxious search of food and drink.

"So, I was right to assume it was Miss Susan's dress you had on the other day?" Corazon observed, as he lowered himself onto one of the couch's comfy seats, stretching his arms out casually along its back.

"Yes. As I already told you, she's the same Susan who helped me out in my escape, Corazon. And, unlike my Mother, I do not consider her my maid, but my friend!" Bella responded, while also making herself comfortable.

Against protocol, she chose the only available spot right next to him, on the same divan. The knave did not mind her choice in the least, enjoying her close presence, but was still rather surprised at the gesture, considering where they were. He at once lowered his hand off the back of the couch, to be sure there could be nothing inferred, no etiquettes broken. As he did so, he smelt a faint hint of her feminine perfume.

Just in time too, as yet another of Bella's family entered the room.

The newly arriving young woman floated into the room with a regal gate, her nose held high in the air, as if the stench of refuse surrounded her. Although Corazon had witnessed a lion's share of rich ladies in fine clothes, this other Bolton girl was dressed in what was unquestionably, the most opulent looking gown he had ever seen.

Her delightfully extravagant garment was made of a luxurious dark green velvet, trimmed with fine, bright white, French lace and included the requisite, very tight bodice and full skirt. Advantageously, the included whalebone corset enhanced her extremely slender waist but could do nothing to help the lady's sad lack of bosom. It was pleasing to note, however, that the large ruffle attached around the garments open, scooped neck, almost as if added intentionally, did at least provide some impression of size.

Her extremely long blond hair, hanging down as low as the top of her skirt, was partially tied up in a plat, looking very regal. The stately woman moved so smoothly and graciously; one might have mistaken her for the lady of the house. Her lack of visible age, obviously denying her that pleasure. A sister then, perhaps?

"That's my elder sister," Bella confirmed, whispering conspiringly, while holding her hand up to her face, as if the presence of her sibling was a big secret.

Bella's sister was definitely older than her sibling and looked the part. She was closer to her mother in look and, like the Duchess, had a somewhat harsh, unfriendly stuffiness about her. This was verified when, upon reviewing the occupants of the room, she instantly appeared quite uncomfortable in Corazon's presence. Rather reluctantly, she continued forward to stand awkwardly in front of the pair, who rose politely to greet her.

"Welcome home, dear sister," she stated in a soft, high voice, edged with a slight whimper, as she respectfully tilted at the waist to kiss each of Bella's cheeks in the customary way. The waver in her speech, betraying her evident uneasiness.

Observing closer, Corazon could see that the girl's face was slim and refined, but starkly pale, like the nearly bleached blond of her hair. The cheeks of her face were indrawn, quite unlike the youthful chubbiness evident in those of her younger sister. Instead, the tall woman's fragile bones stuck out, giving her a slightly, sickly appearance.

But despite her gaunt look, the new arrival clearly possessed the Bolton family beauty. And with just a few more pounds added to her overly skinny frame, she might very well eclipse her younger sibling's attractiveness. As it was, the woman remained just shy of a perfect package.

"Good morning, Melissa Anne." Bella answered, looking up at her sister, while returning the greeting. She used her formal name because of Corazon, but in the house, she usually called her May, in accordance with her initials, M.A. Bella always thought her sister's name was too stuffy for its own good.

"Oh, so we're being formal today, are we?" May chided. Then, looking beside Bella at Corazon, she continued, "And who do we have here, another friend of yours?" she asked this with such a condescending tone, it was almost malicious.

"My name is Corazon, dear Lady," the knave answered, before Bella could respond. She was still so shocked at how badly her new friend was being treated by the various members of her family. "I am here, but only briefly, for some refreshment, after having escorted your sister safely home. She had a relatively busy day, yesterday."

"Did she now?" the hostile tone remained, "Well, it serves her right, running off like that! And in the maid's clothes to boot." the casual use of words, betraying a hint of her, still very recognizable, youth.

"May happens to be three years my senior, Corazon and she loves to tease me." Bella said, almost reading his mind, "But she also looks out for me. And, as we all know, I sometimes need it." May nodded in agreement, her expression softening at her sister's kind words.

As the three of them took their seats, comfortably across from one another, Bella's tone changed, "You see, she only does it because she really has nothing better to keep her occupied. She should be married off by now, but it seems," and now she stared angrily at her sister, getting back at her for her ill treatment of Corazon, saying vindictively, "she is so skinny, there has yet to be a young man brave enough to ask her." Melissa Anne's expression turned, from one of slight disgust, to that of pure hatred in one quick moment.

"How dare you speak to me that way, Anabelle?" May stated, both shocked, and hurt.

"Yes, how dare you address your elder sister in such a manner!" the Duke had entered the room and had evidently heard the latest exchange between his two daughters.

"And why on earth are you sitting in the same seat as that..., ruffian. Come quickly Bella and sit here. Right next to me."

Squire Bolton had taken a seat, opposite the pair, in a light brown leather chair and patted the top of a taupe coloured chez lounge next to him.

Grudgingly, Bella stood up, taking a quick glance at Corazon before making her way over next to her father and dropping into the chosen armchair in a huff. Shockingly, surely only to rile her sister, May stood, revolved on the spot and sat next to Corazon on the seat Anabelle had just vacated. The only difference being, making sure to leave plenty of room between her and the stranger.

"Father!" argued Bella, "Did you see what she just did?"

"Indeed, I did child. And your sister, as the eldest, has every right to sit anywhere she wishes."

He looked behind him towards one of the other entrances to the vast room, as if expecting someone, "Now, where on earth is your Mother?"

Speak of the devil, for at that very moment, the Duchess retuned with a very young woman in tow, dressed in a black and white pinafore and carrying a tray of tea and cakes. The platter was obviously unbalanced and looked much too heavy for the young servant to carry. But Bella's mother made no attempt to support the maid in her plight, taking the first available chair opposite the knave. Her assistance limited only to an indication upon which table she wanted the refreshments served.

Without hesitating, Corazon stood up, his tall frame dwarfing anyone else in the room and swiftly extending his hands, assisted young Susan with her labours. For, by the look of recognition on Bella's face, this was certainly the Susan that had been the topic of recent discussions. And by the colour of the young servant's hair, Corazon could see why. For its auburn red was an exact duplicate of young Anabelle's.

Bella had also made a move to get up, but his quick, lithe movements easily ensured everything made it safely to the top of the table without further trouble. The young servant looked very grateful, smiling a warm bout of thanks at the knave but saying nothing, as was proper etiquette for the situation.

"Well, I'll be!" stated May horridly, unbelieving that a guest of the house, regardless of his unpleasant look, would assist their serving staff in such a way. Her voice grinding in such a way, one would have guessed she had just stepped in horse waste.

"Perhaps, Lady Melissa Anne," Corazon offered in return, "you would rather she spill the tea down the front of your gorgeous gown?" the knave's polite teasing dropping, the already frigid temperature of the room even further.

"Oh, my!" exclaimed the Duchess. May just sat still upon her chair, flabbergasted.

With the excitement over, Corazon carefully returned to his seat beside the disgusted May. It was then several more, quiet minutes while Susan served the tea. Once their drinks and cakes had all been properly served, the maid departed swiftly through the closest exit, an expression of sheer relief on her plainly pretty face. Corazon again thought sorry for the staff of the house, rapidly understanding full well, why young Bella had run away.

"Okay then. Now that we are nice and settled, why don't you tell us what happened yesterday." the old man began, sipping his tea.

"Well, it's this way, Father…"

"No, Bella," the Duke rudely interrupted, cutting his daughter off so sharply, he might as well have slapped her. "I was not talking to you. Let the young man tell the story." Bella looked furious, her cheeks quickly reddening, but nevertheless held her tongue.

Corazon firmly believed that Bella had every right to relate her own story and had assumed she would have been allowed to do so. For it was clear to him that she was the only one qualified to relate the tale. But obviously, based on the present company, he could see, attempting to step in to insist that she do so, would be fighting a losing battle. Therefore, looking at Bella first for permission, and receiving a shrug of her shoulders as consent, he began.

"Your coachman and Bella…" he had barely started when the Duchess cut him off.

"How dare you speak of my daughter with such familiarity, Sire! She is Lady Bolton to you, Sire!" the woman screeched as she spoke, hurting his ears.

"Yes, my dear wife is quite correct," followed up the Duke, in his pretentious tone, "Sire, I must ask that you address my family by their formal titles when you are in my house."

"My apologies, your worship," Corazon apologized, honestly, "it will not happen again."

After taking a small drink of hot tea to lubricate his dry throat and a short moment of silence, he started again, "Your coachman…, Johnson wasn't it?" receiving a brief nod, he continued, "and the Lady Bolton had just entered a clearing on the edge of the forbidden wood.…"

"The forbidden wood!" shrieked her mother, once again, this time really spilling her tea, "what on earth were you doing there, child!" then, without waiting for an answer and patting herself dry with a napkin, she added, "See I told you Fredrick, our Anabelle was not safe! Not safe at all! Running all around the countryside alone like that! Not safe at all!"

"Calm yourself, my dear and let the man talk, will you?" but his voice betrayed an edge of fear at the knowledge that his youngest daughter may have gone near the fearful forest.

"Certainly, your worship, with your leave, I will continue." Corazon waited politely.

"Go on!" the old man said, casually waving his hand, while his wife continued to hyperventilate beside him.

"As I was saying, the carriage carrying Lady Bolton arrived in the meadow clearing, just shy of the wood and there...," he briefly hesitated, "it was set upon by four bandits."

Again, the Duke cut him off, "The girl was just out for a simple afternoon ride. Why on earth would there have been bandits! And in the middle of the day, no less? You must take me for a charlatan, you rogue!"

That's not all I take you for, thought Corazon, before saying out loud, "I am simply relating the tale, your grace. Everyone is aware, I'm sure, that that area of the county is known for its most unsavory characters. And it was at twilight, don't forget. Shall I continue?"

"Go on then, finish it!"

"The group killed your driver before I had even arrived on the scene. Your daughter..., excuse me, the Lady Bolton, was rough handled out of the coach by the leader of the gang and made to stand aside, while his men searched through it for...," and he hesitated thinking of the right word, valuables perhaps, no, "treasure."

"Treasure! Hah! they wouldn't find any treasure in that jalopy of a wagon." the Duke chuckled at his own joke.

The knave smiled at the man's ignorance, and said deridingly, "And so you consider your youngest daughter, worthless, your grace?" enjoying the indirect insult.

"Oh, poppycock, young man, you know that is not what I meant at all!" turning red with embarrassment and looking quickly over at Bella, "Just continue!"

After that outburst, a strained silence reigned over the room, the only noise a familiar ticking of the large grandfather clock in the far corner of the room and a light hiss of wind from outside. Corazon purposely extended the silence, helping himself to a small piece of cake and swallowing some more tea, before continuing.

"Well, that was about the time when I came upon the edge of the wood and, observing the scene in front of me, immediately recognized the danger M' Lady was in." the knave nodded his head towards Bella, who was just dying to say something. "Using the various tools of my trade, I subdued the hooligans... and rescued your daughter."

"Tools of your trade? What do you mean?" this question from May, who was now on the edge of her seat, listening intently to the knave's story and enjoying every bit.

"Why my knife and bow and arrow, of course, M' Lady." Corazon replied, as if it was obvious. Boy, these people might have money, he considered, but they certainly needed a little education on the ways of the world.

"You mean you killed them?" this one from the Duchess.

"It was either them or your daughter, your ladyship."

This time no one corrected him on his wording. He was about to tease the woman further with; 'perhaps, you would rather your daughter had been brutalized?' but stopped himself. This family had had enough.

"You mean to tell me, young man, that you killed four men..., singlehanded?" the Duke was awestruck.

"Indeed, your worship," he addressed the old man, directly, "As it happens, I do possess some skill in that area."

"What area?"

"Why, hand to hand combat, good Sire!" he replied, finally maddened at the man's stupidity.

"And what were you, Sire, doing near the forbidden wood in the first place?"

Another obvious question from the Duke, but to ask it then was not the time, for young Bella had obviously had enough.

"What does it matter why he was there! Those men were going to rape me, Father!" Bella screamed. "This man saved me!"

At Bella's outburst, her sister stared shocked and open mouthed. But worse, the poor Duchess heaved a great sigh and passed out in her chair. The Duke didn't even notice his wife's peril, nor apparently cared to.

"Bella, I have already asked you to be silent. How dare you speak in that way! And using that word! I will have you confined to the house! Do you understand!" he was livid, his skinny face red with anger.

"But Father," her tone lessened, just hoping to be heard, "Corazon rescued me...."

He wasn't listening, "I told you to be quiet! I have had enough of you and your lies! May, take your sister up to her room, immediately. I will have no more of this!"

As he said this, three more figures entered the cavernous room.

Everyone looked up in their direction as the trio had apparently come in from the main hall. Clearly one of the new arrivals was the mansion's butler, as he was tall and slim and dressed for the role, in black with a green waistcoat. In addition, he looked a little sheepish, at not being there when the young Lady Bolton had arrived and upon noticing the Duchess had fainted, immediately ran to her aid asking for someone to obtain some smelling salts.

The second and most imposing figure, was also a notably tall man. But unlike the first, he was very muscular and dressed in the regalia of the local constabulary, mostly in black. His costume consisted of a dark black waistcoat, over a maroon red tunic, with black hose and knee-high riding boots. His blouse was beige not white, but still possessed flowing sleeves, the portion that could been seen, anyway. For his large forearms were encased in strong, dark leather gauntlets, barely visible under the long black cape that fell heavily from his broad shoulders.

He had dark hair, that matched his uniform and a long face of chiseled features. There was a thin, vertical scar on his chin that extend high enough to produce a partial cleft in his bottom lip. Along with a large hunting knife, that could be seen stashed in his belt, a sturdy and rather elegant broadsword, stored in a sheath, hung loosely from his hip, a single black gloved hand resting gently on its ornate hilt. The strangest piece of attire he wore, however, was a triangular patch of black cloth over his left eye, giving his visage a very frightful, sinister look.

The last man to enter the room was not nearly as impressive as the Chief Constable, and clearly only accompanied him as the taller man's lackey. Medium built and somewhat unassuming, he too was also wearing the uniform of the constabulary, but on him, the dark outfit was nowhere near as intimidating as that of his superior. Evidently, however, he was pleased to be there, a proud look on his thinnish face. For some odd reason, Corazon was also sure the man stared almost exclusively at Bella's sister, May, with her, rather favorably, retuning his look.

The tall, newcomer stated a simple inquiry, "Is this the man, your worship?"

Bella looked first at her father, who nodded and pointed directly to Corazon and then at the mammoth constable's dauting frame. "Who do you think you are, and what are you doing here?"

The Chief Constable was completely unimpressed with the young woman's bravado. But was evidently enjoying what had turned out to be, a most awkward assembly, "M' Lady Bolton, I am simply here at your own father's request."

He smiled wickedly, while staring unwaveringly into her emerald green eyes, "Apparently, he has apprehended a thief who robbed you and murdered your coachman. I am simply here to see that he is put to justice. That's all." saying this with a very deep, yet somewhat charming voice, clearly with no malice intended against the girl.

"What do you mean...?" turning away, Bella looked shocked at the news. Then gaining her courage, once again stared unbelievingly at her father, her eyes drilling right through him.

"Enough!" her father yelled. "You will be silent, girl! Melissa Anne, take Anabelle to her room." her sister stood, attempting to help Bella away, all the while the duchess remained passed out, the butler close by, fanning her. Corazon sat completely still, not saying a thing.

"No, I will not go! This man saved me! He is not a criminal!"

"Bella!" Corazon finally spoke out loud, his voice sounding regal and commanding, shocking the room to silence. "It's alright, I'll be fine. Remember what I told you of the animals in the wood. They always return to feed. I will see you again..., then."

And proudly standing up, he slowly walked toward the door, placing himself in the custody of the constable in black.

"You will never see my daughter again, you rogue!" the Duke shouted as Corazon calmly strolled past him.

The policeman's assistant immediately took possession of his sword and knife, and after placing the knave's hands behind his back, tied them up with strong twine. As he did this, Corazon smiled, remembering that, thankfully, he had left is quiver and bow atop the old carriage. He was absolutely certain he would see them again. He would, however, need to find a new sword and knife.

Bella and her sister watched all of this in abject horror, until the Duke stood up and shoed them violently from the room. Literally chasing them out. Bella looked back at Corazon through the doorway as she left, clearly concerned, receiving only a crooked smile in return. He only hoped she had understood his puzzle. The two girls disappeared into the bowels of the house, leaving only the men. And the swooned Duchess of course!

"Chief Constable, thank you so much for coming, I was not sure you would get my message in time." the Duke added.

"You need not have worried your worship; I came as soon as your emissary informed me of your rather unique... visitor." the tall man's voice had subtly changed pitch into that of a sneering scowl, his obvious hatred of the knave evident in every word.

"Well, I am glad you made it just the same." the old man wiped his brow, "This man is a menace and must be taken care of."

"Oh, don't you worry about that," the Chief Constable said, taking Corazon by the arm and leading him away, "we will take very good care of your friend here."

And turning away, he chuckled frighteningly.

Chapter 5 - Prisoner

The two well-dressed lawmen escorted Corazon back through the Bolton estate's cavernous entry hall and then out into the bright daylight. Awkwardly, the knave squinted against the harsh light, temporarily blinded, while his eyes made their adjustment. It was not long before he could see again which soon revealed where his escorts were leading him.

A large, enclosed midnight black carriage awaited in the forecourt. But it was not a normal coach by any means. Each of the doors and sides of the rather awkward looking brougham, were heavily reinforced with riveted steel and the open windows were covered in thick, black iron bars. The huge wheels were also reinforced and presumably their axels strengthened as well, considering the excessive weight resting upon them. Two extremely large brewery horses sat at its head, the burden of the bulky vehicle requiring their robust strength to motivate it.

This prisoner landau lay in the gravel courtyard just outside the house, its wheels heavily depressed in the loose stones of the drive. Without any argument, Corazon let the two peacekeepers force him inside, subsequently slamming a very solid door behind him. After the relative coolness of the sitting room, the heat of the noon day sun was burning and had warmed the awaiting black hearse to stifling. The knave quickly found himself breaking into an uncomfortable sweat. Now feeling the heat, in more ways than one.

"So, my fine friend," the Chief Constable taunted him, looking in through the window, "uncomfortable isn't it? You don't look so brave or confident now, all trussed up like a pig on your way to slaughter."

Corazon just stared at him meekly, not showing any cards, a small dribble of salty water, from under his brow, running down his face.

"My name is Robertson, Chief Constable, Robertson," the tall man added snidely, "and I take it your name is Squire Corazon."

Corazon continued to ignore him.

"What's the matter, knave? Cat got your tongue."

He waited briefly for a reply, and when none was forthcoming, he continued, "No matter, we will have lots of time to chat later. I apologize the accommodations could not be more..., pleasant."

The man laughed at him again, before turning to his aide. "Hurry up, Stiles, we have a long way to ride!" and without further dialogue, he jumped up onto the driver's couch, waiting for his assistant to mount and take the reign. "I'm afraid it's off to Penbrooke Prison for you, Monsieur."

The Chief Constable cackled again, his voice sharp and loud, as the whip cracked and the horses jumped, yanking at the heavy carriage. It almost didn't move, it was so heavy and so deeply immersed in the gravel, but eventually the strong backs of the horses got it shifted, before the coach moved slowly away from the house and down the gravel drive between the towering elms.

Corazon quickly turned as much as he could and through the barred rear window, looked up at the front of the Bolton mansion, gradually disappearing in the distance. Thankfully, he saw a familiar pretty face, framed in ginger, stare back at him from one of the open windows and smiled. Yes, indeed, he breathed out, spinning around and facing forward, sliding back on the hard bench. Bella had heard what the constable had said and therefore, knew exactly where they were taking him. Tonight, the knave was certain, he would see her again.

***

The ride was extremely uncomfortable. Certainly not like the pleasant, if not fast, trip in that morning. Even the decrepit old coach that the Duke asked to have burned, was more pleasant on the road than this iron contraption. The reinforced suspension, produced a very rough ride and, combined with the fact that his hands remained firmly behind his back, he was unable to comfortably steady himself.

Needless to say, Corazon was not a happy man. But he took it all in stride, knowing that he had already fully recognized the possibility of capture when he decided to return Bella to her home. He had been convinced the Duke might turn him in, but still had been willing to risk it for the sake of the girl's safety. Regrettably, he had not been wrong.

It had been a rather unfortunate adult life so far for Corazon, being born into a very wealthy and important family in a neighboring county. Not liking the way his stuck-up parents and siblings behaved or treated others, in his late teens, he had escaped out on his own. To brave the world as an outsider, a renegade. Similar to what young Bella had done yesterday, but in his case, succeeding.

That was why he had known the ways of the court that very morning. That was why he had been able to address and greet the Duke and his wife by their proper titles. He was not some poor, down on his luck, forest dweller by chance. It was his own choice to live in that cave. Away from his past, away from his family and away from the horrible life of his childhood.

As a young man, Corazon had everything anyone might desire; a grandiose home, plush, expensive clothes, rich food, advanced combat training and a fine stallion to ride. But all of that meant nothing to him, living in a house where the servants were treated like cattle, or sometimes worse, and where his parents thought of him only as a trophy, just another fixture for their parties. Children should be seen and not heard, just as Anabelle had said. He remembered it well, for he had witnessed it again that very morning between Bella and her father and was repulsed by it. It sickened him to no end.

Corazon just could not abide in the awful sense of privilege that infused his ancestral home. How it had resulted in his family feeling ultimately superior, thinking themselves more important, over and above everyone and everything else. He didn't think the birthrights or fancy titles helped much either, but it was not only that.

What was worse, was his parent's innate sense of personal power. Supposedly bestowed on them at birth, to devise law and order, all without any need for consultation or consideration for the greater good. Whatever helped fill the kingdom's coffers, regardless whether it be on the backs of the rich or the poor. And it always tended to be the poor who received the bad end of the stick. He had hated the life of the advantaged and, until things changed, or the situation otherwise demanded it, he would never go back.

Instead, he saw himself as a man of the people, an advocate for the common man, the poor man. One who was there to protect those that needed protecting, those who could not possibly protect themselves. And certainly, if a rich girl with a conscience, happened to be in trouble, he was not picky. He would help anyone who asked for it, or even didn't ask for it, as the case might be.

Corazon just wanted to insure there was justice in the world, fair and honest justice. Equality for all men and women, no matter what their station or birthright. And if was not going to be provided by the courts, the lawmakers, or the regents, then he would provide it himself.

This was in exact opposition to the kind of treatment the Duke, this self-righteous Chief Constable and his lacky, were offering him just now. Railroading him on some trumped-up charge, sending him to jail for no reason other than his look. Incarcerating him only because of who he was, where he came from. Entirely, misunderstanding what had occurred and why. Without even caring to know the real truth behind the story.

He would show them. They were no better than the rest of the rich, arrogant and self-important partisans of that country, including the royals. He knew they all stuck together, all thought the same way, all dreamed in black and white. Never opening their eyes to the infinite possibilities or even the potential ones. Never once seeing the good in their fellow man. Only believing the worst. Only thinking of the law, their law, regardless whether it was right or wrong.

All he needed to do now was affect his escape. And if Bella had understood his message, that would be sooner than they might think.

Bella. He had liked that girl from the beginning. Liked her fire, her bravado and her enthusiasm. He liked her spunk and bravery and, most particularly, liked the thought that she had wanted out of her rich, meaningless life, just as he once had. A girl tired of the same things he was. Maltreatment of the common man and the wealthy feeling they were better than all the rest.

Corazon had learned throughout his life that no one person is better than any other. And it is your own personal choice that determines the type of person you are going to be. It's how you feel and how you act that determines who you are. It's not how you treat your superiors that measures your worth as a human being, but instead, how you treat the man serving you, or the beggar on the street, that counts. And certainly not how much money you have, where you are born or which family you were born into. His own family had never learnt that. And, apparently, neither had Anabelle's.

Like him, Bella understood all of that. And in running away from her rich family and birthright like she had done, Anabelle had demonstrated that she was just like him. A real kindred spirt. Someone who fought for fair and equal justice for all. Respect for one another, no matter what their upbringing or heritage.

It was funny that he had met her in that clearing by the wood, put upon by thieves. Normally, it would have been he who had robbed her expensive coach, stolen her possessions and sent her sorry, rich self on her way. To walk home, as he had done to so many similarly wealthy folks in the past.

Then, after having acquired all these forms of the rich man's plunder, he would have immediately given those expensive things away to those who needed it. Starving widows and their families, small, independent farmers with fallow fields, orphans and sick children. The poor and downtrodden of this society.

But yesterday, instead of being the rogue, he had been the one to rescue wealthy Bella from the hands of thugs. Four men so unlike himself in every way. Greedy men only thinking for themselves, with not one ounce of concern for the good of others. Bandits in every sense of the word, for they even robbed themselves of a better world, a harmonious lifestyle. Truly, lost hooligans that deserved their fate, their rampant selfishness ultimately leading to their untimely, but most deserved, deaths.

It was a great shame and a pity that the constabulary of the region could not tell men like himself, apart from those resembling the four thugs he had dispatched so easily, so brazenly. The reason for that was the lawmakers of this region were all the same. Things were always so black and white to them. Those so-called leaders, thinking things easy, only to make them more difficult.

Well, unfortunately the world was not like that. Sometimes things were grey, or even multi-coloured. Meaning, sometimes, it was conscience and empathy, or concern and appreciation for life, that made the decisions for you. Sometimes it was just love. Love for your fellow man. Love for what was right and just.

But the wealthy landowners, county constabulary and rulers of the land did not see that, or even try to understand it. One either upheld the law, or broke the law, regardless of your logic, reasoning or purpose.

At first glance, this might appear to be a very reasonable way of thinking, certainly there was some sense to it, for without it one might say you would have anarchy. And in most instances, they would be correct.

But there are always some laws, particularly the unjust ones, ones that give the rich more money, while continually drawing it away from the poor, that are simply made to be broken. Should be broken. And, if there was to be any justice for the common people, must be broken. At all costs.

Corazon was one of those men who chose justice, pure and simple. He would only break the law where it helped, not hindered the development of society and would do so as often, as frequently and as prudently as possible to maintain his goal of fairness for all. Needless to say, it sometimes it got him into trouble. Big trouble.

Smiling, he cherished all of these thoughts as the iron coach jogged and bounced over the countryside, the sound of the galloping horses, the crunching of the gravel under the wheels and the squeaking of the steel, all reminding him of his ultimate goal. He moved his head against the bars to feel the cool breeze glance against his face, knowing that eventually, all would be well.

***

Gazing out the window, about fifteen minutes into their ride, Corazon noticed that they had driven right through the village of Eastborough, before turning directly north, and venturing deeply into the green hills beyond. The road remained rough and potholes abounded, making the wagon twist and jerk as it made its way higher into the mountains. But they were also beginning to slow, due to the ever-increasing grade. The horses evidently having a much harder time puling the heavy steel carriage up the mounting slope.

This sudden change in elevation brought on a different kind of scenery as well. Rather than pleasant countryside rolling along through the bars, the only things visible were disagreeable rocky outcroppings and scrub brush. For they had long since left the village and meadow far behind and were now quite high in the surrounding hills.

The weather too had transformed, the sun having dipped behind the developing clouds, creating a marked drop in temperature. Meaning the excess perspiration still left on the knave's skin was now cooling, adding an extremely unpleasant chill to all of the other various disagreeable aspects of this most uncomfortable journey.

Corazon still managed a smile, however, when he overheard the Constable's driver complain, "Sire Robertson, this sudden cold is so bitter, might we stop for a hot drink?"

"No, you fool," replied the Constable, "we have somewhere to be. Now stop complaining and get a move on."

Although the man was obviously not impressed with his assistant's complaint, the tone of his voice signified that he too desired a warm refuge, and soon.

It turned out they would both get their wish, for within the hour the coach entered another gravel drive, stopping sharply in front of a rectangular stone building nestled smartly against the sheer rock face of the mountainside. At that location, the various surrounding outcroppings effectively cut down the blowing wind, offering the trio a brief respite from the biting cold.

The low roofed structure, at which their journey terminated, was every bit the antithesis of Eastborough Hall. The main walls were a dark grey granite, all cold looking and morose. The wood trim was painted black, offering no colour to an already drab looking facility. The single-story construction was clearly an institution of some kind and heavy iron bars, similar to those on the carriage, were mounted at every opening

But the building had obviously seen better days, appearing very unkempt, almost abused. The structure had evidently not been altered, renovated or even maintained since its initial construction as was demonstrated by the poor condition of the existing construction materials. The mortar around the various bricks and windows, for instance, was soft and spalling off, the cooler temperatures and higher humidity not helping in anyway. The black trim was completely faded to an almost light grey and, in some places, the aged splintering wood could be seen beneath.

The slate tile of the roof showed signs of wear as well as damage from rockfall and many of the ceramic gutters were broken and hanging loose from the rafters.

A large sign above the main entry stated they had, however, reached their destination. All in all, the grand Penbrooke Prison was a very sorry looking facility. But rather than feel depressed about its current state, Corazon actually laughed to himself.

"The state this place is in, it should be no problem to arrange an escape. That is provided Bella brings a horse!" this he said only to himself, now quite pleased with the Constable's poor choice of venue.

"Well, Corazon."

Speak of the devil. The Chief's voice rang out loudly over the whispering wind. "It's time to disembark from your delightful carriage ride. We do hope you enjoyed it?" sneering rather malevolently as he placed a large skeleton key in the lock to release the heavy door.

"Indeed, my good man, Indeed. It was very pleasant." returning the Constable's jest in an equivalently mocking manner before motioning with his body, "Please lead on."

Once open, Corazon stepped out himself, almost falling in the process. With his hands tied behind his back, it had offset his regularly very steady balance. Once he had recovered, he stood up tall.

The knave's reinvigorated bravado rather upset the Chief and as the knave passed him, he harshly pushed against his back, forcing Corazon forward.

This time, he did lose his balance, falling face first into the gravel. "Oh, my apologies, Monsieur Corazon," the devil said, as he pulled him roughly to his feet, "you must watch your step, the footing here can be a bit tricky."

There was now blood dripping from the knave's lower lip and one side of his face was severely lacerated. But he did not offer the Constable any reply, just moved on ahead through the open door of the facility, that had already been accessed by the Chief's shivering assistant.

"Right through here, Corazon" he taunted, the sound of his voice wavering in the cold, "we have a nice room just waiting for you."

Again, his method of speech was nowhere near as menacing as his superior but the disgust with which he said it added just the right amount of hatred to the statement.

Once inside, they immediately closed the large wooden door, shutting out the wind and frigid cold. Down a short hallway, found the trio in a small reception room, a plain wooden table placed in its center. The heavy furniture's legs were wide and stocky, just like the man sitting behind it.

The prison custodian was an enormously portly man, seated on a stool and looking up at them intently, as if they had been expected. Small beady eyes, under huge bushy brows, looked out of his red, chubby face adorned with a generous set of jowls that shook with every breath. He was so fat and obese that the flesh of his massive, hose encased buttocks overflowed his seat, hanging down rather grotesquely on either side. His fleshy arms, like hocks of ham, lay flat on the table beside a paper book and quill, sitting at the ready, in an inkwell beside it.

"T' what do I owe de pleasure, Const'ble," he mumbled, his voice slurred, his cheeks flapping, "we weren't expect'n yer today?"

"Neither was I expecting to be here, Lucky," the Chief grinned at the warden, "but this knave here, found his way into our laps and needed attending to." adding without pause, "he's here for safe keeping, I trust you can handle that, can't you?"

"D'rn rights, Chief, Sire," the fat man replied, "I'll book'm in right nows then, sh'll we?"

The man's huge stomach prevented him from sitting up close to the table, so he had to lean over to reach the quill and book.

"Name?" he chortled, flesh wobbling.

When their prisoner did not reply, the Constable spoke up for him. "Our friend here is not very talkative. We will have to remedy that," and with a quick turn, he forced his large, gloved fist into Corazon's belly, doubling him over. The surprised blow clearly hurt the nobleman and with a loud grunt, he fell to the floor. Once more, with tears rising to his eyes, he was pulled roughly to his feet.

"His name is Corazon."

"Cora.... what?" the fat man asked, stupidly.

"Corazon," when the warden made a face, the constable spelled it out loudly, "C.O.R.A.Z.O.N."

The big man grunted as he wrote, repeating the letters in time with Robertson's voice. "Thar!" he stated triumphantly, putting a large dot at the end of the name. "E's nah, one of us."

"Your assistance is always appreciated, Lucky" Robertson added condescendingly, the fat man not realizing his jibe.

I 'sume ya'll want ta quest'n 'im, eh?" smiling jeeringly, his fat lips splitting unevenly.

"You are correct, my good man," Robertson making a face, "can I use the regular room?"

"B' ya'll means, Chief, Sire. E's all yers." raising one of his arms and gesturing down the hall, the sagging skin on his upper arm jiggling excessively.

"Won't be long."

And he grabbed Corazon by the shoulder ushering him out of the room. Then, as an afterthought he turned back to the warden, saying, "Hey Lucky, while I question the prisoner, can you get Stiles here a cup of tea?"

His assistant looked on with great appreciation.

"Sure T'ing, Chief, anyt'ing yer say." Getting up from his stool, his flesh flowing off the seat and back into his buttocks, the huge man waddled over to a small fire roaring in the corner, hanging a brass kettle over the blaze, "Shun'dt be l'ng, Stiles, Sire."

Corazon heard no more of their pleasant exchange as he was roughly manhandled down the hall into an open room. Once again, with the heavy hand of Robertson on his back, he almost fell but by now, having found better balance, was able to stumble on ahead without incident.

The room they entered was small, no more than 10 feet by 10 feet, equipped sparingly with two chairs and a bench. On one wall, about four feet off the floor, was a rusted iron shackle buried deep into the stone. Robertson roughly forced Corazon in that direction and lifting his bound hands up toward his shoulders from behind, secured him uncomfortably to the shackle.

The pain was excruciating, as the bastard had not undone his wrists before placing them in the restraint. That left Corazon standing in a very precarious, slightly crouched position, the only way in which he might reduce the agonizing backward tension on his arm and shoulder muscles. Ultimately, ending up facing the floor, the only thing he could do was observe the wear marks in the grey brown stone below, presumably made by one of the rooms previous tenants.

Once he was secured, Robertson turned and grabbing one of the available chairs, pulled it in close, sitting right next to his prisoner's straining form.

"So, Corazon my friend," he sneered at him, light drops of spittle hitting the knave's face, "now that it's just you and me, what shall we talk about?"

Corazon knew then that it was going to be a very long and tedious afternoon.

Chapter 6 – Interrogation and Attempted Escape

It was indeed a long afternoon, the Constable being entirely relentless with his questioning. Time and time again, asking about the knave, his life and his origins, his recent movements and what had he been doing out in the forbidden forest. Corazon remained completely silent throughout the interrogation, not offering Robertson even as much of a hint of his recent activities.

It displeased the tall man to no end and, after about half an hour, Robertson began to get testy. The Constable finally stood up from the chair in frustration, kicking it violently towards the corner, then began pacing the small room, agitation clearly displayed all over his features.

"Well, Monsieur Corazon, if you will not talk to me, how on earth am I to help you?" he stated rather loudly in irritation.

This was a different tactic and wanting the acute pain in his muscles to stop, the knave decided to take the bait, opening his mouth for the first time. "You, are going to help..., me?"

"Ah, so he does speak after all."

His singular response finally eliciting a smile from his interrogator.

"Indeed, I am not mute."

"You could have fooled me."

"What do you really want, Constable? You said, to help me?" then he tried to help himself, his voice tired, "It might help us both, if you were to release me. So that we could sit together... as gentlemen."

"Release you? Gentlemen? But you are a brigand, Sire. I'd hardly call you a gentleman."

"You might be surprised," Corazon stated under his breath. But instead, he said to Robertson out loud, "Well then, let's just say, I'll promise to act like a gentleman. That is, if you release me, of course."

The Constable thought it over a moment, silence again prevailing. The knave's request clearly under his consideration. "I have your word as a gentleman then, you will answer my questions if I release you?"

"Indeed, you do, Constable. I only wish to sit. In a more comfortable position. And relieve my arms of the severe strain they are presently under."

"But my good man, that strain is exactly what is supposed to be making you talk."

"How's that been working for you so far, Constable?"

The tall man thought a moment, "Not very well."

"Well then," Corazon returned, now sure he had the Constable ready to bargain, "shall we try a different way, a more humane way. You might be surprised. One often finds they get more flies to honey than to vinegar."

"Ah yes, you are right, of course. But instead, I could just make it even more painful for you."

"You could and I would just continue to remain silent. It's your choice."

With that, Robertson was sold. And making a move over towards the wall, he expertly drew his knife swiftly cutting the bonds holding Corazon to the wall. Immediately, the knave dropped his arms in relief, letting out a deep breath and, selecting the nearest chair, sat down.

Corazon noticed at once that not only had he been released from the wall clasp, but the stiff twine binding his hands was also gone. This surprised him, and immediately put him on guard. What was Robertson playing at?

Regardless, he took full advantage of this bizarre generosity, spending a short time rubbing his wrists and arms, attempting to relieve the pain and bring some circulation back to his mistreated extremities.

Looking up at the Constable still standing by the wall, he simply said, "Thank you."

"You're welcome." said Robertson, giving him a slight bow of his head. "Now that you're no longer under the stress of the clasp, perhaps you might tell me what you were doing in the woods?"

"It's much too soon for that, I'm afraid."

"Is it, really?" Robertson revealed his cards, "You might be interested to know, Corazon, that I am fully aware you did not kill that coachman. As it happens, I had a personal envoy following young Bella throughout her entire ride yesterday afternoon. One who was there to witness the supposed scene of the "accident". My man did not see everything, but did confirm there were at least three, if not four, different men killed in that clearing. So, I have it on good authority that the story you told the Duke was correct."

"How are you aware of what I told the Duke?" the knave questioned.

"I have my ways." was the only reply he received.

Corazon ignored him, "So, you will also know then, that it was myself who rescued young Miss Bolton from certain death, or worse."

"Yes, I heard what transpired and what that dirty brigand bastard was about to attempt. And for that, I thank you." and again, he surprised the knave, "You see, there was a reason I was having the Lady Anabelle Bolton followed." before Corazon could say anything, he continued, "And no, it was not at the Duke's insistence. You see, I happen to have developed a rather strong fondness for that somewhat, spirited girl. Unfortunately, she does not share the same attraction to me."

"No surprise there," the knave said under his breath, grinning.

"What was that?" Robertson asked coming closer.

"I said, that is a big surprise, Sire, but also a welcome one. However, I could have used the assistance of your... envoy during the battle."

The knave deflected quite well and Robertson, not suspecting a thing, continued.

"From what my associate relayed to me, it was not much of a battle Corazon, but more a rout, a very one-sided affair. Apparently, you did just fine on your own. Polishing off those men quite smartly, without so much as breaking a sweat." he approached Corazon closely, "What I would really like to know is what happened afterwards? And where did young Bella one, stay the night and two, get that dress?" He counted the items off on his long, thin fingers.

Ah, thought Corazon so that was it. The man was jealous.

"Let's just say she spent a comfortable night under shelter and by herself!" Corazon stated, stressing the last part, before pausing, "And considering her outfit was ruined, courtesy of the thug, she could not possibly travel home in what she had. All I did was provide her with a new gown from my collection."

"Your collection? You collect women's attire?" he said it as an insult.

"I collect anything of value that happens to fall into my hands, Constable..." waiting for a reaction before adding, "and then, afterwards, pass it on to those that need it most."

"Ah, I see," Robertson was quiet for a moment, considering what had been said. "You see, Corazon, there have been reports of a country knave that attacks wealthy citizens during their travels, always leaving the owners unharmed, but not before completely relieving them of their fine possessions first. You wouldn't happen to know anything about that now, would you?"

The way he said it, meant it was purely a rhetorical question. Corazon said nothing.

"Such foolishness is not to be tolerated, not in my county anyway. Theft for whatever reason, even a high and mighty one, is still theft." Robertson sneered at Corazon, his attitude at once passing back from friend to enemy. "I think, my unfortunate friend, despite your recent and very much appreciated heroics, that we will have to hold you. At least until we can get more specific information about your exact whereabouts for the last several weeks."

And smiling wickedly, he walked over to the rooms closed door, knocking on the inside, while adding, "I hope you don't mind, but my good friend, Lucky here, will take great care of you."

And then he opened the door, exposing the obese guard standing ready with a rusty set of iron manacles.

The portly man swept past him and proceeded under the Constable's protection to rebind Corazon's wrists. As he finished, Robertson turned back to Corazon, concluding their conversation, "I should think that the experience of a few days in one of the cells here, may result in you being just a tad more talkative."

"What happened to the honey, Constable?" Corazon asked, once more in manacles.

"Oh, my friend, I think we both left that back at the Bolton estate."

And then, with a swing of his cape he left, leaving Lucky to take the knave's arm and escort him out of the interrogation room and down the passage towards the cells.

The hall stank of sweat, urine and feces. It was also moist, water constantly dripping down onto the floor through holes in the roof, making large puddles in the stone. As they passed several doorways, Corazon could hear many uncomfortable sounds, bouts of teeth chattering and various inmates talking to themselves. Sometimes, only haunting silence. He decided to take a moment to make conversation.

"So how long have all these fellows been here?"

"Theys been 'ere a long time, mate. Sort 'a like yous gonna be," laughing, the warden's jowls and breasts shook, as he inhaled noisily. "Stops the chats and get in 'ere," offering an open cell door and directing Corazon to enter with his plump fist.

Thankfully, the tiny compartment was empty, just one of the many spare holding cells around the perimeter of the prison. The small room had a little barred window that revealed the darkening sky outside, while letting in a brisk, chilling wind. A hard bed of mouldy straw was the single piece of furniture that adorned the, not so cozy, chamber. As Corazon made straight for the cot, looking forward to a rest no matter how awful looking the accommodation, the warden stopped him.

"Uh, uh, pretty boy. Yous going thar," and he pointed with a chubby, sausage finger, to another iron loop, except this one was high up on the far side of the wall. He manhandled the knave over and lifting his bound hands above his head, connected the manacles to the clasp. Thankfully, this time Corazon's hands had been bound in front so, while his weight hung from the contraption rather painfully, the position was much more bearable.

"Th's way," the guard mumbled, "yous won't be goin' no place." chuckling to himself as he put the key in his tunic pocket. "Yous 'ave a grit nigh' now, ya 'ere"

Then he slammed the cell door closed with a metallic thump and disappeared up the corridor, his flesh slapping loudly as he did so, a scurry of rodent feet running haphazardly in his wake.

There was no lantern within the cell but gratefully, there was a large torch burning right outside, used to illuminate the passageway. The dim orange flame cast its glow eerily through the barred door, providing Corazon with a small measure of light in which to investigate his very meager surroundings. The room was completely barren save for the bed, all of the slightly moist, grey stone walls giving the place a very dreary atmosphere. There was a dark puddle of moisture in a small depression off in one coroner that reeked of human waste, obviously having been placed there by the room's previous occupant.

Corazon stared out the window at the last vestiges of the failing sun, feeling the shadows of the night press in against him, making him shiver even more. He was glad, however, that the fools had not robbed him of his clothes. For they sometimes did that in places such as this, so he counted his blessings. He tried in vain to pull his hands free, his efforts only serving to cut and chafe the already sore skin on his wrists. But on the final tug, before giving up, he could have sworn he detected a scraping sound of metal on concrete. That was promising. He would rest a while, before trying again later.

Night fell and the evening air became even colder, keeping Corazon wide awake. His arms were beginning to hurt once again, his legs now feeling the effort of keeping himself upright for the many hours since he had last seen the obese guard. He was very pleased to have participated in tea at the Bolton's, for the small amount of cake and fluid had sustained him throughout most of the day. But now his stomach growled with hunger.

There was little sound except for the constant tap-tap of dripping water and the occasional light flare of the wall torch's flame outside the room. He was sure it had been several hours since he had heard the constable and his assistant ride away. The law men having left the heavy carriage in the prison's forecourt and each taking only one of the two large horses in order to hasten their journey home. Corazon was, indeed, all alone.

After a few more hours and no sign of Bella, he began to get worried. Had the girl not heard him? Did she not know where the prison was? Could she not, because of her father's anger, find a way to sneak out of her house? These were all questions running through his mind as he slowly began falter, slipping downward, his legs giving out. Straining to keep his head up, his vision centered on the opposite side of the room.

Looking longingly at the old threadbare hay of the cot, Corazon wanted only to lie down and take some pressure off his aching arms. That was the case, until another sound reached his ears. A soft, rustling noise, that appeared to be coming from that side of the chamber. He stared intently at the surface of the bed, suddenly noticing an undulating movement within the loose straw. In the half light, for just a moment, a small brown field mouse exposed his furry nose, its whiskers twitching before plunging back inside and burrowing deeper.

Perhaps, it's a good thing I was not able to use the bunk after all, supposed Corazon, immediately returning his thoughts to his present predicament.

The knave could not even slump down for rest even if he wanted, as every time he tried, the pressure was just too great on his wrists, bringing him out of his stupor and cutting into his skin even more. Eventually, after several bouts of semi unconsciousness, he felt a warm dribble seeping down the inside of his arm, the minor flow of blood itching his skin. It soon became like ice in the bitter cold, irritating him even further. Where on earth was Bella?

Then, outside, he heard the sound of a horse tentatively approaching on the gravel. It began quietly, the animal clearly being driven gently over the loose stone surface. He smiled, breathing a great sigh of relief, believing young Bella to have finally arrived. Ultimately, the noise of its advance stopped, and instead he heard only the stallion breathing and then, what was surely the light crunch of feminine feet on the crushed rock surface.

Corazon detected her moving sideways along the wall of the prison, away from his window, the sounds of her footfall diminishing. In an effort to alert her, he yelped. But the exclamation came out as just a dry hack and the attempt felt flat. For he realized he had not had a drink since the tea that afternoon, almost 12 hours previously. Clearing his scratchy throat, he tried again, this time louder, his groan wafting into the night like a hoot of an owl. One with a very sore gullet!

His second attempt, apparently successful, alerted the visitor and soon afterward, the footfalls retuned. His heart jumped in his chest as he detected the soft, beautiful voice of Anabelle Bolton, who had indeed come. Just as he had requested.

"Corazon? Is that you?" low but inquisitive.

"Bella, I'm here, come to the window."

Within moments he could see her ivory forehead, crowned in ginger, between the window bars of his cell. Then she shifted, the hallway torchlight providing just enough illumination to see the top portion of her pretty face, bright red cheeks and a bit of chin as she struggled to look inside.

"It's too high, Corazon, I can't see you. What am I to do?" her voice was strained, unsure.

"Bella, listen to me. You brought one of you father's beautiful stallions, didn't you?"

"Of course! Although he doesn't know it, they love me even more than him and will do anything for me." he sensed she was smiling.

"Okay, listen, I want you to attach a section of rope to the bars on the window and then connect it to your saddle. Because of the lingering moisture, the structure here is weak and with enough force, you should be able to pull the bars free. Can you do that?" he himself had begun struggling at his manacles once again, finally feeling the bolt of the wall's iron ring, loosen.

"Of course. Just give me a few minutes," her reply immediate, before she disappeared, the sound of her feet on the ground signifying she had returned to the horse.

Corazon continued to struggle, blood now flowing freely from several new cuts in his wrists, but the cast iron ring was coming free, he could feel it. As he looked up to notice Bella's small, soft hands wrapping twine around the bars, he finally felt the steel break away completely and he fell to the floor, free at last. It was blissful to be able to rest there on the pavement, even though the place stank, and crimson blood was flowing even more copiously around the manacles still binding his arms. He jumped up to try and see out, stepping up on the side of the cot to do so.

Outside, Bella had everything prepared, the rope now bound securely to the bars at one end and her magnificent steed's saddle on the other. She jumped up on the animal's back and spurring him on disappeared into the dark. There was a huge whinny then Corazon saw the rope go taught and the bars screech and bend in their casing. After a brief flash of dust and some movement, the metalwork seized, holding fast.

In his anxiety to escape, Corazon called out rather loudly, "Come on back, Bella and try again, except this time take more space."

He saw her canter back to the window, a smile on her full face. "It's going to come apart this time for sure," she said, before once again encouraging the horse, the two of them prancing energetically away into the dark.

This time they got up quite a bit speed, before feeling the sharp counter pull of the rope. On this second attempt, the bars bent and twisted, the loose, moist concrete mortar finally giving way and violently ripping an opening, as the whole cast iron assembly was torn completely from its support.

Far off in the dark, Corazon heard the stallion nicker in complaint, but they had done it! He jumped down and moving the cot as best he could with his shackled arms, he moved it below the ragged window opening. Then he climbed back up and thrusting his arms out, began pushing wildly against the wall, forcing his body through the tattered hole. He got some of the way through until his shoulders forced him to stop. He squirmed and shifted, twisting and shoving, trying his best, but just could not get through. Corazon now desperate, moved in a different direction, trying again, but still, it was no use.

"Bella!" he shouted looking down at her.

"Yes, Corazon?"

"Throw me the rope."

"But the bars are still connected to it." she commented, not understanding.

"Fine, throw me the bars then."

Anabelle didn't actually plan to throw the bars, but fingering out what he was after, went to find them. They were lying a short distance away, the frame and bars still in one piece, tied to the rope. Lifting them up off the ground, which was quite hard for her considering her light frame, she trotted the horse over to Corazon's awkwardly hanging body, handing him the heavy frame. He gripped it tightly in his manacled hands and then said.

"Okay my dear, once more. Spur him on and pull me out. Just like you did the bars."

"Oh, Corazon I can't do that! I'll pull your arms off!" Bella cried, scared.

"No, you won't, lass. I'll be fine. Just do it!" Corazon's voice was forceful, so sure of himself.

She looked at him with a renewed concern in her face, but reluctantly cantered away, spurring the stallion on one final time. The rope lost its slack and suddenly Corazon felt a pressure in his arms like no other. The pain was far worse than any of the foul treatments the police had given him that day. He screamed loudly, stupidly holding on. But instead of popping free from the opening, all the added force did was jam his shoulders even further into the small opening, tearing his clothes and flesh very painfully against the stone frame.

Stubbornly and rather foolishly, he kept his futile grip on the cold steel. Just before his arms were torn from their sockets, but not before dislocating one of his shoulders, he let go of the iron and let it fly away into the night.

"Stop!" he yelled into the dark, and she did, immediately dropping the rope and trotting the stallion back to his window.

She looked up at him with tears in her eyes, "You see, I told you. I've hurt you."

Corazon eyes were watering with the agony burning in his shoulder and initially he could not move, "Yes, my dear. It was my fault. I suppose I was just so anxious to get out of here. We'll just have to find another way."

Reluctantly, after gaining some strength and gritting his teeth against the discomfort, he squirmed backward. As his one shoulder was already dislocated, he was able to contort his body, extracting himself rather painfully from the confines of the window. And not before cutting himself even further, just barely managing to get back safely into the room, cradling his heavily damaged arm.

"What are we to do now?" the frightened young woman asked from outside.

"Well, Bella, my dear," for the knave had thought of the only viable alternative, "how do you feel about portly men?"

Chapter 7 – Escape for Real This Time

The night remained cold and dark and Corazon remained tightly secure inside his cell in Penbrooke Prison. The walls remained upright and unmoving with Bella outside and the knave in. The open window no longer had any bars, but it had proven much too small for a successful departure. Something else had to be done to change all of that. Something rather unexpected... and likely very unpleasant. But not for him.

What Corazon had said at first, did not make any sense to Anabelle. Her brow furrowed as she considered his statement once again. *Why did he ask me my feelings about portly men? He was slim and muscular, far from portly?* Then she thought about it more closely, and realizing the truth, cringed.

With a disbelieving look on her face, Bella asked, "Corazon, what exactly are you suggesting?" all the while, unfortunately, knowing exactly what he was suggesting.

"Do you see the lights at the main door?" he asked, politely ignoring her question.

"Yes, what about them?" she did not want to do it.

"I'm going to ask that you head inside there." again, ignoring her.

"But isn't there a guard?" she asked tentatively, knowing perfectly well there was, but wanting to delay the inevitable as much as possible.

"Yes, indeed there is, Bella and that's where you come in." pausing slightly before continuing, clearly detecting the hesitation in her voice, "I need you to use your youthful feminine whiles to get him to open the door, or perhaps just get the key. Your choice." he stopped before confirming. "It really is the only way."

"You really want me, Anabelle Bolton, to sweet talk a prison guard?" she questioned, disbelievingly, her highbrow status finally peeking through.

"Well, my dear, if I'm going to get out of here tonight then, yes. I just can't fit through this small opening. Unless you happened to bring a large rock hammer along with you this lovely evening?"

"Well, no, I didn't," tugging anxiously at the bodice of her dress in fear, "but what am I going to say?"

"That's strictly up to you, Bella, my Sweet. I really can't help you there."

"My Sweet," she repeated, dreamily, "I like that."

"Well, if you manage to get me out of here, I'll call you that all the time." Corazon said, smiling to himself, despite the pain wracking his body, "Now get going."

"Alright, hold your horses." she said, now a bit more resigned as to what was in store.

"Ah, that reminds me. Make sure you leave the horse where he is within easy reach. Just in case."

"Will do," she looked back at him, through the window, or at least his shadow through the window, "you're absolutely sure, there's no other way."

"My dear, if there was, I would have told you already." and with another smile, he gave a final order, "Now go!"

***

Bella pulled the stallion by the reigns, leaving the broken opening of the knave's cell, making her way towards the front door of the prison. There was not a soul about, and it was relatively quiet, the night crystal clear with only a light wind. Walking slowly, delaying the inevitable as much as she could, Anabelle looked up at the star filled sky. Noticing firsthand that, from up here in the mountains, the stars appeared brighter, more magical, twinkling like diamonds on black velvet. The view was spectacular, peaceful and filled her with renewed purpose, spurring her on.

But in moving along the wall, she also detected the sounds of the prison's other various inmates chanting to themselves, crying or even screaming in their sleep. The darkness, the unfamiliar place and its disturbing sounds, all acting together to heighten her dread. Upon reaching the buildings front doorstep, she hesitated once again.

Tying her horse very loosely to the closest post, Anabelle found herself automatically straightening her skirt and hair. While seemingly strange, it also felt necessary, the actions natural and therapeutic. Mentally prepared once again and rustling up her courage, she placed her hand on the lever, trying the door. It was unlocked, the entry swinging open easily. This must bode as a good omen, Bella thought, and without further uncertainty, she made her way carefully inside.

The walls were whitewashed, but incredibly dirty. Blazing torches in the numerous iron wall brackets, provided ample light for her passage, staining the walls even further with black soot. Sandy footprints on the stone floor betrayed signs of recent activity, but at that time of night, there was absolutely no one around.

Upon reaching the last corner in the passage and turning into the reception vestibule Bella saw, in his usual place behind the table, the obese warden, Lucky. Sitting there asleep, his abundant fatty deposits once again, greatly overflowing his seat, gravity pulling the prolific excess towards the ground. He had one arm on the table and another on his cheek, his bald head bent over, his eyes closed. His snoring was so loud, it might have woken the dead, and with each new chortle, a small dribble of spittle oozed from his fatty, lopsided lips. Behind him, a fire roared in the hearth, providing a welcome breath of heat to an otherwise deathly cold room.

Thank goodness he's asleep, thought Bella. Now all I need to do is find the key.

She tiptoed towards the table, being careful not to make any noise, although with the warden's constant snorting and wheezing, he might not have heard her anyway. She had already spied the ring of skeleton keys, attached to the fat man's belt, and making her way around the far side of the room, she gently bent down reaching over to grab them.

All at once, the obese man sat up with a chortle, sniffing and rubbing his nose.

"Eh?" he asked, stretching his arms and yawning, "Wats dat smell?"

Evidently, the sleeping guard had detected Bella's expensive French perfume, its strong floral scent, waking him up. Even though she had put it on for Corazon, Anabelle immediately cursed herself for wearing it.

The drowsy warden finally noticed Bella, who had quickly and smartly straightened up, "Wats yous doin' 'ere, missy?" rubbing the sleep from his eyes, the girl backing slowly away, 'Dis 'eres a prisn' fer de male pris'ners."

With a loud groan and his flesh wobbling, he now stood, making a face as he did so, clearly thinking hard, "And, anyways 'tis the middle of da nigh', Wats yous 'ere fer?"

Well, here goes she thought. Using the sweetest, most feminine voice she could muster, she cooed, "Oh my, what a handsome man. When I saw you there asleep, I just had to come over to see if you were alright."

"'M fine, missy. Dar's nutt'n 'rong. Wats yous want?" then he added, realizing, "yer not supp'sed to ev'n be 'ere, missy."

"Oh, I know, good Sire, but I got lost on the trail and all the pretty lights brought me to you. Such a strong man." and, very reluctantly continuing her charade, she batted her lashes, "It is so nice and warm in here." she said, fanning herself.

"'deed, tis, missy, 'cause I keeps da fire goin' all nigh'," and he pointed to the hearth, the flames raging.

"Can you help me?"

"Wat's yous need, missy?" the warden looked at her with renewed interest.

"I need a room for the night and a bed to sleep in." was all she said, pointing down the hall.

"Awe, dunt 'ave nutt'n like dat, missy. Dis place 'eres for men. Bad men. Beds down d'er 'ere full o' mice. Nutt'n for a gran' lady like yerself."

After a short pause, and for the first time that night, he smiled leeringly at her, "but me 'ave me own room backs 'ere." pointing the other way, past the flickering blaze, with one of his sausage fingers, Per'aps yer wou'd like dat, eh!"

"Oh yes, Sire!" she said happily, clapping her hands together, "It would be so warm. And so cozy."

Smiling as seductively as she could manage, Bella added an invitation, "Would you like to come with me?" as an afterthought tilting her head and twirling her hair on one of her fingers.

The stout man's eyes nearly popped out of his head. Had he really been propositioned by this gorgeous young maid? Whatever the case, right or wrong, he was certainly going to take advantage of it. It was like a gift from the gods.

"Comes 'long den, missy, 'll show yous da way." with that he turned, ambling towards a door on the far wall.

"My that's a fine set of keys you have there," Anabelle said, pointing to the ring on his belt and following closely.

"Ah, dee's da keys to da kingd'm der, missy." lifting the ring off his belt and jingling them in front of her. "Ya like?"

"I do," she replied, with a wide smile, showing her pearly white teeth. "I assume your own room key is on that too, isn't it?"

"'Tis 'ndeed, missy." lifting a silver key and holding it up, "Dis da, one. Want 'a lock usselves in, do yer?"

"Well we wouldn't want to be disturbed, now would we?" another bright inviting smile. But by now, nervous perspiration began to build heavily on her brow as they neared the warden's suite.

"'Spose not?"

The warden continued towards the door, using the chosen key to open it. Swinging it wide open, he swiped at the air, with a flapping arm and hand, to show off his lair. The brief action only serving to highlight his malodorous, sweaty form.

The room was indeed cozy, containing a small, comfortable looking four poster bed, with large pillows and a nice thick duvet. There was a rough wooden desk in the corner and two black iron wall sconces, torches burning brightly to illuminate the space. A small round carpet covered the majority of the floor, and together with a painted ceramic water jug and bowl on the side table, gave the room a very homey feel. Considering the occupant of the chamber, it was surprisingly clean.

"'Ere 'tis missy, me 'ome away fr'm 'ome. Yer like it?" the chubby man exclaimed, very proud of himself.

"I love what you've done to the place," Bella commented, entering before him, slowing making her way gracefully over to the bed, touching every surface. Before sitting on the end closest to the door and wrapping her right arm seductively around one of the wooden posts.

"It's all so manly." stated Anabelle. Shifting her skirts a little and trying to expose more leg, she added invitingly, "Come, please, sit by me."

Saying this while using her left hand to tap the top of the coverlet encouragingly.

The warden's eyes widened, completely disbelieving his good fortune. Without hesitation, his jowls and other bodily flesh jiggling grotesquely, he hurriedly waddled his way across the chamber, sitting down heavily on the far end of the bed as directed. Beside his prospective conquest, but thankfully not too near.

Bella could now, however, really smell the chubby man's excessive body odour, his dirty clothing, and see his moist, puffy skin. Shifting uncomfortably on the bed and lightly rubbing her nose at the stench, she swallowed, her own perspiration building, her mouth dry.

But now, Anabelle was now closer to the door than he was, and it was time to make her move.

Coquettishly, she asked, "Kind sir, can I see your wonderful keys again? I just love the way they sparkle."

The warden lifted them up, holding them tantalizing in front of her, "Yer do like 'em, dun't yer, I knowed it."

She reached out to take them, but the warden snatched them quickly away, "Ah! Ah!" he said, shaking a chubby digit at her, "not yet, missy. I's wants a kis' f'rst."

Smiling rather crudely, he exposed his rotten teeth, several of them missing.

Bella cringed at the thought, smelling his horrid, sour breath. This rancid fragrance, combined with the unbearable scent of his intense body odour, almost made her gag, but she kept her cool and her fanciful expression. If that's what it was going to take to get Corazon out of here, then so be it.

"Certainly, good Sire," she said.

Slowly, holding her breath and bending over, she touched her lips lightly against his cheek. His flesh was moist and soft, the full day's stubble itching her lips as she planted a light, dry kiss on his disgusting, flabby flesh. With the hard part over, she quickly sat back, holding her hands out expectantly.

"Ah!" the guard was blushing, profusely, "I's like dat. 'Ere, missy," he said, finally handing her the key ring, "play t' yer 'arts cont'nt."

She carefully pried the ring from his large sweaty hand and immediately stood up.

"'Ey! We'r ya goin', missy." the fat man said, frowning.

"Just want to freshen up a bit, that's all." Anabelle said, heading toward the water jug. The warden seemed satisfied with her response and lay back on the bed, placated.

Bella was now standing, with her paramour sitting relaxed and unprepared. It was time to move. Quickly, she changed direction and was nearly halfway across the room, before the warden even noticed what was happening. And before he had even popped up and yelled, "Wah!", Anabelle was through the door.

Shutting it with a loud bang, Bella heard the warden grunt angrily behind it, followed by a hard thump, as having obviously moved too swiftly for his extra-large frame, the man had tumbled off the bed onto the floor. She already had the silver key in the lock before he had even recovered, and the strong door was safely locked by the time he began his lumbering gait to the entry.

With a hard, wet splat, he slammed his fat body, against the wood, now locked fast, yelling, "'Ey, Missy wats up? Taut yer w'nted cmpn'y."

"I do, big fella, I really do. Just not yours." laughing hysterically, rubbing her lips on her sleeve, she tore down the hall towards Corazon's cell, the warden still banging furiously on the locked door.

Bella swiftly made her way down the very hostile appearing cell corridor, lifting her long skirts high to keep them out of the dirty puddles. The action did not save her from the cold drops attacking her from the ceiling, spattering her from above, several dripping on the back of her neck and making their way into her clothes. Again, she heard the terrifying wailing and shrieking of some of the inmates, now echoing hauntingly in the enclosed space. The frightening sounds giving her the chills.

Passing one cell, a rough, dirty hand sprang out, reaching for her, accompanied by a stifled moan. As Bella swerved to avoid the outstretched arm, she ended up rubbing along one of the walls, covering one sleeve of her gown with a wet, green slime, making her shiver. She really wanted nothing more than to find Corazon and get out of this horrid place.

Finally, she saw the knave's face pressed against the bars of one of the rooms, his wonderful but very scratchy voice, urging her on.

It didn't take them long to find the right key. Soon the inner door of the cell was open, and the knave had her in his arms. Their embrace was hard earned, the warmth much appreciated after the earlier events of the evening. Suddenly he groaned as, in her eagerness for his touch, she had hugged just a bit too high and too hard, hurting his dislocated shoulder. Standing back abashedly, Bella apologized, looking distractedly on the ring for the key to open his rusty manacles.

"It should be one of the smaller ones," he quipped, regretting his frail outburst, just wanting to hold her tight again, thanking her for her efforts. But nothing more was said for the moment, the rather frantic search to get the cuffs off their new priority. Sure enough, the second small skeleton key they tried, finally loosened the damned fetters, freeing Corazon completely.

"Well, my Sweet, it appears you were successful. I trust it was not too difficult or disturbing for you."

"Well, I..."

Without further pause, Corazon bent down to kiss her, cutting off whatever she was going to say. Their eager lips touched only briefly, but with the satisfying moisture of cherished lovers. Separating reluctantly, they looked into each other's eyes, the orange glow of the torches enhancing their breathless features. Bella was absolutely enchanted and in a swoon.

The moment did not last. "Let's get going, we have to get away from here."

With his good hand, he softly touched her face, then holding the same arm at her waist, Corazon guided her back out of the door, and away from the cell.

And then they were off, running back down the passage toward the front entrance, all worry about the excessive moisture forgotten. As the pair passed the reception hall, they could hear the warden knocking on the rear chamber door, still anxious to be let out, "Missy, Missy, whr' 're yer?"

"Well, we won't be needing these anymore." Bella laughed, dropping the ring of keys on the table.

They were all ready to head out the door, when she stopped, grabbing Corazon's good arm, her pretty face flushed and suddenly concerned, "Will he be alright? Cooped up in there?" motioning to the locked door.

"He'll be fine, my Sweet. Let's go!"

"No, wait, Corazon." Bella said, holding both of his hands for emphasis, "What if nobody comes by for days? He'll die without any food or water. And who will feed the rest of the prisoners?"

Suddenly, Corazon realized that he had, indeed, finally met his match. For young Anabelle had just bested him in her concern for others and it melted his heart.

"Okay, you win, my Sweet," seeing her smiling at his acknowledgement and loving her for it. "Go outside, loosen the horse and be ready to ride. I will join you in a second."

Running from the building, Anabelle turned backward, and smiling brightly, blew him a kiss before disappearing out the door.

Corazon reacted immediately, first reaching for the ring on the table, then walking over to the wooden door. Behind the thick, hard wood, the fat man continued to yell, apparently still hoping his potential concubine might return. The knave fumbled with the keys, before finding the right one. Then, waiting for a break in the warden's incessant pounding, inserted it smartly in the mechanism, unlocking the door.

Leaving the ring in place and without waiting, he ran back around the heavy table, down the hall and out, not knowing if the portly guard realized he was free or not.

Just before exiting Penbrooke Prison, while clenching his teeth and grimacing strongly, Corazon rammed his dislocated shoulder hard against the wall surrounding the doorway. In much a similar way to what he had done once or twice before, against the wall of his own cave, after some of his previous, more strenuous, *excursions*. With a loud click and a stifled scream on his part, the bone popped smartly back into its socket. While the action did nothing to relieve the pain, or the various cuts and bruises on his body, it did allow him to move his arm again. Holding the opposite hand over the shoulder, he made a few circular stretching motions to verify its functionality. With that accomplished, he ran out of the putrid prison.

As instructed, Anabelle was already on her horse and ready to leave. Jumping up in front of her, he brushed his lips rather frantically against her cold cheek, before grabbing the reigns. With Bella holding tightly to his waist and without a break in the action, Corazon immediately spurred the animal to a gallop. After a random spray of loose gravel, they headed down the trail towards town.

Free at last!

Chapter 8 – Returning Home Again – Bella Tells Her Story

As before, almost like déjà vu, it was time to get young Bella home, but this time it would be under the cover of night. The long ride ahead of them, however, would also provide the couple, ample time to get acquainted. As he was quite interested in the details, Corazon began their chat by asking Anabelle what she had done to escape from the Bolton house that evening.

"Well, Corazon," she said, squeezing his waist as they continued down the trail, "after you had given me your clue at tea that morning, which by the way, I had worked out almost right away," she said whispering in his ear and smiling into the wind, "I knew, if any rescue was to be attempted, I would have to find some way of getting out of the house that night. But even more important, was to first find out what that nasty piece of work Robertson was going to do with you. And where he was going to hold you."

"After May and I had retired to my bedroom upstairs, my sister demanded I get undressed, so she could put me to bed. Avoiding her edict, I walked to the window, with an excuse that I needed some air. May, originally upset that I was not listening to her, suddenly agreed that it was a great idea, as it might help to clear my obviously troubled mind."

"This gave me a chance to put my head out the window and listen to what was going down in the courtyard, as they loaded you in that ugly contraption. It looked like a hearse you know, well at least to me anyway." she added getting a bit off track.

"You are right of course, Bella. It did look at bit like a hearse. Please continue."

"Anyway," continuing with her story, "It was only when I looked out the window that I overheard them say they were taking you to Penbrooke." Anabelle took a breath, sucking in the fresh night wind.

"Well," she continued, after a fashion, "as it was, I didn't even know what or where that was." at this she jabbed Corazon lightly in the ribs. "Imagine, I knew you wanted me to meet you, but didn't even know where to go?"

"It would have been most unfortunate, had you not figured it out." the knave replied in concentration, guiding their horse down a tricky part of the hillside. "So, what did you do, then, my Sweet?"

"Ah," she confessed. "you must give me a little bit of credit, my darling. What I did was spend the rest of the day, trying to find out."

They went over a slight bump, pausing her story.

When they returned again to a smoother ride, Bella went on, "After various discussions with all of the house staff, who knew nothing of Penbrooke or prisons in general, I finally went down to the stables to speak with Carson. Now, I learned from Susan..." she got off topic again with, "You know, Corazon, I think Susan and Carson are a couple."

"You only think?" replied Corazon.

"No, I know!" and she smiled at him even though he couldn't see it.

"Okay, where was I...Oh, yes! It seems that our Carson had somewhat of a shady past, growing up in the poor area of the village. His mother was a single parent and, while doing her best for him, he was often forced into resorting to petty theft, just to get by. Well, my Father bumped into him one day in the market, or shall I say he bumped into my Father. And quite on purpose, I'm afraid. But before he could pinch his purse, my Father, feeling sorry for him...."

"Your father felt sorry for him?" the knave asked, cutting her off and taking his own tangent, "The same father, I met today?"

"Yes, rather funny isn't it? The way he is with the staff sometimes, you would never know he had a good side." the happy thought causing her to sigh, loudly. "Anyway, he offered him a job. I assume in an attempt at getting him on the right side of the law. I think Carson appreciated it, and his mother was very pleased to see that her son was now working for the Duke. Even if it was only as the stable boy."

"Where was I going with this? Ah, yes, now I remember. While young Carson had never been to Penbrooke himself, he certainly had friends that had and from their tales of woe, lucky for you, he could, somewhat reluctantly I might add, accurately describe its location to me."

"When he asked me why I wanted to know, I just smiled demurely, stating that I had heard terrible stories about the place and wanted to avoid it at all costs. He looked at mc funny, not believing a word. But then, after a pause, he actually asked if I might accompany him over to the stables for a moment."

Anabelle laughed, "Now, normally, a lady of the house would never, ever do such a thing. In fact, May would have fallen faint if he had ever asked her. But as I'm sure you've already learned; I'm made of thicker stuff. So, I agreed, walking along with him to the rear of the property. There, in the back field, sat the charred remains of the coach you and I had such a great time in." giving the knave a friendly shove.

"But that was not what he wanted to show me. Carson went inside the tack room by himself, leaving me out in the sun, standing there for a several moments, still wondering what his request was all about. Then the boy returned, a strange smile plastered on his face. And do you know what he held in his hands?"

"I haven't the foggiest idea?" although Corazon already had a bit of an inkling.

"Why, it was your long bow, and quiver of arrows! He said he had found atop the old carriage!" by now she was chuckling. "It turned out he didn't get rid of them with the coach but kept them instead. He was very curious as to who they belonged to and had a sense that I might know. I took them from him, thanking him, saying I would see to it that they made their way back to their rightful owner.

Then he asked me quite excitedly, using my formal title "It was that knave, wasn't it, Lady Bolton?".

"Well, so what if it was." I replied, not giving anything away.

"Well, if you ever do see 'im again, tell 'im I'm impressed. And if 'e ever wants a 'and with anything, I'll be there for 'im." by now, he was smiling from ear to ear, "You see, M' Lady, 'e helped my Mother once, when she was down and out, and I never got a chance to thank 'im."

"Fine young man, that Carson," the knave commented, "and your imitation of his accent is fabulous."

"Now you're just teasing me."

"Perhaps. You didn't happen to bring them along with you?"

"What? Carson?"

"No, my bow and arrows!"

"Of course not, silly! They're safely hidden away in my upstairs room, back home." Bella added giggling, "In my hope chest!"

"Your hope chest, umm!" his voice raised an octave, teasing her once more.

"Oh, stop it, you knave," hitting him lightly with her fist, "do you want to hear the rest of the story or not."

"Fine, my Sweet," he flirted, "please, do continue"

"Anyway, now that I knew where you were, I had to get there. So, I arranged with Carson's help to have a horse saddled and waiting for me that night. He was more than happy to assist me and knew to add a length of rope and a saddle bag with some food. Hey, that reminds me, here."

And reaching into the bag beside her, she grabbed a slice of bread wrapped around some cheese, handing it to Corazon. As he could not take his hands from the reign, she fed him. Slowly, bit by bit, until he was done.

"That was delicious, Thank you, Bella. Or shall I say thank you, Carson." teasing her yet again.

"Your welcome, Corazon," she said in a very high and mighty tone, getting back at him.

Snack time over, her story continued. "The trick was going to be for me to get out of the house that night. So once again I called on my faithful servant..., no excuse me, my friend, Susan." Bella continued to munch on her own sandwich, as she spoke. "Now as you've no doubt seen, Susan and I share one thing in common, our gorgeous red hair."

"If you do say so, yourself?" teasing her endlessly, this time at her self-complement.

"Oh, you rotter." Anabelle returned, elbowing him once more, the words coming out muffled, her mouth still partially full of food.

"Okay, okay," he held up his hands in surrender, "Yes, my Sweet, I had noticed that rather unique, common trait. Very convenient." he was mocking her again and thoroughly enjoying himself, "but as a Lady, you know you mustn't speak with your mouthful."

"You don't give up do you?" she yelled, hitting him again, this time a little harder, while she downed the last of her bread and cheese.

"And your right, it was convenient..., is convenient." Anabelle pressed on, enjoying relating the tale, "Therefore, we dressed Susan in one of my nightgowns and she crawled under the covers in my bed in my place. When my sister, May, who was acting as Father's watchdog came in to check on me, she would see her and not me. Leaving me free to escape... to rescue you." Bella squeezed him tightly.

"I crawled out through the window, onto the roof and around the back of the house. Then, climbing over the eve, I shimmied down the downspout and across the lower wall. It was then just over to the ivy encrusted trellis and down to the ground. This was the exact same method I had used the previous day, during my own personal escape, the day you found me. It was quite an adventure doing it all in the dark, but eventually, I made it safely to ground."

"After that, it was easy. I headed over to the stables and retrieved, Winter here." Bella said this while reaching beyond him and patting the neck of the stallion. "Carson had him all done up for me as promised and immediately we headed out. Carson also promised to wait up for me, just in case, the dear fellow."

"Anyway, the ride itself was refreshing. A bit wild at first, considering Winter had been stabled all day and wanted to stretch his legs, but as we reached the hills just beyond town, we had to slow right down in order to climb the steep hill. Once we made it on the trail to the prison, there was really nowhere else to go, but up. On approach, I brought Winter to a trot and that's when you must have heard me, coming across the gravel. I had no idea where you might be, but then you called out and well, you know the rest."

"It also means I have to get back as soon as possible, so that poor Carson can get some sleep. And I can switch places with Susan again. Before my Father or sister finds out I'm gone."

Corazon ignored her plea and instead asked, "Tell me, Bella dear, what's up with your sister, anyway? You two appear nothing alike. Is that nose in the air thing just an act, or is she always that stuffy?"

"Oh, pay her no mind her, Corazon, she has an excuse. May's just had a bit of a rough time with life, is all." Bella sounded sad, "My mom relies on her far too much. That, and the time she was engaged but unfortunately missed the ceremony.

"Why? How? I thought everything for you rich girls was set at birth?"

"Well, in this case, for Melissa Anne as the eldest, it was. She had been promised to a fine young gentleman and his family, when they were small. May was all set to get married and they had even begun to plan the event. My Mother getting intimately involved with its preparation and everything. But then, tragedy struck." she swallowed, remembering the tale.

"What happened?" Corazon asked, his voice tentative, unaware of how delicate the subject might be.

"One day her fiancé was out shooting. They were out on our back quarter, near the cliffs. His horse threw a shoe and he lost control. They struggled, attempting to stay on the path, but with all the loose soil, the two of them fell into the ravine. The next day, the search party found them at the bottom. The horse was dead and May's fiancés neck was broken. It was a tragic accident. Poor Melissa Anne was bedridden with grief for months. I don't know if she will ever really get over it."

"My mom certainly never got over it either. So, it's not really May, she used to be a great joy to be around, she's just had a really rough time."

Then Bella's voice brightened, "Although, I do have it on good authority that she has finally found a new suiter. A little bird tells me, that Melissa Anne's in love with that constable's assistant.

"You mean that wimp, Styles?"

"I guess if that's his name, then, yes. I know, it is unfortunate, but my sister seems to like the wimpy type. What can I say? Probably because she wants to rule the roost, I guess."

Then Anabelle's tone changed, "The real problem of course is, Father. He will not allow the marriage, until this..., Styles, is it?" Corazon nodding, "Is better placed. If he could get the role of chief constable, Father might allow it, but as it appears Sire Robertson's not going anywhere any time soon, May is out of luck. That's why she mopes around a lot, puts on airs." Bella paused contemplating, "It really is sad to see them together, when they can't be together, you know?"

"I know the feeling." Corazon stated under his breath. Then louder, "It must be really difficult, for them both. I remember noticing some eye contact between them when I was taken away the other day, I just had no idea."

"Yeah, so you see. That's why she's a bit put out. May's really quite nice, when you get to know her." Bella admitted, concluding the tale.

"Well, hopefully, things will work out in the end." Corazon offered.

"Perhaps, I don't know how, though." Bella conceded, grudgingly.

All their talking had brought them to the edge of Eastborough village. There were almost no lights and there was no sound, except a few hooting owls in the distance. Even though it was the middle of the night, the streets were deserted and there was little chance they would be seen, Anabelle still directed him towards the service road, winding around the rear of the village next to the river. Just in case.

After a short climb out into meadow country and then a hard gallop along the main carriage road, they arrived back at the Bolton estate, just as the sun rose in the east. The ride had taken much longer than they had anticipated, and daylight was upon them. The pink and orange shade of the sky was magnificent, and despite the lateness of the hour, they stopped for a moment looking at it, sharing it together. In the background, the birds began to chirp, as the rays of the rising sun slowly illuminated the surrounding lands.

"Come on, let's hurry!" Bella encouraged, "People will be waking up soon!"

They left the road and headed across country, around the back of the estate, using the path along the edge of the ravine. Evidently the same ravine in which poor May's fiancé departed this world. The verge of the cliff was quite rocky, small scrub brush and other spindly trees hanging precariously over the precipice. Corazon ensured they stayed well clear, the two of them thinking of what had occurred that fateful day, giving them both the shivers. Soon, however, they were back on more solid ground, past a small wood and eventually, the gravel drive leading up to the rear of the great mansion.

Close by, after the final turn in the path, were the estate's huge stables, towering two stories over the surrounding countryside. It was a massive enclosure, accommodating up to twenty, full grown stallions and numerous carriages. Above the stables, on its second floor was a rooming house, presumably where the stable boys and other servants resided, and beside that, a huge barn, storing all of the food and livery for all of the Duke's fine creatures.

Upon reaching the complex, Corazon tugged lightly on the reigns, slowing Winter to a gradual stop. Bella jumped down first, eager to be home, just as a lone figure came running out of the shadows to meet them. It was young Carson, who apparently had remained awake, despite the hour.

"Oh, M' Lady, it is so good to see you 'ome and safe." after assessing she was alright, he turned and looked up at Corazon, just as he dismounted.

"And to you good Sire, welcome. Anytime you need me, I will be 'ere to 'elp. I know what you did for my Mother and I, when we were down and out with nowhere left to go. And I appreciate it." the young man reddened, with his honesty, "Thank you so much, Sire. I must admit, I'm very glad to see M' lady was able to rescue you."

"Yes, quite right, so now M' Lady and I are even." Corazon said smiling, Carson not really understanding the reference.

"But now, M' Lady," Carson encouraged, "you must get back to the 'ouse, daylight is upon us and the 'ousehold awakens!"

"You are wise as well as kind, young Sire." the knave replied, "You put away, Winter here and I will accompany the Lady home. You and I will see each other again. I'm certain of it."

Corazon handed the reigns to the stable boy and the couple headed towards the mansion, their feet crunching lightly on the stone drive.

They didn't run but instead, walked at an accelerated pace, Anabelle lifting the soiled skirt of her dress, to allow their rather hurried passage. She also directed their movements, being the one who knew just where to go and soon enough, they were at the side of the ancient stone building. The adjacent wall was covered with a trellis, liberally festooned in ivy, trailing all the way up the lightly coloured wall to the roof of the main floor. It was here Bella stopped, turning at once to Corazon.

"Well, this is it?" she said breathlessly.

"You know I can't come with you, but you know where to reach me."

"Oh, Corazon!"

As she said this she leaned forward, as he bent down, the two of them moving together. Taking one another in each other's arms, they kissed, their lips embracing each other with excited warmth and moisture, lingering only slightly longer than protocol. Regretfully, they broke apart, already missing each other.

Anabelle stared up into his eyes and as the brightening pink sky highlighted her pretty face, Corazon appreciatively retuned the look, the dim sunbeams highlighting her fiery, red hair.

"When will I see you again?" Bella asked, her voice trembling, but not with the cold.

"Anytime you wish, my Sweet." when she made a face, he added, "just close your eyes and remember. You will see me then."

She smiled, but then asked wantonly, "No, my love, I mean for real?"

"We'll have to see. After all, we both have our duties to perform." smiling warmly at her and brushing his fingers lightly through her auburn hair.

"Yes, our duties." Bella said it with distain, looking to the floor.

Corazon placed a hand gently below her chin, raising her face to his, "Well, take care, my Sweet, and good luck!"

"You too." almost sniffling as she spoke, then they were kissing once again, their eagerness and affection for one another boundless, somehow still unfulfilled. This time they lingered far longer than any etiquette allowed. The two lovers making their own rules.

It was hard to tell who broke away first, but it was Corazon who spoke.

"And now, I must be off."

Before Bella could say anything, or utter another word, the knave slipped swiftly away across the gravel, over the verge and through the trees. Bella watched him give her a quick wave as he disappeared, moisture rising to her eyes, a tear running down her freckled face.

With fresh determination, Anabelle turned and immediately began climbing the ivy trestle, ascending almost as swiftly as the knave had crossed the stone drive. Bella then quickly retraced her steps across the ramparts of the manor, eventually reaching her own bedroom window. Reaching in, she opened the glass frame and slipped into the room, tears gone, a smile now firmly affixed to her face.

"Susan, dear, I'm back. Wake up." she said this in a low voice, so as not to wake anyone else.

But Susan was not asleep, the chamber maid immediately bounding from the bed, throwing the covers to the floor.

"Oh, my goodness Bella, do you know what time it is? I'm late for my rounds! What kept you?"

While she asked all of her questions, she scooted around the room like a mad woman. Then calming down a little, she came over to her friend, grabbing Anabelle's shoulders and looking her wildly up and down.

"Forgive me, M' Lady. You're all right, aren't you? You were able to save your gentleman friend?" her questions posed, rapid fire.

"Yes, Susan, I'm fine," grinning and turning pink, Anabelle added, "and yes, he is fine too. And safely on his way home."

"Oh, that's marvelous, but oh, look at the time, I have to go!" and without a second thought, Susan ran towards the door, opening it and preparing to leave in a rush.

"Susan, dear," Bella called out, still quite softly so as not to wake the house.

"What?" Susan responded excitedly, turning back to her friend.

"Don't you think, you had better get changed first?" and dropping her eyes, Anabelle stared at Susan, the girl still outfitted in one of her nightdresses.

The young maid looked down at herself laughing heartily, before it morphed completely, changing into one of almost semi-hysteria, "Yes, M' Lady, you're right. Of course, you're right." then she started looking around frantically, "Well, where the devil are my clothes?"

Bella, laughing with her friend, helped Susan find her clothes and somehow got her dressed, forcing her out the open door and back to work.

Once her friend had gone back, rather worriedly, to her duties, Bella relaxed, while she slowly removed her own dirty clothes. Because of the stains, she knew she would have to find somewhere to hide them, while she figured out how to get them cleaned. Hastily, she chose under the bed, as her coverlet fell right to the floor and no one but Susan would ever think to look down there.

Once the incriminating outfit was hidden, Anabelle slipped into the abandoned nightgown, noticing the material of the hastily discarded negligée was still warm with her friend's residual body heat. She then climbed directly into the bed, gratifyingly, slipping under the warm covers.

Pulling the sheets up tight to her neck, Bella lay back against the abundantly soft pillows, also still warm from previous use. Then closing her eyes, she remembered, and smiling widely, drifted off to sleep, just as her sister, May ran into the room, shaking her awake.

Chapter 9 – Another Visit from the Constable

Later that morning, the two Bolton girls were sitting in the grand reception room, sipping hot tea. They were dressed in their typical finery, the blond May, even more so than her younger sibling. To match her hair, she wore a dress of finely gilded, gold silk that, while providing a warm welcoming glow to her pretty face, unfortunately blended in too well with the yellow tones of the room's surroundings.

According to May's preference, the gown had a low neck, exposing the white flesh of her cleavage with just enough of a frill to disguise her rather smallish chest. She sat demurely, with her white nylon encased legs crossed, breathing in and out, slowly and methodically, as if practicing, staring across the low wooden table at her little sister.

Anabelle in contrast, wore a relatively simple affair. The bodice of her dress was striped in blue and beige, with off the shoulder sleeves, a full skirt and delicate, snow white lace trim. Like her sister's, her hose was white to match the lace of the dress, the materials sheer surface, exposing just a hint of her soft skin tone beneath. Regardless of the outfit's plainness, its cut properly accentuated the young woman's perfect curves, auburn hair and alabaster skin.

As a result of her lengthy, nocturnal excursion however, Anabelle's eyelids were extremely heavy and all she really wanted at that moment was a good, long sleep. Thankfully, as was protocol for wealthy young women of her day, they always participated an early afternoon nap. Normally, Bella thought this odd custom unnecessary, even trite, but today she looked forward to this particular afternoon's brief sojourn.

After noticing her sister's drowsiness, May commented, "Well, my dear," expertly placing her cup back in its saucer, her pinky finger extended beautifully. "I'm surprised you're tired. Considering, after all the excitement of yesterday, Father had us both in bed so early."

Evidently, her sister was quite observant, noticing Bella's fluttering lashes.

"Oh, it's nothing, May," Bella returned, yawning, "You know my sleep habits change daily. I had a bit of a rough night, is all. Thinking so much about my recent experiences, I suppose. I barely slept a wink."

"But Anabelle, dear, when I checked in on you, and I did check in on you, you were always sleeping so soundly."

Her observations clearly describing, the sight of the sleeping Susan, left in her place.

"That's probably only a few of the times I actually did sleep, May. I don't know, why does it matter?"

"I'm just concerned for you, Anabelle dear. After your scary adventure with that evil rogue." May leaned forward, an expression of disbelief, or was it desire, on her face. "I was glad when Father had him arrested. Such a devilish man!"

"May, darling," Bella retuned, her patience waning, "do not comment on what you don't know. Sire Corazon is a good man. If not for him, I wouldn't be here sipping tea with you."

"Oh, don't be silly, Anabelle. The Chief Constable wouldn't have arrested him, if there wasn't something wrong with him." emphasizing the 'something'. "I was just glad he came in when he did. Just in time, it appears."

"Now look who's telling stories, May. You're just glad he came, because he brought Master Styles along with him."

At this poignant observation, her sister's white cheeks turned bright red.

"Oh, don't be silly, Anabelle," May responded, rapidly wafting herself with her hand, as if to shed the heat rising to her face, "I don't know what you're talking about."

"Don't worry, May, I won't tell Father. Your secret is safe with me." smiling warmly at her embarrassed sibling, her voice more agreeable "I think it's nice to have someone you can dream about."

"Oh, Anabelle, stop it! You are embarrassing me." her fanning movements, accelerating furiously.

As she said this, their father entered the doorway, deeply engaged in conversation with the Bolton's trepid looking butler. So, rather fortunately, he was completely oblivious to their recent exchange. After roughly dismissing the thin man with a wave, he moved into the room, taking his normal seat next to the fire.

"Good morning, girls." he stated simply.

"Good morning, Father!" the Bolton women returned in unison.

"Had a nice sleep, did we?"

May was about to respond to the casual comment, but was prevented by Bella uttering a stifled laugh, a deceitful smirk obvious on her face. Attempting to hold back her laughter only made it worse and she ended up just releasing a loud exclamation and breath of air, shattering the relative silence of the room.

"My goodness, Anabelle," her father bellowed, continuing before either could answer, "First, it was the theft of my prime riding team and your dangerous jaunt into the country, in that poor excuse of a carriage. Followed by your poor choice to bring home that forest brigand who attacked my driver. Now, you burst out laughing upon my simple inquiry. What on earth has gotten into you, young lady?"

Bella listened quietly to his rant, the smile slowly draining from her face. Deciding, however, it was best not to rile her father further, she replied as evenly as possible. "I don't know, Father. Perhaps I've just been confused lately, a bit unsure of myself. I firmly believe that after a good day of rest, things are bound to improve."

This seemed to placate the old man, at least temporarily. The clear evidence of this being the room's immediate return to quiet. The two girls sat quietly, demurely drinking their tea, looking anxiously at one another, dying to speak but refusing to do so with the Duke present. The tick of the grandfather clock, the roar of the fire and the tinkling of china, the only sounds. It was as if an unexpected chill had entered the room.

All of a sudden, the morning got much livelier.

A loud crunch of gravel outside and a subsequent hard banging at the front door, woke them all from their subdued revelry. The added clicking of the butler's shoes on marble, along with a muffled but energetic conversation at the door, supplemented the excitement. As a denouement, the two very different speaking voices raised in volume before a scuffle erupted, after which there was an obvious clatter of heavy riding boots, stomping towards them down the hall.

The three, now very attentive Boltons, looked toward the entry, just as Chief Constable Robertson burst into the room, interrupting their morning solace.

"And what is the meaning of this?" the Duke stated, rising from his chair.

Flustered, the butler entered shortly thereafter, harping. "I told him your grace, that you were busy and that he had no invitation. But he insisted."

"That's alright, Simon," the Duke motioned to his man, giving him a wave. Turning to face the constable he asked again, "I asked you Sire, what are you doing here at this time of the morning, interrupting our breakfast?"

Robertson almost sneered at the Duke, before remembering his place. "Your excellency, I have come to report some rather startling news. The criminal we apprehended with your assistance yesterday..., has escaped."

"You mean the man that attacked my daughter?"

"Yes, the same."

"He did not attack me, Father," Bella had also risen from her chair, "he saved me."

The Duke spoke to her, without turning, "Hush girl, can't you see I'm speaking to the Chief Constable?"

Standing in support, May moved over to stay Bella's arm, the two sisters holding each other, while their father continued speaking.

"Well, what of it, man? He was in your custody and care. What does his escape have to do with myself, or my family?" the Duke asked, incredulous.

"After we left you yesterday," the Constable continued, "we secured the man in Penbrooke Prison. In fact, I took him there myself. Apparently, after being locked up securely, the man escaped in the middle of last night."

"That is all most interesting, Chief Constable, but I repeat, what does that have to do with my family?" the Duke said impatiently.

"Well, your grace," Robertson replied, "it's this way. The man escaped with the assistance of someone from the outside. The iron bars of his cell window were torn from their frame with a horse and rope. Further, when the opening turned out to be too small for his exit, his accomplice then subdued the guard, obtaining the keys to the cells and released the man, after locking the warden in his parlour. The two then made off into the night. The warden only realized he was free a few hours ago and sounded the alarm."

Throughout the entire time he was speaking, Robertson's one good eye glanced accusingly towards Bella.

"That is all fine an well, but I ask once again, what does any of this have to do with me?" and finally, noticing the direction of the constables stare, added, "and I would very much appreciate it, Chief Constable, if you would look at me, when addressing your Duke."

Robertson quickly averted his gaze, looking back towards the old man. "Apologies Your excellency. But I have it on good authority, that it was a woman who assisted this man's escape."

"A woman? Subdue a guard? That's preposterous." and then it struck him, "You're not suggesting it's one of my daughters?" he looked disgusted at the very notion.

"She was reported to have red hair, your grace." and again he looked beyond the Duke at Bella. She just stared defiantly back at him, unmoved.

"Are you accusing my, Anabelle? My dear Constable, you must be joking?"

At that moment, through the rear door, the maid Susan, walked in the room, carrying a tray with more tea. Enabling her to witness what had become a rather heated exchange.

"Unfortunately, this is no joke, your grace. The description we have was... quite exact."

"Chief Constable, my Bella has been in bed all night. Isn't that right, girls?"

"Yes, Father," this from May, "I checked on Anabelle multiple times, throughout the night, and she was always fast asleep."

"Yes, your grace," Susan spoke out of turn, knowing she would regret it later, "I saw M' Lady off to bed myself. And she never left her room, until I saw her this morning."

May gasped loudly at the maid's uninvited outburst, but the Duke, in his excitement, completely missed Susan's break in etiquette. Bella just stood there, hands on her hips, silent.

"There you have it! From both my daughter and her servant, Chief. Anabelle was in bed, here at Eastborough Hall, throughout the night. There is no way she could have been this so-called accomplice of yours." he paused, looking back at the girls briefly, "Candidly, I'm shocked, as to how you could even think it possible."

Then getting really angry, the Duke stepped forward, "In fact, I believe I want you, and your wild accusations, out of here! Right now!"

"Simon, come here!" the Duke yelled, as the butler hurried over, "Escort the Chief Constable from this house. Frankly, Chief you have disappointed me. I believed, when I assigned you this role, that you would be professional and diligent. It appears you are neither."

"I make no excuses for my behaviour." Robertson purposely dropping the Duke's title, "Your daughter was involved, I'm sure of it."

Turning red, the Duke continued to blast Robertson. "You have the gaul, Sire, to come in here and accuse my daughter of criminal acts! My youngest daughter! How dare you! You are to leave my house this instant or I will report you to the crown!" now visibly shaking, "Get out of here, now!

The two sisters had never seen their father so incensed. For that matter, neither had the Constable. He backed down immediately, his shoulders dropping, realizing his fight was a losing battle. The timid butler grabbed his arm to escort him out, but he shook him off rather violently, at once making for the door.

"I will leave, now your grace. But understand this, you have not seen the last of me." and he stared with his one, evil eye beyond the Duke, directly at Anabelle, with a look of vile disgust, that shocked even her.

Turning, he stomped out. With a slam of the main door and the sound of a baying horse and hoof beats on the stone drive outside, he was gone. Simon the butler, just stood there in the opening, looking shocked, the Bolton family all stood there, stunned by the Chief Constable's accusations.

The Duke broke the sudden silence, "Susan! Simon! Out of here! I wish to speak with my daughters..., alone."

The two servants immediately rushed to the exits, thankful to be given their dismissal without further reprimand.

The Duke turned back into the room, looking at the two sisters, still standing and still holding tightly to one another. "Sit down girls," when they hesitated, remaining cautiously upright, he raised his voice, "I said sit!" and they did.

"Now, tell me, what is going on?"

"There's nothing going on Father, the constable...."

"Chief Constable, Bella."

"Chief Constable, then. He is merely misinformed."

"But what of his allegations, the descriptions, what of your red hair?"

"Father don't be silly, a lot of women have red hair," observed May perceptibly, "Look at our Susan, even she has red hair. And it's almost exactly like Anabelle's...." her voice trailed off as if something had just occurred to her.

"What? Are you now accusing our Susan of assisting with this brigand's escape?"

"Not at all, Father," stated Bella's sister, quickly coming out of her short contemplation, "I'm just saying that it could have been any red-haired woman in the county that helped that man."

"So, the two of you know absolutely nothing about this then?"

"No, Father!" they said together.

"Why then, do you think the Constable came looking here?"

"Chief Constable, Father." Bella teased.

The Duke looked at his youngest daughter with daggers in his eyes, then relaxed, a grin crossing his face.

"We have no idea," May said for the two of them, before adding, "and we appreciate you defending our.... Bella's honour."

The Duke reddened again, except this time with appreciation, "Well, thank you, my dear, I would never do any less." hesitating slightly, before he finished, "However, I think it highly peculiar that Chief Robertson would accuse you of such a thing without cause. Highly peculiar."

Sitting slowly back down, he placed his hand on his head and took a sip of tea, now long gone cold, making a face, "And where is that fool, Susan?"

"Susan!" he yelled, "Bring us some more tea, on the double!"

And with that spoken summons, all the excitement of the morning was forgotten, and things returned to normal.

At least as normal as they ever came, in the great and formal house of Bolton.

Chapter 10 – The Constable's Plans

Robertson left Eastborough Hall in a seething rage. Whipping his horse to a gallop, horse and rider sprinted down the wide avenue between the elms. He knew for certain that the younger Bolton girl was involved but had apparently played his hand too early. The story the warden had recited to him earlier that morning, reeked of exaggeration, but held true in one key respect. Men like him never forget a pretty face. And the fat oaf had described his unrequited love perfectly. From the hair, to the skin, even to the light brown freckles on her face. Anabelle Bolton had been at Penbrooke Prison last night and had ensured the escape of that charlatan, Corazon. It was undeniable.

Spurring his horse further, he turned back north, around behind the estate, passing the huge stables before racing wildly across the countryside, eventually reaching the riding trail running along the ravine. It was his favorite ride, relishing the exhilaration of speed and power as he recklessly ran his mount full speed along the precarious pathway, only inches from certain death. In fact, hadn't the fiancé of the eldest Bolton girl, lost his life by falling from that very track? He didn't care, he was angry and had to relieve the tension of the failed confrontation, by taking a risk. Wasn't life all about risk? For what was life without risk? No risk, no reward, was what his father always used to say.

His father, what a great man! A Chief Constable before him, he had also once been tasked with the protection of the people of

Eastborough, apprehending the lawless, punishing the wicked and upholding the law of the nation. That's just what he was doing now, his job. Upholding the law, irrespective of condition or reason. Robertson believed, like his father before him, that the law was the law and he intended to sustain it, regardless of the costs.

He knew that sorry rogue, Corazon had been the one attacking the wealthy caravans. And, regardless of whether or not he hurt anyone physically, he certainly hurt them in character. Embarrassing the affluent and important citizens of the county, by making them walk home, sometimes only in their undergarments. He also hurt them financially, by making off with their various possessions.

That reckless knave was nothing but a common thief. What he ultimately did with all those expensive things he walked away with, was anybody's guess. It was rumoured, he delivered the goods to the needy citizens of the town, farmers having trouble paying their taxes, or widows who could not put food on the table. The townsfolk said he was a man of the people, helping the downtrodden in their time of strife. What were a few jewels and fancy outfits taken from the wealthy, they said? The rich could always get more, and furthermore, no one was ever hurt in the process. Humiliated perhaps, but what man couldn't use a touch of humility these days. Especially the rich. Corazon always provided, when and where it was needed most. They even had a name for him, calling him the Knave of Hearts.

But Robertson didn't care. He had no interest in the reason or the circumstances surrounding this criminal's actions. Because for him, an upstanding lawman of the county, theft was theft and he was not going to stop until he saw that crook put away for his blatant disregard of the law. No matter what it took.

But it was not only his crimes, that now bothered Robertson. There was something more, making his mind seethe with additional hatred. The man's worst offence, in the Chief Constable's mind, was that the no-good knave had become taken with young Bella Bolton and she equally enamoured with him.

Robertson boiled with jealous rage at the thought of the two of them together.

For he had loved the young Anabelle Bolton from the first time he had seen her. He remembered it well, for it was on the day of his assignment to Chief Constable and so, in his mind, she was destined to be his.

It was a proud day. He had already been working the county police force for years and was a fine upstanding constable, after being inspired by his famous father. So, it was no surprise, that upon his father's untimely death, at the hands of thugs like that devil Corazon, Robertson had been summarily promoted into the role of Chief. And by the Duke himself no less. Certainly, there had been many other candidates, including that idiot, Styles but the heart-breaking death of his father had given him the sympathy vote, ensuring his successful coronation.

The advancement ceremony had been a huge affair and most of the town had attended, most particularly the family of the Duke. The first time Robertson had seen young Anabelle standing there on the dais, he was smitten and vowed that, one day, she would be his wife.

But try as he might, their union was not any closer to fruition now than that day on the platform, several years previously. Bella had shown no interest in him at all, never once paying him any attention, even at the celebration following his promotion.

Strangely, the younger Bolton girl never seemed to behave per her station, the young woman always looking for something different, something just out of reach. And it was her desire for something more that gave him hope. A girl who's mind wandered like that would be looking for a different kind of suiter, someone special, someone outside of the rich and wealthy circle. But as it was, he was mistaken, at least as far as he was concerned, his interest clearly being of no consequence to her. For she never once even spoke with him, until these recent days and then it was with hatred and loathing.

Because now something else had gotten between them; that rascal, Corazon. Well, Robertson vowed, he would make sure he saw the man eliminated as a threat. He remained certain that, in removing the knave from the equation, it would finally open the door for him with Anabelle. Without her fancy thief to pine over, young Bella might possibly seek solace in the arms of the Chief of Police. Robertson remained cautiously optimistic that the smallest chance still remained for himself and Anabelle to unite. Even if it was a fleeting one.

And because of that minor possibility, he was slightly upset with himself today. Especially with the extremely harsh looks, he had bestowed upon the poor girl. But he couldn't help it. He had been so upset and irritated by her rash acts. Not only had she defied her family, she had chosen to rescue that criminal! And from within his own custody, no less! He had been livid!

Despite her actions, however, Robertson remained completely infatuated with young Bella; her beautiful auburn hair, her soft skin and bright eyes. Almost to a point, where it began affecting his reason. And now, because of that man, that thief, that knave Corazon, any potential consummation of his love was in jeopardy. He had to get rid of him. Take him out of the equation, if he was to have any hope at all.

Arriving at his own manor house on the edge of the village, he dismounted swiftly, handing the reigns to the stable boy, standing at the ready. Robertson's large house was in no way as grand or luxurious as the Bolton estate, but it did have over 20 rooms on two levels, running water and was made of stone, serving as both his prime residence and his place of work.

A portion of the lower floor had been renovated to provide a headquarters and assembly area for his various constables. A place where they might come and receive their instructions when called for. It also housed his personal study, in which he planned his daily activities and organized the security requirements for the local populace. The small, rather humble estate had belonged to his family for generations and he, being an only child, had inherited it upon the death of its patriarch.

Arriving in a huff, Robertson stormed up the steps, dropping his weapons on the entry table and heading directly inside. Per long established protocol, upon entering the main section of the house, his own butler approached and asked him what he required. But today, he just waved him away with his outstretched hand.

"Don't disturb me right now, Jacob.... No wait," he corrected, spinning to face the slightly dishevelled man, "there is something you can do. Send a messenger out to Styles, Martin and Ashbrook. I need them to assemble in the lower hall before 3 pm. Today!" and then he physically pushed the man out of his office. "Now be quick about it!" and then as an afterthought, "And get me a drink! The good stuff, I'm parched."

***

When the three junior constables had assembled at the requested time, Robertson addressed the group, a plan now firmly in place.

"Men, we have a dangerous criminal on the loose. It is high time we reacquired him."

"What do you mean *reacquire* him?" Ashbrook questioned, unfamiliar with the events of the day before.

"Styles and I arrested him at the Bolton estate and sequestered him in Penbrooke Prison yesterday. He was broken out of there, last night."

"Broken out! On the first night? How?"

"The thief had an accomplice. One with whom he had obviously made prior arrangements. In the dead of night, that person travelled to the prison, and then managed to lock up the warden and make off with his keys. The culprit is, therefore, back on the loose and is now in need of re-apprehension.

"What about the accomplice? Don't we need to round them up too?"

Robertson raised his eyes at the incessant questioning.

"The problem there, is that we have no firm information on the alleged accomplice. So, we are not to worry about her...."

quickly correcting himself before any of them noticed, "I mean, them, right now."

He began to sweat slightly, at his embarrassing blunder. "What we really need to do is concentrate on the man who's escaped. The dangerous thief."

For justification, he added, "You are all aware of the recent robberies that some of the wealthier members of our town have suffered at the hands of the so-called, friendly thief?"

"Yes." Ashbrook laughed, "He sends them home packing, with no clothes on!"

"That's quite enough, Ashbrook!" Robertson gave him a nasty look. The man quieted immediately, "Well, our fugitive is one in the same."

"You're sure, that this man's the same one? The so-called Knave of Hearts?"

"Of course, I am sure. Would I have called you here, otherwise?" Robertson's blood pressure began to rise, a flush seeping into his cheeks.

"Do you know where he's gone to then?"

"Not exactly, but I have a general idea. You three are to go to the edge of the valley, near the main entrance to the forbidden wood and find his lair. It's probably somewhere just inside the forest perimeter."

The instructions stunned the three men.

"The forbidden wood? Why there? That place is haunted." Ashbrook's voice trembled, a look of abject fear on his face.

"It is no more haunted than this house, you fool." Robertson declared angrily.

"It's just what their saying, Chief." attempting to appear nonchalant, but clearly remaining fearful.

"I don't care what anybody says, and Martin has already been there, haven't you, Martin?"

Martin nodded, as it was, indeed he, who had been the one who had followed Bella on her carriage ride the day before. He did not speak further, however, clearly not relishing returning to the questionable location himself.

"Ah," stated Ashbrook, still not completely satisfied, "so that makes it okay, then. You're sure we have to go out there?"

"You need to go out there, because that is where he lives, I am certain of it. You are to comb the forbidden forest for that man's lair and bring him back here. Dead or alive." then Robertson added, something none of the three appreciated, "and you will do it tonight!"

"Tonight! Can't it wait until morning?" this from Styles who had remained silent throughout the conversation.

"No, it can't," Robertson replied, staring with his one good eye at Styles. "You will do as I command and head out there immediately."

"But, Chief...!" from the one with all the questions.

"No buts, Ashbrook, you go tonight. All of you!" then he made the command a little more bearable, "Jacob will outfit you accordingly and provide fresh provisions." smiling wickedly, "I would hate to see any of you catching a cold, now."

Then he added the ultimate carrot, "Should you succeed in returning him to me, as I have requested, each of you will receive 5 pieces of silver for their troubles."

While this promise put a temporary smile on the face of each of the junior constables, it was with great reluctance that the trio left the ready room and entered the back area of the house to prepare themselves for a night of searching. Jacob had prepared them all a nice hot supper, making the thought of roaming the cold forest by moonlight, a little easier to swallow.

Once ready, they left Robertson's house at sundown, riding into the east. As he watched their horses disappear into the falling darkness, the Chief Constable, mused over their lack of discipline in the matter. He must find better men, more dedicated personnel, men who would care more for the safety of their community, than for themselves.

But that was a consideration for tomorrow. All he wanted now was for them to apprehend Corazon and bring him to justice. And he firmly believed they would find him.

And when they do, Robertson mused, I will remove the troublemaker for good. After all, how hard could it be to find one, lone marauding bandit?

***

It turned out that it was quite difficult. Quite difficult, indeed.

The first party searched for days, returning cold and miserable half a week later, two of the officers having suffered injury by wild animals, and finding absolutely nothing of the escaped Knave of Hearts. The second posse Robertson sent, expertly supplied for a week living in the woods, had no luck either. They too, could not find a single trace of the criminal Corazon, even after looking almost twice as long. But the Chief was determined, sending out yet another team of lawmen, to chase down the escaped bandit. After the failure of this third search party, and several more injuries, however, Robertson began to get frustrated, resigning to try something else.

The clear failure of his staff obviously did not please the demanding Robertson. It was clear now that Corazon was cunning enough to evade even the prime of the Eastborough constabulary. So, if the thief couldn't be caught and brought to justice, they would just have to think of something else.

One evening, about a month later, Robertson considered the situation further by the fire. *If I can't imprison or kill him*, he mused, *I will destroy him a different way. By annihilating his character as a sympathetic rogue and saviour of the common man. I will make him the most feared man in the land, so that no one will think of him as kind or merciful anymore. I will tear apart the reputation of this so-called people's thief, this Corazon, so that he will be hated, reviled and feared by all. Including his blushing, Lady Bolton.*

His new plan went beyond the boundaries, breaking the codes of all that he had been taught and stood for all his life. However, Robertson was so blinded with hatred for the man of the people, and so consumed with lust for a girl he could never have, his mind had distorted and changed.

His final plot would end up taking a very nasty turn, in such a wrong and unrecognisable direction, that it would eventually see his life completely unravel and to end in his ultimate undoing.

But before that, he had one final card to play, he just needed the right timing for it to occur.

Chapter 11 - Market Day

Several weeks had now passed since the infamous *incident in the wood*, as Bella's father, kept calling it. Life had indeed returned to normal, or some semblance that might have been considered normal, for an aristocratic family at Eastborough Hall. There gratefully, being no further visits from either rebellious, knaves of the wood, or Chief Constable Robertson.

After that morning of Robertson's visit, with the clue of the red hair, May had eventually worked out her sister's subterfuge. And under constant questioning, Bella had finally admitted that, with Susan's help, it was indeed she who had left the house to rescue the imprisoned knave. At first, May had been appalled at even the thought of what her sister had done. But after seeing the love in Anabelle's eyes, and realizing that deep down, she too had been attracted to the handsome knave, she vowed to keep it all a treasured secret. After that point, the two sisters had become inseparable.

Anabelle and Melissa Anne, now the best of friends, talked incessantly about their male acquaintances, although strangely enough, neither of them had seen Styles nor Corazon in quite a while. The two girls, however, were happy enough just discussing their chosen suiters, as if talking about the two men helped the ladies remember who they were and what they looked like. Quite often during these conversations, one of the sisters might stare off into the distance, a cheeky smile or longing look appearing on their pretty face, while her companion just watched in awe, providing much needed support.

But being sisters, potential gentlemen friends were not the only thing they spoke about. There were many subjects that caught the girl's attentions; what was in or not in vogue, the latest fashions (May was well up on these) or any other happenings around the local village. Whatever the chosen topic, the two female siblings were now so excessively giggly that the Duke began to tire of their constant, girlish snickering.

"Girls, please! Keep it down," he stated sharply, one morning over breakfast, the three of them sitting in the sunroom. "While I'm very glad the two of you are finally getting along like sisters should, I simply abhor the foolish noises you make." making a face, the Duke summarized, "If you wish to laugh like a bunch of hyenas then, please, do it elsewhere."

"But Father," May interjected, still chuckling, "we're only having a bit of fun. Give us that?"

Today, Bella's fair sister was dressed all pretty in pink, her cheeks bright red to match and her small chest heaving delightfully with each new smile.

"Yes, Father." Anabelle entreated, also dressed very stylishly in a light purple, full skirted frock that accentuated her near perfect features. "We're only doing what girls do at our age. Surely, you appreciate that?"

"As I said, I do appreciate that the both of you are now getting along, and that young girls tend to do what they do, but you must try to keep your exclamations to a minimum."

When they both smiled back lovingly at him, his expression softened, "Under the circumstances, I hasten to think what my next bit of news for you might bring. I would wager it will just make things even worse."

"Oh, tell us Father, what news?" the two girls stated in harmony, before rushing over, and siting themselves eagerly on the round rug at the Duke's feet, both looking up in fervent anticipation.

Looking down at his two beautiful daughters, the man could not but help love them, immediately describing their upcoming adventure. "Well, my dears. You know today is Thursday?"

"Yes" the young women replied in unison, looking at each other in interest, eagerly awaiting their father to continue.

"And you know what happens on Thursday?"

"Carson washes the horses?" May chimed in.

"No, silly," said Bella, lightly sticking her elbow into her sister's ribs, "it's market day!"

"Oh, yes, market day! How grand!" May giggling at her own stupidity.

"Does this mean you're taking us to town for market day, Father?" Bella questioned expectantly.

The Duke, seeing how anxious his two daughters were, purposely hesitated, still looking down at them, letting them stew.

"Well?" the sisters said together, clearly on the edge of their seats.

"Well, of course darlings! Your Mother and I thought it about time that we went as a family into town. And what better time than for market day. We haven't been in a while and your Mother insisted." he smiled warmly, or as warmly as a Duke could smile.

"Oh, Father, that's just delightful. We haven't been to market day for ages." May was impressed.

"I know. That's exactly what your Mother said," then changing his tone added a warning. "but girls, remember what has been happening on the roads in recent days. There is a mad group of men on the loose, attacking wealthy caravans on their way to and from town. Which is part of the reason your Mother and I have waited so long between town visits. We must be cautious."

"Oh, Father, we'll be fine!" this from Bella. "Were not very far from town. Surely, only folk coming in from far away need worry." then she smiled mischievously, "And we all know the Chief Constable is a *personal* friend of yours."

"Well, be that as it may," completely missing the young girl's sarcasm, "I understand that sometimes the brigands work fairly close to here. And remember, these men are not like that friendly knave person, who just relieves the people of their belongings. These horrid men actually kill people." he was silent as he thought about it more, "Perhaps our friendly knave has gone bad and the two are one in the same?"

Then, considering the frightened look he saw forming on his daughter's faces, the two of them looking at one another puzzled, he added, "But I'm sure your right, Bella. We should be just fine. However, we will be extra diligent, nonetheless."

At the talk of brigands, attacks and Corazon, her friendly knave, Bella's mind wandered back to her own adventure near the forbidden wood, that now seemed such a long time ago. She thought of her rising fear at the death of the family driver and the abject horror she had felt during her attempted assault. But then there were also the remembrances of her joy of being saved, yet still shocked at how easily Corazon had rather brutally killed all those men. And then afterwards, the two of them and their time together in his lair, of her cold shower in the flowing water of the stream, of her new dress and of her subsequent return home. Then the continuing escapade at the prison and finally, the kisses the two had shared on her doorstep. Every part of it flashing by like a fanciful dream.

Recently, with all the time getting reacquainted with her sister, she had almost forgotten about how much fun she had experienced on her previous solo journey, out from beneath the protection of the Bolton family estate. Suddenly wondering what Corazon was doing right now. What he was thinking about. Was he thinking about her or was he out, helping folks in need? Could he really be one of those horrid thugs as her father suggested? Or was he simply just relaxing in his mountain side home, taking his own shower, standing in that refreshing stream of cold, cascading water? Her eyes were blank with reminiscence, when her sister returned the elbow.

"Bella," May prompted, "Father asked you a question."

"Oh, yeah?" finally coming out of her reverie, "Yes, what is it? Oh, sorry, Father, I must have tuned out for a moment. I apologise."

"My dear one must never 'tune out' when one is being addressed or spoken to. It is most unladylike."

"Indeed, Father. I am truthfully sorry. What was it you asked?"

"I had just asked if you were going to wear that nice morning gown to the market or if you wanted to change into something, perhaps a bit more appropriate. I know your sister plans to."

Bella's sister, May was already up and heading to the door, intent on getting changed for their planned day out.

"Oh, yes, Father, sorry. I will also want to change. Can't go to market in this outfit."

"I thought as much," the Duke responded, "well, be off with you then and don't take all morning, I wish to leave before eleven."

And with that final instruction, Bella jumped to her feet, heading swiftly out of the room, right on the heels of Melissa Anne who was now almost halfway up the stairs.

"Good," stated the Duke to himself, "now I can have a half an hour of peace and quiet," and sliding back into his chair, he relaxed.

***

They didn't get out of the house until almost noon, with May fussing about which of several travelling outfits she had to wear. The two siblings did eventually return downstairs, appropriately dressed in respectable, but still relatively ornate, clothes. Nothing, however, unexpected for young women of their standing.

May's gown was a light ochre colour, with the standard lace bustle around the top of the bodice, selecting her beige, button up, riding boots to accent the costume. Anabelle had on a dark teal dress, with ivory accents, but with the addition of a bold sash of deep orange around her middle. It added just the right amount of flair to an already quite spectacular travelling outfit. Her boots were black and high heeled complementing the rest of her ensemble extremely well.

"You look far better than I do Anabelle, I should have picked the red." May complained, as the pair met up at the top landing.

"Oh, hush you fool, you look fantastic. We can't wait another moment for you to change a third time. You do want to go to the market sometime today, don't you?"

And the two of them laughed as they descended the stairs, arm in arm.

The four Boltons left the estate in one of their best enclosed carriages, but thankfully with all of the windows wide open. The family crest, gilded in bright gold, adorned the doors of the black beauty, its glossy piano finish gleaming in the sunlight, reflecting the surrounding trees and landscape off its shiny paintwork.

The Duke selected young Carson as driver and footman, with two of his finest stallions set to draw the apparatus on its way into town. Choosing Winter as one of the pair of horses had been Anabelle's idea. She took the time to pat him appreciatively on the neck, before finally moving around to climb inside.

"Come inside dear," the Duchess demanded, "you'll catch a cold."

"Oh, Mother, don't be so silly, it's such a beautiful day." Bella responded, "And besides, all the windows are open anyway." Prompting the Duchess to stare around her as if just noticing for the first time that the coach was already wide open to the elements.

"Oh posh, dear," she stated, feeling quite stupid, "just get aboard."

"I'm coming."

As May was already seated inside facing rearward, Bella settled in comfortably on the seat next to her, facing their parents. She looked them over appreciatively. The Duke and Duchess had aged considerably well under the circumstances and, although both were greying a bit on top, they maintained just the right amount of vigour to make life interesting.

"Well, Carson my boy, let's be off," the Duke ordered, knocking the top of the cabin with his cane. Within moments the horses whinnied, the carriage wheels rotated on the gravel and they were on their way.

**

Market day, as one might believe, was the busiest morning in the village of Eastborough. All manner of citizen, animal and vehicle stormed the narrow, cobble stone streets, all in an effort to get the best location in the central square. The ambient noise was calamitous, voices yelling, birds squawking, cattle mooing, pigs grunting, horses braying and cartwheels squeaking. All of the various sounds echoing nonsensically between the houses and balconies overhanging the closely-knit streets.

But even more obvious to the traveller on market day, were the many different odours overpowering the village. Some quite pungent, almost enough to make one gag, like those of the rapidly perspiring livestock and their offal, but others, so fine they even tantalized the senses. The delectable aromas of the street food vendors, those of sweet fruits, fresh baking and cooked meats, all creating a virtual cornucopia of wonderful fragrances for the hungry soul.

The town rose early on market day and by the time the Boltons arrived that morning on the village's outskirts, some of the merchants had already sold their share and closed up for the day. Still, that didn't stop the remaining farmers and shopkeepers, all eager to empty their baskets, while filling their coin purses. So, the town remained busy, almost at a fever pitch, business booming.

The central square of Eastborough was extremely large, consisting of a vast quadrangle of flat cobbles. All the village's main roads lead directly towards it, before efficiently encircling its rectangular plan. The stone spire of the local parish church graced its north side and a slowly meandering river passed by to the south. East and west saw the bulk of the main commercial streets of town that now, at the height of market, were bustling with happy shoppers. Almost every citizen was in the square or just outside it, spending, trading or just browsing the various stalls and shops. It was absolute bedlam.

Carson could not get the large brougham and team much closer than a few streets away, so he had to change direction before finding a place to stop just shy of the riverbank. Normally, the presence of the coat of arms of the Duke afforded a little bit more courtesy and priority for its occupants. But on market day, it provided no more special attention than a loaded ox cart hauling fruit. Meaning the four Boltons were soon forced to dismount and make their way in closer on foot.

"Bella and I are going to go on ahead, if that's okay." May called out to her parents who were struggling hard to keep up with their younger brood. "We will meet you for a late lunch at the Dog and Partridge."

The place she referred to, was a local pub serving reasonable and well-prepared food, which for the rather picky Boltons, was their usual eatery. At most times, it sat in a quiet corner of the square, a perfect location for the stuffy Duke and his wife. Of course, today, the place would be anything but quiet.

"Fine, dears!" the Duchess responded, stopping to let a vendor, pulling two pigs behind him, to go ahead of her, "We will meet you there at two!"

But the happy sisters, now arm in arm, were already too far ahead and within moments had disappeared into the seemingly endless crowds of busy vendors and anxious shoppers.

"Oh, Bella, dear, isn't this just grand!" May chimed contentedly, "A day in town, and on market day, no less."

"Indeed, it is, May," Anabelle responded, smiling brightly, holding tightly to her sister's hand, "I have been dying to get out for so long, I'm so excited."

"Do you think we'll meet up with anyone we know?" a vague hint of expectation in her voice.

"Who's to say, darling, you never know on a day like today." Bella responded cautiously, furtively glancing up ahead.

Making their way down the high-street, the two sisters soon turned the last corner, around a large butcher shop, to finally face the vastness of the main square. There were people and animals everywhere, all vying for their one small section of the once wide-open area, now completely closed in with stalls, tents and tables galore. The noises here were even more intense, the clamour of the people, animals and machines all adding to the building din. And, as if that wasn't enough, every 15 minutes, the chime of the church bells rang loudly about the square. The cacophony of sound attacking the ears of the young women was absolutely marvelous!

Several street vendors very close by were offering bar-b-queued delights of all kinds, the smell of roasting foul, making the girl's mouths water. Those succulent scents, combining with all of the other overpowering smells of the market, assaulted the Bolton's nasal passages with all means of fragrance, raising their spirits even further.

"This is wonderful!" screamed May, over the constant noise, still holding tightly to Bella's arm.

"It's not only wonderful, it's breathtaking!" came her sister's reply, at an equally loud volume, the only way to hear with all of the furious activity going on.

"Where shall we go?" May asked, just as an old woman came up to them offering a small, handmade trinket, her wrinkled palm extended.

May held up her own hand as if apologizing, but Bella, stepping in and seeing the woman was poor, pulled out a bright copper coin, offering it into the beggar's outstretched hand.

"Why bless you, missy. Here." she said, handing Anabelle the trinket.

"No, thank you," replied Bella, politely pushing it back towards the old maid, "you keep it, that money is for you. You keep that lovely thing. Sell it to another."

And bowing, the grizzled woman let them pass, thanking the girls profusely.

"That was a nice thing you did, Anabelle." commented May, now regretting she hadn't chosen to award the old woman herself.

"She needs that copper at lot more than I do," Bella replied.

"You know, you're quite right, little sister." May looked very contemplative, like she had learned something. Bella just retuned a slight smile.

Moving on, and weaving through the eddying masses, they circled around to the opposite side of the square, eventually arriving on its far north side, in front of the church steps. Suddenly, May stood straight up, stopping. Now quite breathless, she grabbed rather urgently at her sister's forearm.

"Bella, look!" and pointing urgently with a trembling finger, she said, "There's Sire Styles. And he's just sitting there."

Sure enough, sitting there on the stone steps of the cathedral, staring blindly into the crowd, was constable Styles. He was rapturously engaged in the subtle enjoyment of something locally roasted. Completely unaware he was now being watched, he munched rather appreciatively on a leg of cooked meat, partially wrapped in plain paper, while copious amounts of fat dribbled down his severely pointed chin. So enamoured was he with his tasty lunch, the young man didn't even notice the two Bolton women approaching.

"We should go over, Anabelle, if only to say hello," May said, still breathless, except now it was not from exertion, but from the welcome sight of her would be beau. Despite his thin, awkward frame and rather greasy looking face. "It would be rude not too."

"Oh, May do we have to?" but it was rhetorical question, Bella already knowing they would. For it if had been Corazon they spotted instead, May would have been certain to acquiesce in her favour. That, and considering her sister was already anxiously dragging her over in Styles' direction, the pair headed over towards the cathedral stairs.

When Styles finally realized it was the Bolton girls that approached, he nearly jumped out of his skin in disbelief, dropping his unfinished dinner quickly in the gutter. Standing up and awkwardly wiping his soiled face on his dark sleeve, he rubbed his oily hands furiously on his thighs, already very unsure of himself.

"Why M 'Ladies" he gasped, his face reddening, still chewing a piece of half cooked flesh, "I am honoured. Truly honoured." he continued furiously rubbing his dirty hands on his legs, the stain of the grease darkening his hose.

"Why hello, Sire Styles," May said demurely but almost with anticipation of something more, now equally red. "It is very nice to see you again."

"I am sorry that I cannot offer you some of my lunch," he said foolishly, looking at the half-eaten chunk of fowl, lying in the gutter, now covered with dirt, "perhaps a drink?" his stark voice was flat as he pointed to a vendor close by, looking only at May. The man might as well have been in a hypnotic trance.

"Yes, perhaps I can offer you a drink, as well, M' Lady."

This offer, directed only at Bella, was articulated by a new voice, a much deeper voice, spoken by none other than the Chief Constable himself, coming up on the surprized trio from behind.

"While my illustrious second," nodding his head towards Styles, "treat's your enchanting sister to some refreshment, perhaps you, Lady Anabelle, might care to honor me with a small drink? To your health of course?"

When May started nodding energetically, taking Styles' dirty hand, Bella had to admit that the two of them looked very cute together. Far be it for her to get in the way of their unrequited love. But even so, Anabelle had never really liked the Chief Constable and didn't particularly relish the thought of being alone with him.

She had always felt he was too overly demanding of his men, maintaining such a high opinion of himself, ever since that first day she met him, when he was initially appointed chief. The man's huge ego easily outweighing any of his other positive, or negative, personal traits. However, under today's circumstances, Bella really did not appear to have much of a choice, thinking only of her sister's happiness. So, rather reluctantly she conceded.

"Well, Sire, providing that it's alright with my sister," and May nodded again, holding Styles arm tightly, "and it appears it is, I will acquiesce to one drink." turning to face him properly before adding, "But it would have to be here, at the Dog and Partridge."

For the entrance to the quaint pub was visible, just down the front street.

"Excellent choice, M' Lady." then rather forwardly, Robertson took her unoffered arm, escorting her immediately away from her sister. May having already begun a very intimate conversation with Styles and seeming to have forgotten all about her younger sibling.

"Thanks, May," said Bella, quietly to herself, "leave me to the wolf while you tend the sheep."

"I'll meet you back here in half an hour, dear" Bella yelled out load, back at May.

Her sister nodded again, nonchalantly swiping her hand at the departing Anabelle. Evidently already too enamoured talking with Styles to bother with arranging a future rendezvous with her new best friend.

"Only half an hour?" Robertson looked down at the girl as if slighted, his large eyepatch gleaming in the sun, "That seems a bit unfair. It doesn't give them much time." stressing the word them, but Anabelle knowing perfectly well what he meant.

"Sire, you speak out of turn." Bella retorted angrily at the Chief, "I am only accompanying you for my sister's sake. If not for her, I would not dare been seen with you."

The jibe hurt Robertson, but he continued in a very polite way, regardless of the young woman's apparent rudeness, "My dear, it is only a drink and you certainly have nothing to worry about. After all, I am the Chief of Police."

"And that is the second reason, I'm happy to accompany you. You are an upstanding citizen after all, with a reputation to protect. And therefore, would not dare to try anything..., untoward." ending with a slight stress in her voice.

"Untoward, M' Lady, how could you even think that." producing a wide smile, "I do, after all, have a reputation to protect." the sarcasm clearly evident in his voice.

"Yes," she teased, harshly, "a reputation of locking up innocents and letting the real criminals go free."

"If by any chance, you refer to the young knave, Corazon, you are very much mistaken, M' Lady." Robertson continued, just a slight hint of anger in his voice, as the pair strolled leisurely toward the pub's front entrance. "The man you refer to is a criminal and a menace to society. Robbing the wealthy, people just like your father and mother, then making off with their possessions and leaving them to their own devices." smiling again, as they entered the tavern, holding the door open for her, "I am sure you would not want, nor enjoy that happening to your own family now, would you?"

"Of course not," Bella sighed, "but I have it on good authority, he uses the spoil of his escapades to help the needy and downtrodden. That must count for something?"

"Is that so?" Robertson raised his single visible eyebrow. "You of all people should know, that in terms of the law, it is really of no consequence what he does with his rewards. Theft is theft, and that man is nothing but a sorry thief."

Anabelle remained silent as they walked deeper into the pub. As expected, the place was seething with people from all walks of life and extremely busy. But the proprietor, noticing it was the Chief Constable who entered, immediately found them an open table, sweating slightly as he pulled out the chair for Bella.

"M' Lady." he said simply, then stood close by while Robertson took his own seat. "What can I get you, Sire," he asked, clearly uncomfortable.

"A wine for the lady… and the usual for me," was all Robertson said.

"Right away, Sire, coming right up," running away towards the bar as if burnt.

"You certainly do appear to have a way with people," Anabelle quipped, "what did he do to you, to cause him to act in such a fashion."

"Oh, it's not what he did to me." Robertson replied slyly, "No, the gentleman over there is an ex-convict. One whom I put away, sometime during my earlier days on the force. Now that he has been released, he runs this establishment." providing a quick sweep of his arm. "Apparently, he inherited the business from its previous owner. Also known as a gentleman of somewhat, questionable repute. Merely mentioning to him that I am watching him very closely, appears to have put him slightly on edge whenever I care to visit. It certainly helps on days like today, though. We would not have got a table otherwise."

"Oh, you never know. We may have done," smiling cheekily at him, motioning her head toward an empty table for four, in the corner, by the window. "That table there is permanently reserved for my Father and his family. And that includes me."

Robertson, not realizing, looked at bit sheepish but continued, unabashedly, "It is very nice of you to have accompanied me, M' Lady, I have been looking forward to getting you alone, for quite some time."

"Well, it's not as if I had much of a choice, is it."

"Well, no, but here we are..."

Their discussion was momentarily interrupted by the barman who had returned with the drinks. A small goblet of red wine for Bella and a large chalice for Robertson. Filled with what was clearly a hard liquor drink, its wheat coloured liquid, sparkling in the silver vessel.

"I must say you are looking very striking today. Teal blue isn't it?" he continued without an answer, "And the addition of the bright coloured sash. Certainly, makes a statement, wouldn't you agree?"

Bella answered immediately, "Indeed the colour is teal, and yes, I wanted to wear something elegant, yet still ensure I stood out in the crowd. I felt it might be easier for my family to find me that way. Is that so bad?"

"No, not at all. I like a lady who knows what she wants."

"And what do you want, Chief Constable? You did not invite me out here to introduce me to your barman friend."

"You cut me to the quick, M' Lady. What makes you think I want anything from you at all?" saying this as if hurt.

"Oh, don't think I'm such an innocent. I may be young, but I wasn't born yesterday. I saw the way you looked at me the last time you were at our house and it was clear then, as it is now. For your look is the same."

Bella put her cards on the table, "You believe I was the accomplice who aided Sire Corazon in his escape, don't you?" her eyes sparkled beautifully in the lamp light, despite her angry tone.

"It does not matter what I believe, but what I know, young lady." Robertson's voice retuning to its sinister edge, "Yes, I do think you had something to do with it, in fact, I am certain it was you." he stared back at her, with his single good eye, "As I said to your father the other day, the warden's description of the knave's accomplice was very clear. Right down to the freckles on your pretty little face. He even spoke of that tiny scar over your left eyelid." pointing a long, extended finger to her face, almost, but not quite touching the spot. Bella turned away, as if attempting to hide it.

It was true. It was a very small scar, one Anabelle had received earlier in life, falling out of a tree one sunny afternoon, at the ripe age of six. It showed up very clearly, in bright light, as a short white slash on her already very fair skin. But what the Constable said next disgusted her, only reinforcing her already negative opinion of the man.

"He must have seen it when you provided him that kiss, he was so longing for."

Bella jumped up out of her seat, preparing to leave, "you despicable, disrespectful man, how could you?" she was mortified and hastened to the door, but the Constable was up in a flash, physically grabbing hold of her arm. The force of his grip was quite strong, raising tears to her eyes with the pain. Instead of squealing however, she stopped, and biting her tongue, turned to face the evil man.

"What do you plan to do, Constable, arrest me?"

"Oh no, not at all! Unfortunately, from prior experience, our fair warden does not make a very good witness, particularly in a court of law. However, from your guilty expression and violent reaction, my suppositions are correct, and you are the knave's accomplice."

"I was not reacting to your accusation, but to your rudeness, Constable!" Bella stood firm, unmoving. Still, the tall man did not remove his hand.

"Sit down, my dear. I have not finished with you yet." Robertson sneered in her ear, assisting her slowly back to her seat at the table. "You have not yet told me where I might find your... friend?"

Sitting down again, he finally released her. Bella rubbed her arm where he had, most assuredly, bruised her, "You are a very foolish man, Constable. When my Father hears what you've have done, he will have your job!"

"I am not afraid of you father, Bella. You see, I am appointed by the state. If I was to report you for what you've done, the scandal would be enough to destroy him and let me keep my position. Imagine it, a local constable turning in the daughter of the Duke, the same man that appointed him."

On seeing his wicked smile and listening to his reasoning, Anabelle slumped in the chair, admitting defeat.

"Miss Bolton, you have no doubt heard of the ring of bandits recently found to be attacking wealthy citizens. You and your family need to be on the watch, for who knows when they might strike next?"

"Is that some kind of threat, Chief Constable?"

"Absolutely not, my dear, I am merely pointing out one of the possible perils of your journey, as you return home." Robertson paused, enjoying himself, "You may also have heard that your knave of hearts has recently disappeared and is no longer offering his spoils to the deserving poor. It appears your friendly, Sire Corazon has gone rogue. And now attacks to harm, rather than just to steal."

"You're a liar! That band of thugs is not lead by my Corazon!"

Flinching at her use of the word *my*, he responded in kind. "Are you certain of that, M' Lady? After all, if I'm not mistaken, you have not heard a word from him since my last visit to Eastborough Hall, well over a month ago."

"And how would you know that?" she asked unsure.

"I just know."

"Well, you're wrong." Bella replied strongly, "I do know him, and Sire Corazon would never hurt me or my family. Or any other rich family.... Steal from them maybe, but hurt them, never! You're looking for the wrong man!"

"So sure, are you? Why don't you just do us both a favour and tell me where he lives."

"Not on your life. I would never give him up to you. No matter what lies you've concocted." glaring at him defiantly.

"Well, my dear, I cannot have a thief, now turned murderer, on the loose. If you will not tell me, then I will have to find him myself."

"Good luck with that, Constable." and this time she stood determined to leave, hovering next to her seat just briefly. "I am going to leave now, and you will not touch me. For if you do, it will be the last act you perform as Chief Constable."

"Such spirited words, young Bella. Very well, my dear, but hear this." Robertson remained seated, "No matter what you believe, I know your gentlemen friend has gone bad. I also know he resides in the forbidden wood. I know he rescued you near his hideout and I know you spent the evening there. Alone with him." his inference was deliberate.

Bella did not rise to his bait, "You'll never find him," completely red faced, she was now almost yelling, a few heads in the room turning to see the ruckus, "and it's Lady Bolton to you, Constable!"

Anabelle could not believe this gaul of this cad and, not about to listen to one more word from his hurtful, disgusting mouth, she began walking swiftly toward the tavern entrance. The welcoming light of the afternoon sun beckoning to her.

But the Constable was fast, also standing and appearing directly in front of her, taking hold of Bella's arm once more in his vice grip, squeezing hard, much harder than before. He spoke directly into her ear, the warmth of his alcoholic breath feeling hot and moist on her neck, making all her little hairs stand up, "I will find him, my dear, Lady Bolton and this time, when I do, he will not be going to prison. He will be going to the gallows!"

Finally releasing his grip, he allowed Anabelle to run from the room, tears in her eyes. His hand flexing, Robertson watched her go, the once angry look on his face now contemplative, almost sad. Exiting the tavern, the girl turned towards the church, clearly in search of her sister and the rest of her famous family. She was welcome to go, for he had more important matters to finalize.

It was now obvious that the two of them would never be together and, if he couldn't love her, he thought, why not hate her. It would be easier that way. His feelings still made him unhappy and this situation with the fool Corazon only made it worse. Perhaps not worse, as he would be able to see at least one of them put away for life. And if need be, once the blasted knave was out of the way, perhaps he would decide to put Anabelle Bolton away too.

Determined he would be the one to do it. For if he could not have her, no one could.

Chapter 12 - Bella's Mistake

Bella ran as fast as she could, back along the cobbled street to the steps of the cathedral, looking for Melissa Anne. Spotting her from a short distance away, it was clear that May was still rapturously engaged in a dialog with Styles. The two of them, pleasantly seated on the stone steps of the church, munching on some fried meat. Deep in conversation, their heads almost touching, the couple were holding hands, clearly enthralled with each other's company.

While the last thing Anabelle wanted to do was mess up her sister's rare opportunity, she was so upset about her encounter with Robertson that her selfishness got the best of her. She ran right up to the pair, the previously shed tears finally drying on her face, "May, we must get back to Mother and Father, it's almost time we met up. You've been with Sire Styles long enough."

Looking up at her as if stunned, the expressions on the couple's faces clearly showed that her rude interruption was most disagreeable. Rather reluctantly, they discontinued their revelry, May speaking first.

"Bella dear, can't you see that Styles and I are... engaged?" May's voice was most unpleasant.

Anabelle, reconsidering her approach, was about to usher an apologetic reply, however, quickly stopped herself upon scanning the market further afield. It turns out, her decision to interrupt the love birds was well timed, for coming towards that side of the square, having spotted Bella's very bright outfit, were her parents.

The Duchess, wearing an extremely bright smile on her face, evidently well pleased to have found her wayward daughters.

This altered her response quite readily. "May, Mother and Father are coming up behind me."

Disbelieving, her sister bent her head around Bella's body, to look.

"No silly, don't look! They'll see you. Just stand up smartly and come here. I'm sorry, Sire Styles, but my sister will have to finish up with you some other time."

The frightened junior constable helped May quickly to her feet, his gangly legs suddenly quite weak at the thought of being discovered by the Duke.

"My apologies, M' Lady." he said as he looked directly into May's eyes with fervent longing. Clearing his throat, he added, "In order to avoid you any potential embarrassment, I will perhaps sneak away, while the opportunity presents itself."

After making sure May was safely up and staring one last time at her beautiful face, he turned to go. Suddenly remembering, he spun back toward her, grabbing the remaining greasy food from May's outstretched hands, who had completely forgotten it was there, "You're done with this, I'm sure, M' Lady." he quipped, finally preparing to leave.

"Oh, dears!" they heard their mother's call from the bottom of the steps as, with May now upright, the Duke and Duchess had spotted both of them, "Please come on down, it's time for lunch!"

Gratefully, Styles remained partially hidden by Bella's motionless form and had not yet been noticed. May, adamant that this time, she was not to be denied, moved sideways behind her sister, hiding herself again briefly from her parents. Brushing her lips urgently against the young man's cheek, but only for a second, she said her goodbyes. Her young suiter, thoroughly embarrassed, turned bright red almost instantly. Puffing out his chest and smiling rather stupidly at May, he dashed away up the steps, disappearing through the front door of the Church. Presumably to make a getaway from one of its side entrances.

"Darlings, thank goodness. Where have you been," the Duke rambled, mounting a few of the stone steps towards his children, "Your Mother's been frantic!"

"Oh, Father," returned Bella," wiping the last of the salty water from her face, "Not to worry, we've been here all the time." looking over at May conspiringly.

Her sister nodded, just as her mother noticed Bella's tears. "What's that, dear, have you been crying?"

"Oh, posh Mother, it's just all the smoke from these food vendors. I can't abide the stuff. It makes my eyes water. That's all."

"Well come along then ladies, let's get inside where it won't bother you." the Duke offered.

As the four of them dismounted the stone steps, May turned, offering a rather longing look up at the church doorway. Reaching out, Bella grabbed her hand, helping her down and together they made their way towards the pub. Anabelle was nervous that the Constable might still be there, but knew she could do nothing about it, as her parents were keen for some afternoon refreshment, their destination set.

"I do hope our regular table is available, on this very busy day." the Duchess chimed in.

"Oh, darling, you know it will be available. It's available for us every day, whether we use it or not," the Duke assured his wife pleasantly.

"Oh yes, dear, perhaps your right." his wife replied, as they entered the busy establishment.

The inn's proprietor, immediately noticing it was the Duke, promptly rushed to the door to escort them in. He glanced rather strangely at Bella, who he had just seen, wondering why she had returned so soon, but said nothing. A quick scan of the room revealed that the Chief Constable was long gone, permitting Anabelle to breathe a great sigh of relief.

As they sat down, the waiter presented them with menus while the rest of her family broke into normal discourse. However, Bella remained quiet, completely stressed about her entire conversation with Robertson and what he had said about Corazon. As she sat there thinking it through a second time, there was really only one decision she could make. Before the drinks had come, Anabelle had made up her mind and, as the barman placed the four goblets of wine nervously on the table, she knew exactly what she had to do.

She was going to find out once and for all what was happening. And, that meant yet another ride into the forbidden wood.

***

The family finished their lunch and shortly afterward, the Duke demanded they return home. With the Duchess having shopped for what she had been after, Bella in a state of extreme nervousness and May pleased with her short, but meaningful rendezvous with Styles, there were no complaints from any of the Bolton women. While the Duke thought this rather odd, he welcomed their lack of argument.

Their walk back to the brahman was short, as Carson had managed to move it slightly closer to the village square as the day progressed and traffic lessened. As the four of them entered, Bella noticed all of the Duchess's packages stacked atop the carriage, nicely wrapped and loaded for the trip home.

The return journey was as uneventful as the mornings inward trek had been, the family arriving back at the Bolton estate shortly before five, with the sun just beginning to lower in the west. The two girls ran inside ahead of their parents, while Carson took away the coach and the two very tired horses.

May, anxious to let Bella know all about her escapades with Styles, was literally loopy with excitement, as the two sisters mounted the stairs up to their rooms.

As an answer to her sibling's request, Anabelle offered, "Now May, while I would just love to hear all about your afternoon, right now, I don't feel very well. Can I ask that you tell me all about it, tomorrow?"

Melissa Anne, a huge pout poised on her thin face, was stunned with disappointment. Disbelieving that Anabelle, her new best friend, knowing how important it was to her, would be so mean as not to share in her joy.

So, in order to save face, May turned angry, responding, "Well, you look fine to me, Anabelle Bolton. I just think you're jealous of Styles and me." putting her hands on her hips, "Frankly, I don't care what you do with yourself. Go, have your rest! Perhaps I might tell you tomorrow, but perhaps I won't."

When no protest was forthcoming at her threat, May stomped off down the hall, "I need to get out of these travelling clothes anyway," turning around briefly, calling back to Bella, "I'm sure Susan will be very interested to listen to all the *intimate* details." May making sure to stress the intimate.

"May, I'm sorry," Bella said, holding up her hand in mock protest. But it was too late, for her sister was already heading away from her down the passage, calling loudly for their maid.

As soon as she was out of sight, Anabelle wasted no time, running straight to her room and quickly shaking off her elegant travelling gown. Looking around, she grabbed for one of her more practical travelling outfits, slipping hurriedly into the light beige, heavy cotton, riding costume. While still doing up the buttons, Anabelle ran toward the window. The late day sun was streaming through the glass, illuminating her way, making bright, distorted patterns on the bedroom carpet. As she had done many times before, Bella mounted the frame and hopped out onto the roof. Carefully maneuvering across the various ramparts, within moments she was at the ivy encrusted trestle and down to the gravel drive, once more.

Anabelle ran urgently to the far side of the path and keeping to the lengthening shadows of the surrounding shrubberies, she eventually reached the stables.

"Carson, Carson!" she called lightly, hoping the boy was close by, obviously still working with the team they had just recently returned with.

"Yes, M' Lady?" was his shocked reply, emerging from the large building, wiping his hands on a dirty cloth that had surely seen better days.

Looking up to see Bella standing there dressed in what was obviously a travelling outfit. He stared, "Why, M' Lady what brings you out 'ere? I thought you 'ad gone inside to gossip with your sister." suddenly, realizing what he had just said, with profound mortification, he turned a humiliating pink. "Oh, please pardon me, M' Lady," he stammered, bowing, "that was uncalled for."

"Oh, don't worry about a silly thing like that, Carson." Anabelle retuned, chucking at his awkwardness, "You're absolutely correct. That's exactly what I should be doing right now." Bella remained slightly out of breath, "And I know I'm going to be in for it later, knowing what I'm about to do is foolhardy in the extreme. But regardless, I need you to get Winter ready for me."

"But why, M' Lady? Where on earth are you going?" he looked at her with a slightly troubled expression.

"I'm going to see if I can find, Sire Corazon. There have been some nasty rumours floating about and I must find out exactly what's going on?" grinning at the open mouth of the stable boy. "Close your mouth, Carson, you're catching fly's. It's not polite, in front of a lady."

The young man stood up straight, wiping the silly look of surprise off his face, "Yes M' Lady," and running inside, within minutes he returned, leading out the faithful stallion, saddled and ready.

"Is there anything else, M' Lady." he asked, helping her mount.

"Why yes, there is one more thing," Bella said, looking down at him, "I'm going to ask you to cover for me, in case I'm missed. Can you do that?"

"I'm not sure," the stammer returning, "what on earth would I say?"

"Oh, I don't know," she said riding off, "tell them we're seeing each other, or something?"

Anabelle left the young Carson, standing in the bright light of the stable entrance, looking so red, he might have been mistaken for a large radish.

***

Bella made good time. Even though Winter had gone all the way into town and back again drawing a heavy coach and was tired, the fact that Carson had provided him food and water, gave him a second wind. On his own, he was very fast, and the young Bolton girl delighted in the cool air flowing through her hair, as they raced over the fields. She turned north early to avoid the ravine, then cruised east, away from town and toward the forest, just as twilight fell.

There was little noise, except the sound of Winter's heavy breathing and his shoes clomping on the dirt of the pathway. As it had been a dry day, the two left a small trail of dust in their wake, accelerating faster in the direction of the dark wood. The night was cool and not having an overcoat, Anabelle shivered as she urged Winter onward.

So, intent was she on her final destination, that young Anabelle failed to notice a second plume of dirt rising off the road behind her. Whomever, or whatever, it was that occupied the same path, remained unseen, as they continued riding into the darkening night.

Upon reaching the meadow near the edge of the wood, Bella slowed and, now at a slow trot, approached the darkening treeline. There was still a hint of illumination left as she entered the wood and for that she was glad, for she would need it to find Corazon's lair. But after several more minutes, the young girl realized she had forgotten the way and stopping, looked around the glen in frustration.

"Corazon!" she yelled, now knowing she was lost, "Corazon, are you there?"

There was no reply, just the sound of Winter's heavy breath, the wind in the trees and the distant hoot of a screech owl.

Remaining stationary on the forest path, the light smell of loam and pine filling her nostrils, she breathed in a deep breath of the fresh mountain air in an attempt to sooth her trembling spirit. But, just on the edge of the next light breeze, amongst the natural forest fragrance, she detected something else. Sensing a deeper, vaguely musky and no doubt unfriendly, animal smell. One that for no apparent reason, made Bella even more uncomfortable and on edge. Certain she would not want to meet its owner. She glanced around nervously, unsure of herself, a rising fear building in her heaving chest.

"Corazon!" Bella tried again, this time with a little more urgency, "I need to speak with you! If you're out there, please it's me, Bella!"

Still no response, and by now the trail had become very dark. The woods' many shadows lengthening, the early evening darkness, closing in like a veil of thick, grey smoke.

Anabelle shivered. Winter, neighing in protest pulled hard to return them back to the meadow, where they might at least share the last vestiges of daylight. She pulled on the lead, reigning him in, attempting to calm him, "It's okay, boy, everything's fine."

Patting his moist neck, he seemed to relax briefly, before lightly stomping around once more.

"Oh, perhaps your right, Winter, you might know better than I," she said quietly to herself, as the horse continued to fight her, "this is just unladylike foolishness."

Bella resigned at once to leave and return home, for that was the only thing she could do.

"Perhaps foolishness, yes, but certainly, not unladylike." the knave's voice, coming from out of nowhere, frightened her silly, making her jump. Winter also bucking with fear at the new sound.

"Now, that's a good boy," Corazon said gently, emerging from the shadows and patting the horse, calming him almost instantly, "to what do I owe the pleasure of this rather..., nocturnal visit."

"Oh, Corazon," Bella sighed from above, her fear abating, her chest still heaving, "am I glad to see you!"

"And I you, my Sweet." he smiled widely, "but I would suggest, before our hungry forest friends come out to play, that we get out of this cold wood and indoors, to a place more comfortable for us all."

Saying this, he led them a few minutes further down the trail, then off through a familiar sidetrack and, finally, into the clearing bordering his cliff side hideaway.

"Winter can come inside, also, if he wishes," leading the horse and rider around the stone abutment and through, what looked like, a weave of twine and nettles covering the entrance of Corazon's lair.

In passing, he commented, "I made this up last month when the Chief Constable's goons started looking for me."

"You mean Robertson has already sent men here?" Bella asked incredulously, as Corazon helped her down off the horse, after entering the foyer of the large cavern.

"Why of course, my Sweet," Corazon commented nonchalantly, first tying Winter up on a knoll post, then offering his arm and directing Bella further inside, "Didn't you think he would begin looking for me right away? The man's sent at least three groups out to find me, already."

"Oh, Corazon!" she gushed, hugging him, "I'm so sorry, I didn't know. I thought you were safe here." then she looked up into his eyes, a small tear visible on her rosy cheek.

"Well, I am, for the moment."

The knave lightly brushed the saltwater away with his thumb and bent to kiss her. She pressed forward and up, accepting his lips anxiously, wantonly, feeling the slight coolness of their moisture due to the cold outside. They soon warmed however, their two bodies sharing heat, as they embraced warmly.

When they parted, Corazon answered kindly. "Not to worry, darling, those fools would never find me here. They have absolutely no skill as trackers. Even with my lair right in front of them, I'm sure they would just wander right on past."

He made a swinging motion with his arm, before taking her waist and guiding her into his sitting room, the light sound of the falling waters at the back of the cave, soothing her.

As before, there was a bright, roaring blaze in the hearth meaning, contrary to the antechamber, Corazon's lounge was toasty and warm. Bella dropped into one of the seats, her paramour taking another opposite and for a moment they just stared at one another, appreciatively.

"Tell me, my Sweet, why are you here? Certainly not to warn me about that fool Robertson."

"Well, No... I mean yes, but...." Bella hesitated, staring at him, at his ruggedly handsome face, wonderfully illuminated by the fire, "Oh Corazon, I missed you terribly!" saying this as she sat forward.

"And I you," he returned, graciously, also bending toward her, "but tell me, what brought you out here, and at this time of night? There's obviously something else..., I can see it in your face."

Breaking their rather intimate eye contact, Anabelle suddenly straightened up, glancing down to the floor and hesitating, yet again. "You're right it's true, my love, there is something more. Seemingly, there is nothing I can hide from you. But before I tell you, can you answer me a question?"

"Certainly, anything." considering, "my love... I like that.... What is it?"

"Can you tell me why of late, you've not been your normal self." Bella stopped gathering her thoughts, "What I mean to say is..., why haven't you been out stealing from the wealthy to give to the poor, like you always have?" then adding, breathing harder, "People are saying you've stopped providing spoils to the downtrodden of the village."

Without stopping, she concluded, releasing all the tension in her body, "Some are even saying you've taken up as a leader of highwaymen, robbing people for pleasure, and killing for sport. Oh, Corazon, please tell me, I must know!" Bella finally stopped, breathless, obviously eager for an answer.

Corazon, silent throughout Bella's rant, looked at her with his large blue eyes, pausing briefly before he spoke. "Ah, I see you have been listening to the rumour mill again." and he chuckled, settling in his seat, as if to tell a story.

"My Sweet, have no fear, your beloved Corazon has not gone rogue, nor taken up killing rich people for fun."

The knave placed his hands together, peaking his fingers, "It goes like this. Apparently, there is indeed someone out there leading a team of highwaymen, intent only on robbing and killing their prey. And truth is, for some unapparent reason, he happens to dress just like me..., thus the confusion." casually shrugging his shoulders.

"But Corazon, if it's not you, then who?" Bella was visibly upset, apparently not hearing or believing Corazon's innocence. "If not you, then why have you stopped helping people?"

Corazon smiled again, being patient with the girl he adored, "My Sweet, that's an easy one. After I left you, I continued my various exploits, alleviating the fancy folk of their excesses and passing them on to those more... deserving. But after I learned of this new team of cutthroats, I had to change my tactics. Instead of relieving the wealthy folk of their possessions, I have spent the last several weeks, engaged in various attempts to assist them when under attack."

Bella sat mesmerized as he continued. "I have so far, only been able to stop two of these attacks, as I initially had no idea when or where they might occur. However, I have slowly begun to track the men, discovering their preferred..., shall we say... locations of assault. I am certain that, in the future, I will eventually be able to stop them, permanently. Most of the time, I have at least been able to ward off the citizens. The only problem now is that when they see me, they think that I am the one who is after them. It is all truly quite a mess." Corazon paused briefly, "That is the reason why I have not had a chance to help the poor folks lately, monetarily anyway. I have been too busy preventing calamity."

Bella stared waiting for more, but when none was forthcoming, she jumped out of her chair, vaulting onto Corazon's lap, wrapping her arms around him, squeezing him hard and planting a rather rough kiss on his cheek, "Oh Corazon, I knew it. I knew you were not the one. I knew you were innocent. Oh, I'm just so glad it's not you!" and she hugged him even tighter.

Corazon looked down at Anabelle, her arms tight around him, smiling. Liking the feel of her light weight on his lap, the scent of her hair, the sweetness of her breath, the rising and falling of her chest, the smooth fairness of her skin. But what's this?

In grabbing hold and caressing Corazon, Bella's sleeves had pushed upward, exposing her delicate forearms. But what he saw there was not the pinky whiteness of her tantalizing skin, but only nasty black and blue bruising all up and down her left arm as if it had been stuck in a wine press. He looked at her in shock, delicately lifting the damaged appendage and inspecting it further.

"My goodness, Bella what has happened to you? Certainly, this is no accident?" he was shaken at the display of violence, "Who in their right mind would stoop to harm such a delightful creature?

"Robertson." Anabelle stated, her voice flat, looking down, "He did this to me."

"When?"

"This very afternoon. At the inn in the village."

"This afternoon? The swine will live to regret it," Corazon growled, his voice straining, becoming angrier, "But surely, you were not with the Constable, alone?"

"Yes, I know it was stupid, but it was market day. May and I had become separated from our parents. We bumped into Styles on the steps of the church, who clearly wished to speak with May. Well, she wanted to talk with him as well. I was content to stay and perhaps get some food, when Robertson showed up out of nowhere. He asked me to have a drink with him and, rather stupidly I agreed, thinking my sister would appreciate some time alone with her...," Bella almost said fiancé but then changed her mind, "gentlemen friend."

After that she stopped. The room almost silent for a moment, the fire crackling, Corazon stayed still, listening intently.

Eventually continuing, Anabelle began to cry, "He led me away to the Dog and Partridge, where he told me all kinds of sordid tales about you and what you were doing." she hesitated, "I didn't believe a word of it."

"Ah, hah!" stated Corazon simply, chuckling, "But you did, my Sweet. Otherwise you would never have come out here tonight."

"Oh, Corazon," she bellowed, "you're right of course." Bella, unable to face him, stood up, and walking away in shame, began pacing the room.

The knave, slightly upset about no longer having the beautiful girl close to him, let her rave. "I've always thought the best of you, but some of the things he said..., they kind of made sense, in a way. And that's why I had to come to see you. I needed to know for certain that it wasn't you."

Her burden released and no longer ashamed, Bella spun back to face him, "But now I know the truth."

"But that does not explain your injury. Did the Constable ask you anything else during your discussion?" the concern plainly affixed to his handsome face.

"Well, of course he did! He wanted to know where you were. Where to find your lair. This house!" flinging her arms, Anabelle was truly crying now, tears flowing profusely down her pretty, freckled face. "When I refused to tell him, he grabbed me, telling me he'd find you anyway. Telling me, he'd find you... and kill you!" the flustered girl took in a deep breath, "Oh, goodness! I came here to warn you, Corazon."

Corazon remain seated not saying a thing, the only sounds Bella's continued blubbering and the friendly popping and snapping of the wood in the roaring fire. Then it hit him.

"You came here by yourself, didn't you?" he asked, slightly concerned.

"Yes, the only one who knew I left was Carson, our stable man." Bella whimpered.

"Good man, that Carson. Did anyone follow you?"

At this simple question Bella started, her tears stopping as if dammed, regarding Corazon with dread, "What do you mean?" a look of abject fear, replacing her sadness.

"I said, did anyone follow you here, tonight?"

"Well, not that I know of." then she broke down again, nervously edgy, uncertain, "Oh, Corazon, what if someone did? I was so anxious to get here, I wouldn't have known even if they had. What if I've put you in danger! I'm so stupid!"

"No, my Sweet, you are far from stupid," Corazon stated, rising and approaching her slowly. Once again, he took her carefully in his arms, tenderly encircling her with his strength, feeling her fragile body tremble.

"You have only been misled. That fiend Robertson scared you on purpose. Told you all those stories, knowing full well you would come out here to prove them wrong."

The knave stopped, thinking a moment, "But no matter, even if he did, for prudence sake, he would have sent only one man."

They separated, Corazon holding Anabelle at arm's length, gazing at her distractedly, appreciating her exquisite beauty despite the tears. "And that man, if he did come, will still have to go back and report. Considering it is the dead of night, the earliest they might be expected to return is sometime tomorrow, likely afternoon. And when they do, I shall be ready."

Then the knave brought the very beautiful, youngest daughter of the Duke close, kissing her one more time, avidly and passionately. Relishing her taste and her warm fragrant breath on his face as their noses touched, "but speaking of night, Anabelle Bolton," he said quietly, "you need to get back. Your precious family might be worried."

Guiding her gently out of the room, again tenderly wiping the residue salty wetness from her face, "Come along, my Sweet, it's late. By now Winter will be well rested, and I will ride with you..., all the way home."

Arm in arm, they headed out together.

Chapter 13 – Discovery and Escape

As it was, one of Robertson's goons did in fact, follow the young Lady Bolton on her twilight ride out into the forest. It was the complainer Ashbrook, and at first, he had been rather reluctant to obey his superior's seemingly odd instructions. Until he saw the young Bolton woman making her way east all alone, at such a late hour, just like the Chief Constable had predicted. And not only that, but of how very deliberately she rode and with such a look of sheer determination spread across her pretty face.

Setting out after her, the junior constable had followed at a fair distance, the entire way. Ultimately spotting Bella entering the wood, exactly where he and his fellows had previously searched endlessly for that blasted knave. Shortly thereafter, the young woman began calling out the thief's name and so, dismounting and leaving his horse, he crept up slowly through the underbrush, always on the lookout.

It was no surprise that he had a bit of a reputation amongst his brethren, for not being the cleanest of Robertson's constables. As Sire Ashbrook's family considered themselves lucky if he bathed once a month. Needless to say, his personal odour was often extremely pungent, sometimes detectable at quite a long distance, provided he was upwind. It was his job therefore, to always stay downwind of the people he followed, and he continued to do so that evening. Although the winds infrequent gusts were quite variable that night and once he was sure the girl might have noticed him. Thankfully, he remained discrete and unseen.

When the knave did show up rather suddenly that night, he surprised not only the girl, but also his watcher. The startled Ashbrooke had to take several breaths to calm his heart, before following the two, at a safe distance, along the heavily beaten path. He spotted them turning off the main road and, when they had gone a sufficient distance beyond, he marked the path by cutting a large chip off a nearby stump with his knife. He then followed even more cautiously, eventually seeing the pair enter Corazon's cave.

Ashbrook kicked himself as to how many times he and his colleagues had gone by that very spot but, due to its unique and very expertly applied camouflage, they had not been able to detect the grotto's entrance. The tables had now turned, giving him a warped sense of pride that he could finally return to Chief Robertson with some good news. Able to hear the two chattering lively inside, unfortunately he could not detect any specific words, although could tell by their voices that the girl was upset and, at one point, the knave became very angry.

It didn't matter, the junior constable had seen enough. Breaking off and heading back through the trees, he set few more additional markers, before making it cautiously back to his horse, which he found unharmed and just where he left it, patiently feeding itself on the grass of the meadow. Within seconds, Ashbrook had mounted and was off at a full gallop, not wanting to wait another minute next to that terrible wood and the horrid creatures that lived within it. The night was cold but clear, and a bright, full moon cast a warm cerulean glow over the countryside, leading him safely back across the fields and down the road towards town.

Wouldn't Chief Robertson be pleased, Ashbrook smiled. Tomorrow an entire posse of constables would return en-masse and then, that wicked scoundrel Corazon would be all theirs.

***

The following day, after saying goodbye to Bella at the Bolton estate and travelling the rest of the night on his long walk back home, Corazon spent most of the morning preparing his final offering for one of the poor of Eastborough. Contrary to what he had told Anabelle, he still had a few items left over from his last excursion and was determined that they should see their new owner before anything else transpired.

After packing the articles away in a large satchel, he decided it was time to take a shower. After all, he had hiked a tremendous distance that night and did not know how long it might be before he had a chance for another one. And just the thought of a cold, fresh wash, pleased him immensely.

He removed his outer garments, quickly hopping under the flowing water constantly cascading leisurely down into the small pool at the back of his lair. Corazon relished in the sharp feel of the cold water against his rough skin, the flow just strong enough for a pleasant bath. At that time of day, just prior to noon, while still quite cool, the falling liquid was at its warmest. He smiled, recalling young Bella in that exact spot many weeks ago, screaming loudly as she stepped under the frigid falls.

Rather casually proceeding to soap himself up under the tumbling stream, he remembered back to all of the work that had been necessary to set up the useful shower in the first place.

Digging of the deep supply trench across the variable terrain, all the way from the river tributary itself, had been quite difficult. But the subsequent process of first finding and then lining it with cut stone, to insure it did not silt up and would always provide a clear flow, was even more time consuming. Then there had been the construction and set-up of the diverter valve, atop the hill over his house and its accompanying control mechanism, to either halt or release the stream at will.

Looking over to the rope and handle far in the corner of the chamber, reminded him of all the effort he had made to get his water feature just right. Of course, there was also the digging of the opening into the roof of the cave, as well as the connection of the final trench to the diversion he had installed. And lastly the final release of the river's supply.

Corazon shivered, not with the coolness of water, but at the thought of something going wrong to the makeshift, wooden diverter he had constructed. For if something happened to that mechanism, he knew that the water flow would increase so much it might eventually match that of the river itself. Surely, flooding the back of his hillside house, with its excessively flowing volume in minutes.

Coming back to reality and finishing-up, after drying off, he got himself dressed, today using a fresh set of clothes. Corazon always did this when visiting his beneficiaries, with the intent to do what he could to raise the spirits of the person or persons he was about to visit, and a new outfit seemed to do it every time.

He strapped on his belt and knife, as well as slinging on the quiver of arrows and his bow upon one shoulder that Bella had politely returned to him the night before. On the other, he slung the satchel he had previously prepared and pulling on his boots, was ready to go. That was when he heard the sound of numerous intruders outside the cave. Intruders that were definitely not those of the forest dwelling variety.

The sound was faint at first, the Constable's men approaching in on foot, supposedly after having left their horses in the meadow. The blasted swine were early, Corazon mused, cursing himself for not having been long gone by the time they arrived.

Tip toeing his way to the entrance and looking through the webbed cover, the knave spied at least two of Robertson's men already moving around the stone abutment. Without hesitation he dashed back into the cave, briefly topping in his lounge and trying to think. It was only then Corazon realized the awful truth. With no other way to exit his home, he was trapped!

More noises continued to develop and eventually, he could hear the Chief Constable himself, cruelly directing his men in their search. The man did not sound happy, so Corazon knew he had to find another way out or he might not last the afternoon.

He could not possibly fight his way out with that many men and he wouldn't want to anyway. Killing junior constables just doing their jobs, was definitely not part of his mandate.

Wracking his brain, Corazon considered his options. How can I get out? Sweat began running down his back, his body starting to warm with mounting anxiety. Moving back further into the cavern, he backed up slowly, hands against the cold rock of the walls, his head pounding. The voices outside, continuing to build, getting closer.

And then it hit him. Something from that morning's earlier contemplations. That was it! The shower!

Quickly turning, now with renewed purpose, he headed to the rear of the cave, the falling water glistening in the residue firelight. Running over to the wall and pulling hard on the rope, Corazon activated the diverter far above. Initially, there was no change, and thinking something was wrong, he tugged anxiously at the control again.

Slowly, the waterfall calmed, its flow gradually diminishing. Dropping his tense shoulders in relief, the knave watched as it turned into a light drizzle and then single drops, before completely halting all together.

With the flow stopped and after taking a deep breath, he began to free climb the rock wall, the rough stone biting harshly into the skin of his hands. He was about halfway up when he heard the sound of the team of constables enter his home, the echo of their voices in the enclosed space, giving them away.

He accelerated his pace, fresh blood developing on his fingertips making the climb more difficult, Suddenly, his right hand slipped, and he was left hanging by one hand, the weight on his arm heavy, painfully pulling at his tense muscles. The added strain was incredible, and he could feel the old ache, from his recently dislocated shoulder, burn.

Thankfully, the excruciating pain was only brief, as on the second try, his extended reach was successful, allowing him to once more grip the wall with both hands. Corazon paused, chest heaving, the blood rushing to his head. But the respite was only temporary and now recovered, he continued upward at an accelerated pace.

At the top of the cave was a small stone outcropping, that he remembered chipping out of the bedrock to provide a channel for the water flow, so that it fell nearer the center of the chamber. Upon reaching it he stood up, looking upward through the empty, supply hole. The opening was wet and slippery, just large enough for him and perhaps his satchel. But certainly not wide enough for anything more. He would, therefore, have to leave his trusty bow and arrow behind. It was a shame considering he had just reacquired it, but Corazon didn't mind. He would still have his knife and anyway, it was far more important to take the satchel, over and above any of his weapons.

Reluctantly, unslinging the bow, he placed it alongside the quiver in the small residue pool of water left in the channel. Giving it a final, almost apologetic glance, as one might do for an old friend, he began his long climb up the chimney. It was very slippery, and he had to brace his back and feet against the slimy walls to make any headway.

Hoping to make it out undetected and initially believing he had, he continued upward into the semi darkness. But at the last moment, he heard a stifled shout from below, one of the constables entering the chamber, yelling for him to stop. Obviously, Corazon had not been fast enough.

There was no going back now. Doubling his efforts, he felt the impact of an arrow close to his feet. Slipping and sliding awkwardly in the half light, the knave found himself losing momentum with the attack, before gaining renewed strength and pushing onward.

It was almost pitch dark in the shaft, just a haze of grey light emanating from up above, making the ascent that much more perilous and difficult. The wet stone pressing into his back, the slime coating his hands and clothes, the residue water droplets dropping into his face and blurring his vision, all helped to make the journey that much more arduous. But the knave would not be stopped and determined to succeed, continued upward.

The higher he progressed however, the more Corazon began to realize that, should he ever lose his grip, there would be no possible way to arrest his fall. He would surely plummet to his death on the rock floor below. Forcing these grim thoughts from his mind and working ever more feverishly, he continued to maintain his careful hand over hand movements up the tube. Gradually, the light above him became clearer and with it, the feeling that his ultimate goal was close at hand.

Several tense moments later, Corazon miraculously emerged at the top, feeling the heat of the sun, first on his arm and then his head, as he popped out of the manmade fissure into the rock filled trench atop the hill. Dragging the rest of his weary body out of the opening, he lay there in the dry riverbed, chest heaving. Enjoying the warmth of the noon day, but mostly enjoying the fact that he was still alive. The noise of insistent echoing voices emanating from down below, however, brought him quickly out of his revelry.

Then he was sure he detected another sound; that of another person coming up the pipe!

What a fool that Robertson was, sending one of his men up after him! Corazon couldn't believe it. But regardless, he would not be caught, not now. He only hoped it was just the one man, because with what he was thinking of doing now, the unfortunate constable would soon regret his rash actions.

Without any more consideration he stood, brushing himself off and briefly scanning the surrounding area. Climbing out of the trench and reaching down, he grabbed a large branch, before making his way over to his home-made diverter. It was a beautiful thing, having worked so well for him over the many years of its operation. Overtime, the wood valve had aged and as he watched the river's water flow past, bypassing the feed trench, he knew what he had to do.

Using the branch as a club, Corazon began hitting the diverter mechanism over and over. While continuing his relentless beating of the dependable contraption he had spent so much time to create, remorse began building inside him with each successive blow. He was not happy with what he was about to do.

Ultimately, the repeated stress on the mechanism was too much for it and the wooden components blasted apart, separating and releasing the heavy flow of water into the channel once more. But now, with no control, the flood volume was almost triple of that flowing previously, the rapid torrent running down the ditch and almost overwhelming it, before flushing through the opening.

The renewed flow was so high that it began to pool, building over the entrance, gallons and gallons of water entering the slimy tunnel from which he had just emerged. Over the rapid tide of the water, Corazon heard a distant yell, soon morphing into a scream, as the one unlucky constable, still in the midst of his climb, was flushed down and then out of the tube. Dropping out over the overhang and down to his death on the floor of the cave below.

Corazon, listened to the man's suffering with deep regret, hating Robertson for forcing him to that extreme, only wishing there had been another way. Shaking his head and holding on to his slime coated satchel, the knave escaped into the underbrush at the peak of the hill. His intent was to eventually circle around, descend and make his way back into the village.

With a heavy heart, he took one more look back at his home, a strange feeling arising in his chest. Certain he would not be coming back to this place, he finally stole away, a sad, desolate look splashed across his chiseled features.

***

Inside the cave, it had been Ashbrook who had been ordered to make the climb. Robertson was adamant with his order, as it had been Ashbrook's arrow that had glanced off the rock, just shy of the knave's foot, as he escaped.

"But Sire, that climb is too high. And what if I slip?"

"You would do better to worry about what will happen to you if you don't go, Ashbrook," Robertson bellowed, "now move!"

It had been several minutes before Ashbrook made it to the outcropping, calling out to the Chief below, "He's left his bow and arrows here!"

"Well, throw them down and get going!"

After tossing down the abandoned weapons, slowly and reluctantly, Ashbrook climbed into the tube above. He actually slipped out twice, falling into the puddle at the top of the outcropping, before perfecting his technique and shimming up the chimney in a very similar way to how Corazon had done it minutes before. The junior constable was about halfway up when the water torrent was released.

The flow started small, splashing Ashbrooke's face, initially making him exclaim in frustration. But as the current accelerated, it ultimately overpowered the man and, knowing he could do nothing to stem the flood now beating against his body, he began to scream, the sound garbled by the rapid flow of water, drowning out his cries.

Eventually, with his breath gone, his hold loosened, and Ashbrook was literally flushed down the tube, impacting hard against the slotted, horizontal stone projection. Stunned, his body rolled off, plummeting the reminder of the way, into the partially dry pool below, his screams ending forever as his head impacted noisily upon the rock floor. Skull smashed, his blood and grey matter briefly fogged the water, before being flushed away down the earthen drain.

But the increased flow was too much for the drain and overpowering it, quickly began to flood the chamber. Robertson, wet with spray, ran from the room, yelling for his men to follow. The group of them sprinted from the cave, now rapidly filling with water surging down from the raging river above. They took refuge behind the large outcropping of rock at the cave entrance, watching as Corazon's remaining possessions were flushed from the opening. Broken and battered tables and chairs, now all useless, rapidly flowing with the raging flood as it searched for somewhere to go.

The flow, diverted by the stone wall, forced its way around and through a small crop of trees before finally making its way overland to a lower part of the river, returning back to the torrent that once supplied it. The cave home of the knave was completely destroyed, now part of a new tributary and water feature, only to be enjoyed by the animals of the wood.

Standing there, soaked through to the skin, the Chief Constable was livid. "That slimy bastard has escaped us again." scanning the group of wet constables to see if there were any others missing.

As he did this, the battered body of Ashbrook floated by, head bashed in, all bloated and pasty white. His junior constable's dead corpse bumped against the newly created riverbank, getting briefly hooked on some exposed tree roots, before washing away downstream.

"Well," Robertson said rather cruelly, a wicked smile forming, "at least the dirty bugger finally got himself a decent bath."

***

Corazon made good time, managing to get away from the forest unseen, as Robertson had his men stay behind, combing the hills searching for him. The walk through the open countryside was pleasant and he took his time, the bright hot sun drying out his rather soggy clothes. "So much for putting on a fresh outfit," he thought to himself, looking down and seeing all the thick green slime, and other dirt from the recent tunnel climb, coating his tunic. "At least I made it out with the satchel intact."

Reaching the outskirts of the town, the knave jogged his way around the perimeter road, before cutting through into the town proper. Stopping briefly at one of the street vendors selling firewood, he eventually entered the village's poorer quarter. Corazon then continued a few blocks further down the sad looking high street, before stopping in front of what looked like something that might have been a shop front in the past, but now appeared as only a sad looking, personal dwelling.

It was a very gloomy looking home, with a sagging roof, a few missing windows and a rough-cut wooden door. The current state of its construction indicating that it would get mighty cold during the county's frigid winter nights, and for that reason alone, Corazon was happy to have made it. The old woman who lived there, not only desperately required the firewood he held in his hand, but in addition, and more importantly, needed what he possessed in his oil skin satchel.

On stepping up to the stoop, he noticed several rusty iron connections hanging down from above, evidently for the missing sign of the building's former business. Lightly knocking twice, the knave entered without waiting, knowing the owner would have already left the door open for him.

Making his way inside the rather small space, Corazon noted, as he had expected, the pitiful remains of a tiny fire glowing in the hearth; really just a few red coals rather than a real fire. Despite the residence's partial lack of windows, the room was stuffy and dark, ugly grey shadows erupting everywhere. The withering flame of the fire produced no real heat, nor light. Hopefully with his gifts, that would all soon change.

The first thing he did, walking over to the fireplace, was to break up the recently acquired bundle of wood in his arms and add a fresh log to the embers. As the kindling was nice and dry, it burst into flame readily, the new blaze, developing some welcome warmth to brighten the extremely cold space. After fanning the rising flames and adding in several more chunks of firewood, he turned to face the home's lone occupant.

The old widow was sitting on her chair by the hearth, covered in a woolen shawl and a blanket, both slightly threadbare and torn. The pasty white skin of her face and hands, now orange tinged as a result of the fire's renewed glow, was extremely wrinkled, demonstrating the advancing age of its owner. The sleeping woman's entire body shifted in grateful appreciation of the crackling blaze.

Corazon knew that the home's owner had once been a very famous seamstress, employed by several wealthily merchants in the community. But when a new tailor came into town from the big city, setting up shop up in the village high street, it became in-vogue to buy clothes from him instead. Without any care, her previous, well-healed customers abandoned the local business, summarily dismissing the seamstress without further thought. Since then, the poor widow had not been able to obtain any work or been able to sell any clothing, because she could not find the money to buy the material to make them. Previously, any bolts of cloth, for creating her marvelous gowns and tunics, had always been provided for her. The poor, single woman's dress making business had disintegrated overnight, eventually leaving her penniless. Even the sign, that used to hang outside her establishment, now lay on the floor at the back of the room, long since abandoned.

Glancing briefly beyond the old widow, Corazon remained amazed at the one thing left in the ramshackle house, that showed any care and attention. It was beautifully preserved, having recently been oiled and lay in the far corner of the lounge, in a position of honour, like a museum piece. The mechanical contraption appeared almost brand new but, evidenced by the extent of wear of its various sockets and gears, it was obviously well used. The metallic parts now sparkled radiantly in the roaring fires illumination, its warm glow giving the apparatus a fantastic, somewhat unworldly appearance. Every time he viewed it, the knave thought the particular combination of wood, copper and brass a most ingenious device, marvelling that it could be run on only the foot power of its skilled operator. The old woman's magnificent sewing machine lay there, silent. Still clearly operational, yet unused for lack of thread and fabric.

The aged seamstress mumbled in her sleep, enjoying the heat, until Corazon lightly brushed her shoulder, prompting her to wake.

"Marm, it is I, Corazon. Come to visit you once again."

"Oh," she grumped, finally opening her eyes "T'is you, eh. Well, what da you want?" then noticing the fresh blaze and warmth it provided, added "'Cor blimey, lad, what's dis?"

Ignoring the questions, he commented, "I see you still have your wonderful machine."

Rubbing her hands appreciatively over the flames, she looked over at the contraption lovingly, as if her only wish was to thread its needle one more time. Just the thought of being able to slide in a fresh piece of cloth within it to create a wonderous and most unique gown, made her smile. If only a little.

"The magic I could create for you, if one only had some fabric and some thread?" she stated dreamily, the brief smile vanishing, a very sad look appearing on her wizened old face, "I could use dese hands God gave me ta fashion clothing once more. But alas, I have none."

"And you're gloomy because of it?" Corazon inquired, nonchalantly, the trace of a smile rising on his lips.

"No young man, I'm miserable because..., I have finally resolved, ta sell it." as she said this, a tear appeared on her cheek, the woman moving her arms about the room. "I must sell it, if I'm ta survive the coming winter."

"But Marm. I have come to give you something that may..., no, will, change all that." Making a clean area and opening his satchel, he emptied its contents onto the small living room table.

For an old seamstress like her, it was as if he had poured out a huge pile of gold and silver upon the wooden tabletop. The woman's eyes widened at the sight, and after releasing a great sigh from her chest, stood up. Doing it so quickly, Corazon believed she might fall over. He bent down to assist her, but she shrugged him away, swiftly approaching the bench to see what he had brought.

A variable treasure trove of priceless gifts awaited her; spools of thread, small bolts of cloth, and fine rolls of trim, just perfect and ready, for a professional hand to develop it into a fantastic garment of regalia, fit for a Duke or Duchess.

"Oi, Lad, what have you brought me?" the woman stared at the loot, holding to the table's edge to steady herself, not believing her eyes.

"I have brought you a new life. Please, use this in any way you wish, to create something wonderful."

She remained speechless, still not believing her luck, so the knave continued, "And on next market day, you can sell it to the highest bidder and buy yourself some food, more firewood and some new windows!

"This means I will be able to keep my machine?" she was now crying again; except this time, they were tears of joy.

"Indeed, it does, Marm."

"And you also provided me this firewood, to warm up my cold old house?" a rhetorical question that required no reply, "My son, you're a treasure, a real treasure." hugging him warmly with abject appreciation.

He accepted the embrace, returning it gratefully, "No, Marm, it's you who are the treasure. It's only the rich folk, that choose not to see it."

"Hey, wait a minute," she stated, stepping back and looking him over, a smile finally returning to her once, perpetually sad face, "Lad, it looks like you could do with some new clothes, yourself."

"You are extremely observant, Marm. For I just went swimming in these." Corazon smiled cheekily, while looking down at himself and the sorry state of his outfit.

She made a face, not really understanding, so instead, replied, "Well, if you ever need anything, I'll be right here."

"I'm counting on it. Because, I'm sure I'll have to take you up on that offer soon enough."

Then he added something else. Something that made her smile even wider, "Remember Marm, this is only a start. There's more to come."

"God bless you, son."

"God bless you too, Marm," saluting briefly, wanting to leave her to her good fortune. "Good day to you. And remember to stay warm!"

As the thankful woman poured over her lovely gifts, in the building heat of her front parlour, Corazon quietly snuck out onto the empty street. Upon shutting the door, he distinctly heard the sound of the sewing machine's foot peddle as the wheels slowly began turning on a new outfit.

Smiling widely, he slunk away up the high street, back to the perimeter road and obscurity. Contemplating his next destination was easy, for he knew exactly who would be the one to help him. "Now it's off to Bella's," he thought. "and perhaps, Carson has something to wear that I might borrow for a while."

Chapter 14 – The Incident

Robertson was not at all happy that the blasted knave had escaped him yet again. With his mood so heavily soured, he resorted to chastising his useless team of constables during their entire return journey back from the edge of the forbidden wood. Eventually, much to the delight of his hired hands, he separated himself from the group, sending them all toward the village and homeward, while he continued on.

Riding by himself, however, he was able to relish in the one pleasing thought of the day. That knave Corazon's home was a complete right off and never again, would the man be able to use it to hide from him.

Upon arriving at Robertson manor, he retreated immediately to his study, placing his feet up on the large cherrywood desk and settling back in his red leather chair, his hands behind his head, thinking. Leisurely, he sipped gratefully at the brandy Jenkins had delivered, delighting in the heat it provided while sliding down his parched throat. The orange tinted fluid's therapeutic warmth allowed him to relax, letting off all of the pent-up steam that had accumulated as a result of his most unsuccessful morning.

Corazon might have escaped him today, but there was always tomorrow. And, after all, there were many different ways one could use to bring a man out of hiding. Ways Robertson was certain, would work quite effectively.

During his long time on the force, Robertson had learned, that in order to be successful, a policeman must not only know his enemy's beliefs and morals, he must also know his limitations. His father had also taught him; know your enemy's key weakness and you will always be triumphant.

The Constable smiled, as he certainly knew this man, Corazon's weakness. And she just happened to live just outside of town, at Eastborough Hall.

***

Corazon made it to the Bolton estate just prior to sundown, working his way along the path at the edge of the ravine, before cutting across the back quarter of the property, through the small woodland. He arrived at the stables just about the same time Carson was bedding down the horses for the night, interrupting the friendly stable hand with a polite request for a temporary place to lay his head. As suspected, the young man was very eager to help, not only providing the knave a comfortable bunk in the servant's quarters above the stables, but also a fresh set of clothes for him to wear.

The outfit, although a tad snug, was certainly better than the dirty garments he had worn throughout the long, eventful day. Carson had agreed to take Corazon's own clothes up to the main house to get them washed, promising to have them back and ready to wear, bright and early the next morning.

The offered cot was quite comfortable, even more so than Corazon had imagined and much better than the rat infested one he almost had to endure at Penbrooke Prison. Leaning back on the pillow, he let all the day's pent-up tension leave his body. Slowly, he sipped at the glass of water Carson had delivered earlier, delighting in the refreshment it provided, while lubricating his tremendously parched throat. With all the walking and hiking he had recently endured, the clear liquids therapeutic coolness, allowed him to relax and unwind, recalling both his successful escape from the Constable and his men and his most fruitful visit to the old seamstress.

It made him feel most satisfied with himself that he could provide what was missing in the lives of the poor of the village. Making his own life seem worthwhile and meaningful. Not to think only of himself and ignore their desperate, ongoing plight, like the inherently rich and local constabulary did. To be able to reach out and supply what was required, enabling the downtrodden to get back on their feet, back to where they could provide for themselves and their needy families.

For a town stock full of poor, helpless people with nowhere left to turn, provides no pride for anyone. Particularly the wealthy residents of the surrounding areas. But fill a village with good and honest citizens, providing services for decent reward, always leads to a successful, respectful and prosperous community. One to be proud of, one where it is an honour to be part of the neighbourhood. And that was all Corazon had ever sought or wanted in a home.

Still, one last thing remained. A final thorn that was preventing this potential utopia from taking place. Tomorrow, he must attempt to permanently deter this group of dangerous marauders from their continued harassment and murder of the wealthy citizens of Eastborough. This band of slaughterous thieves who were menaces to achieving his ultimate vision. He must ensure that he stopped those treacherous fiends from harming any more of the town's elite, one and for all. Because no matter what Corazon thought of those stuck up fops, it was fairness he wanted, not violence. Justice not power, harmony not dissention, equality not indifference.

Settling back in the comfortable bed, the Knave of Hearts began his dreamless slumber, planning his next move.

***

The following morning, after a good might sleep, he ate and bathed in the equestrian servant's facilities. Dressing in his own clothes, now appreciatively washed and pressed, he headed out once again, but not before conveying prolific thanks to his new best friend, Carson. Full of fresh determination to end the threat to the local community forever, he felt he need to be as prepared as possible. So, just before he disappeared, he asked the boy a question.

"Carson?"

"Yes, Sire?"

"As you know, yesterday was quite a busy day for me. And, because of various problems encountered beyond my control, I am without my quiver and bow. You don't happen to have any weapons lying around out here that I might borrow?"

"Oh, no, Sire, there's nothing like that available in the stables. There may be weapons up in the main 'ouse, but they'd certainly not be accessible to me."

The young man looked around almost in panic, wanting so much to please the man that helped his family. He stood still thinking a moment, before he said, "The only thing I could offer you is this," and disappearing behind the main door, he returned with a stout, hard wood, walking stick, about 2 meters long. It's appearance, not to mention the boy's help, made Corazon smile.

"This is absolutely perfect, my boy and will do quite nicely." the knave said this while hefting the heavy wooden shaft, gleefully in his hands, checking its weight and balance, before repeating. "Yes, very nicely."

Carson smiled, pleased with himself. Glad to be able to provide something Corazon could use.

"It is a pleasure, Sire. Glad to be of service."

"Thank you again, good lad," adding with a flourish, "and tell M' Lady hello for me, if you get a chance."

"I will," he replied proudly, as Corazon disappeared without a sound, into the crop of trees next to the barn.

***

"Come along dear, we mustn't be late," harped the Duke, nervously stamping his foot as he waited for his wife to come down the stairs. "Carson has the team ready for us outside. And you know perfectly well, the Magistrate does not like it when we are late."

"Oh, posh dear, I'm coming." the Duchess stated argumentatively, arriving at the door, "And damn the Magistrate. We will get there when we get there. He will just have to wait."

"That's all fine and well for you to say, darling, but the man lives on the far side of Watson's Glen, and that's quite a long way from here." the Duke continued harassing his wife, "In addition, he is a stickler for protocol. It would not look good for the Duke and his Duchess to miss their appointment."

When she finally appeared at the end of the hall, the Duke took her arm and rushed her outside, straight into the carriage.

"Ouch, dear! You don't have to be so rough," she quipped, nonetheless getting inside immediately, so as not to delay her husband any further.

Following smarty, the Duke yelled up to the driver. "Okay, were in, Carson. Away! And be quick about it!"

"Yes, your worship," and putting a light whip to the horses, the young stable man guided the carriage out of the courtyard straight down the tree lined avenue. They soon made the main road and turning south, headed away from town, deeper into the country.

Watson's Glen was a woodland that separated the county of Eastborough, from the county of Brookside, the home of the area's magistrate. It was small as forest's go, but the trees within it were very tall, creating a heavily shaded area over the single lane path. It was a usually fine place to travel through during the day, but even with its reduced area, it was not a place one would like to travel through at night. The recent attacks, however, had changed everything and so it was natural that Carson kept a very wary eye as he approached the wood.

Driving the horses hard in an attempt to pick up some time, the Bolton's brougham had accumulated quite a pace as it entered the treeline, the clear daylight's brightness becoming more muted the further they ventured into the surrounding woods. Carson, despite their rushed schedule, deliberately slowed the horses in the reduced lighting, not wanting to risk anything untoward in the fading half-light.

Suddenly, up ahead, the coachman spotted a newly fallen tree completely blocking the trail. Without much choice, he fully reigned in the galloping team, gradually bringing the coach to an eventual halt.

"Carson what is it? Why are we stopping?" the Duke asked, slight irritation in his voice.

"There is a tree fall over the path up ahead, your grace." Carson dropped the reign, and grabbing the side bar while standing, intended to dismount, "I will 'ave to get down to check and see if there is a way around."

"Well, be quick about it boy, you know we have somewhere to be?"

"Unfortunately," stated a new voice, deep and resonant, "your worship will not be making his appointment today."

The carriage was suddenly surrounded by a group of ill-dressed thugs, each armed with various weapons, from knives and clubs to short rapiers. One, the leader, also had a long sword within easy reach, comfortably housed in a leather scabbard, strapped to his left leg. He was a tall robust man and wore a dark green tunic and hose, similar to Corazon's own. His tall, black boots also vaguely resembled the knave's footwear and his height also almost matched that of the friendly thief. The only difference was that he wore a black mask over his eyes, presumably to hide his identity, or something else. The other four, wore no such disguise, their plain, unshaved faces looking intently at the coach with much interest.

"What is the meaning of this?" the Duke yelled from inside, his head sticking out of the open carriage window. "How dare you!"

Carson who had already made to step down, looked at the bandits in terror. He was frozen in place, not sure how to proceed, when the leader shouted at him, completely ignoring the Duke. "Yes, my boy, please do come down. After all, we need someone left alive to report this unfortunate incident to the authorities."

"What?" Carson asked incredulously, not understanding, but still carefully climbing down as ordered. Eventually, he ended up standing completely still, beside the stationary coach, in front of the access door.

From inside the voice of the Duchess, now with an obvious hint of fear asked, "Darling what is it? Who are these men?" before the Duke could answer, the leader of the brigands spoke again.

"Be quiet, the two of you!"

This outburst promoted a shocked exclamation from the pair inside, the regents not believing someone would dare speak to them that way.

"Sire, do you realize who you are talking too?"

"Of course, I do, you stupid old man. Now shut it, while I speak with the young man here!"

The man's clearly hostile, brash tone elicited yet another gasp from inside the vehicle.

Looking back at Carson, the man said, "Boy, you are free to go."

When Carson didn't move, the man yelled loudly, "I said go! Or you will soon find yourself dead, like these two!" gesturing briefly to the doorway of coach.

Breaking into a cold sweat, Carson did not know what to do. Having no weapons did not matter, as he would never leave the Duke and Duchess unprotected. He was about to say as much, when he heard a small whistling sound. Turning, he noticed one of the thieves, standing on the other side of the coach, had dropped to the ground, grabbing at his throat, the hilt of a knife imbedded within it, dark blood spurting copiously between his fingers.

Seconds later, before the other thugs could even react, a second bandit was clubbed brutally on the head with a large stick, falling to the path unconscious.

A garbled "What?" arose from the leader, as a stone protectible was hurled sharply in his direction, forcing him to jump away from his position in front of the carriage. While drawing his sword, and taking up a defensive position, he stumbled, falling into the thick underbrush.

The third henchman, also on the far side of the carriage, turned bravely to face the unidentified attacker, club raised, teeth barred and growling loudly in anger. There was a short skirmish and after several swipes of the same staff, he too was face down on the ground, out of the fight.

This violent display, all occurred in a matter of moments.

Carson, taking advantage of this time and using the unknown assailant's activities as a distraction, launched himself at the fourth and last remaining rogue. In the resulting melee, this man, whilst having stayed on the coach's passenger side with his leader, had shifted his concentration across the path to the fate of his friends opposite him.

Thus, he did not even see the boy coming. His short sword was only part way out of its scabbard by the time Carson reached him and the force of their combined collision threw the two combatants heavily to the forest floor. The astonished bandit grunted loudly, as he took the brunt of the fall, the wind expelled from his lungs, the stampeding youth dropping heavily on top of him.

There was a frighteningly loud snap, as the bandit's left ankle broke on a rock, his leg having become twisted behind him. The man's horrific scream of pain was however, immediately silenced, Carson wasting no time in slamming a heavy fist into the surprised opponent's jaw, rapidly closing the man's open mouth and forcing him to bite off part of his tongue. Another quick follow through, with a bent elbow to his forehead, knocked the man senseless, blood trickling from his mouth.

Now, only the leader remained, the man still struggling to get upright in the bushes, his actual movements hard to detect within the long dim shadows of the forest.

Carson, now on his knees above his victim, briefly ignored the besieged organizer of the group, spinning to see who had come so miraculously, to their rescue. In the half-light, he saw the new arrival bend swiftly down and retrieve his dagger from the throat of the dead man. He had to use his foot against the corpse's chin to get enough leverage to pull it out, but after doing so, dutifully wiped the residue off on the tunic of the bandit's carcass.

The hero hopped gracefully over the cadaver, quickly making his way around the head of the horses, who being very riled upon the arrival of the assailants, now appeared calm, almost as if they knew their saviour's identity.

As the rescuer approached, the leader of the violent band finally managed to stand up, balancing himself, one foot back on the path, his sword now comfortably in his hand. Realizing he was completely alone, he stood there with a look of abject hatred on his face. Glaringly, he stared across at the man who had, almost singled handily, decimated his would-be assault team.

Carson, also staring at the newcomer, could not believe his eyes. He actually rubbed them, thinking what he was witnessing was either a trick of the light or his imagination. But then, from the direction of the carriage door, he heard the voice of the Duke yell out.

"I don't understand. How could there be two of them? They both look exactly the same?"

For it was true, the two men who now faced one another, one holding a knife and a staff, the other holding a gilded broadsword, were identically dressed. Dark green tunic, scarlet shirt, brown hose and black boots. The man with the knife, showing his handsome chiselled features, the man with the sword, still wearing the black mask.

"Corazon" yelled Carson, at the knave. For he knew him immediately, "Am I glad to see you."

"And I you, son. Now stay down, while I take care of this scoundrel."

"You might need this, Sire," and in saying it, tossed the short sword that he had drawn from the thief's scabbard, its owner lying unconscious beneath him.

In one move, Corazon dropped the wooden staff and expertly caught the heavier weapon, now turning to face his enemy, "Thanks Carson, I always said, you were a good man."

Throughout this entire exchange, the tall, masked man had not said anything, instead just began moving steadily toward Corazon with obvious, deadly intent. A pure hatred in his unseen eyes. As the two combatants closed together, you could tell the masked 'Corazon' was almost a head taller than the real one and was out for blood.

"So, Corazon," the masked bandit finally spoke, the sound of his deep voice resonating in the tight confines of the glen, "come here and we'll see who the true fighter is."

"By all means, you, arrogant rogue,"

But the tall man had already lunged at him with his sword, a true killing blow, plunging downward.

Crossing his sword and dagger together in expert defense, Corazon caught the man's down thrust blade just before it took his head off. Spinning, he pushed his back at the man, forcing the rapier away, stepping back for a moment, to catch his breath. But there was no break, the man immediately charging at him again. Once more the friendly knave going on the defensive.

"You will not leave here alive, Corazon," the man growled, spittle dripping down his chin.

"You are mistaken, my masked friend," deflecting yet another blow, then taunting the man, "but why the mask? Afraid someone will see you? What are you so scared about? Your goon buddies didn't wear any?"

"It is you who should be scared, knave!" and he lunged again, but this time, in his hatred for Corazon or just because he was on poorer ground, he staggered, his thrust passing sideways, the knave easily paring it aside.

But as before, in a flash, the tall man had swung again backhanded, swiping his sword up and under, Corazon barely having time to jump aside. Bringing his defenses up and deflecting the heavy blow, he was not quite fast enough, the large blade cutting a wide-open gash in his leg in the process. The dark red of his blood, looking black on the brown of his hose covered legs.

In pain, the knave jumped back instinctively, battle strain now showing on his perspiring face. Without looking, he tripped on the body of the unconscious thief, Carson now somewhere else, presumably assisting the Duke and Duchess.

Losing his footing completely, Corazon tumbled downward, hitting the forest path hard and dropping his short sword, the wind knocked out of him. The bandit knave was upon him at once, not wanting to lose the advantage. He raised his arms up high, the broad sword elevated far above his head, ready to bring it down in a final, murderous blow.

Corazon watched as Carson, appearing from behind with the wooden staff that he had dropped at the start of the battle, stuck the infuriated leader full force in the back.

The enraged man, screaming in agony, dropped his arms, his left hand grasping at his back, all the while managing to keep his sword held tightly in his right.

The advantage once again his, Corazon wasted no time flinging his dagger. But done in haste, and from his awkward position lying on the ground, instead of hitting true in his doubles neck, it impacted at the top of his enemy's right shoulder. The resulting throw, slit the bandit's garment wide open, deeply flaying his flesh down to the bone.

With a bright spurt of crimson, he staggered back into the middle of the path, carefully watching his two adversaries. Carson ready to inflict a second blow with the heavy staff and Corazon rising from the ground, his sort sword once again in hand.

Realizing he was now outnumbered, the leader of the thieves continued to back away and up the trail. His left hand now crossed over his chest, holding tightly to his right shoulder, in a vain attempt to staunch the huge flow of blood from his nasty wound.

"This is not the end, Corazon!" he shouted, pain evident in his voice, "Next time you won't have a little boy to help you!" and then he spun, running up the trail. Some distance away, taking a swift jog and disappearing into the thick of the underbrush.

"Shall we follow 'im?" Carson asked.

"No, let him go. We must be sure the Duke and Duchess are safe."

Carson dropped the staff and ran toward the carriage, having completely forgotten about his masters. Corazon followed, the wound on his leg smarting, but not nearly as bad as the one he had just inflicted on his enemy. The two arrived at the door just as the Duke was climbing out, having witnessed the entire exchange.

"Young man, we are in your debt," holding his hand out to Corazon, then looking up and realizing who it was, he gasped.

"Wait a minute! Why, you're that man the Constable took away from my home, so many weeks ago! You're the one who attacked my daughter! Killed my footman!"

"With all due respect, your worship," Carson stated, in Corazon's defense, "this man just saved your life. It was not 'e who killed your footman, nor attacked your daughter. 'E just saved us all. If not for 'im, you and your wife would be dead."

The Duke looked at the two men disbelieving, not understanding Corazon's presence, nor contemplating young Carson's hostility. But then his wife stepped out of the carriage, hair disheveled.

"Oh, Sire, I am so glad you came along. You have now saved both our daughter and ourselves. How can we ever thank you?"

The Duke's distrustful tirade suddenly evaporated, his wife comments finally enlightening him to the truth. Immediately changing tact, he apologized.

"I apologize whole heartedly, young man. My wife is correct, you and Carson here, have just saved us from these brigand murderer's and we are in your debt." he hesitated a moment, glancing around at the sprawl of bodies.

He was about to speak again, when Corazon cut him off, stating it for him, "Your grace, we must get out of here and indoors. As the forward path is blocked, I suggest we return to Eastborough Hall where we will all be safe."

"'E is correct, your grace," Carson confirmed, "It is the safest bet. We should return 'ome. Immediately."

"I suppose you are both correct. Let's get a move on then," he said, ushering his wife rather hurriedly back into coach.

The Knave of Hearts

Carson returned up top and, after seeing the Duke and Duchess safety seated in the carriage, the knave jumped up on the upper seat to meet him. Initially, Corazon took the reins, then thinking twice about it, handed them back over to Carson.

"This is your job lad. I'm just glad you were here. I thought I was a dead man." Patting the younger man on the shoulder.

"Never, Sire. Not on my watch," and the two grinned at one another.

"'Ere, you might need this?" Carson added, passing him several small bolts of raw cotton. We keep it 'ere for emergencies. You might want to bind that wound."

"Thank you, again son, don't mind if I do."

Taking the material, Corazon tore off a piece, swabbing his leg. Then using the rest, bound the wound tightly, suddenly feeling much better.

Carson wasted no further time, dragging the team swiftly around and, at a gallop, they headed out of the forest, back towards the Bolton estate.

As they drove ahead, the two of them heard the Duchess speaking from behind, "But darling, isn't the Magistrate going to be upset we didn't make our appointment?"

Amidst all that had occurred, her Ladyship's completely pedestrian comment, immediately sent the two drivers laughing and laughing hard, both pleased to be able to release their restrained stress and adrenaline. So much so, they laughed all the way back, until they reached the oak tree lined avenue and their first view of the magnificent, beige stone house, awaiting them at the top of the drive.

Chapter 15 - Another Visit - Exposed

The two elder Boltons and their escorts made it home safely, without any further incident. Upon arrival, Corazon dropped down from the driver's bench, his leg smarting as he did so, to help the two beleaguered regents from the coach. As soon as they had disembarked, Carson moved away, to dismount, and eventually stable the horses, anxious to get back to his normal routine.

The carriages early arrival home, however, caused quite a stir amongst the staff. None appeared ready to welcome the Duke and Duchess. The surprized help, of course, not expecting them back until much later that day.

Their butler Simon was the most ill prepared of all. In panic, and racing down the stairs to receive them, he ended up leaving his jacket in his room. The flustered Duchess, not noticing the oversight, upon entering the mansion demanded the immediate attentions of Susan, in order to provide her some tea, before heading off for a rest. However, the red-haired maid was nowhere to be found.

And so, with Corazon's assistance, the disheveled group headed toward the parlour to find a seat, rest up and get their bearings.

All of this activity, generated by their parent's early return, also prompted their two daughters to quickly make their way into the front sitting room. Both women anxious to discover the reason for all the noise and sudden change of plan. Upon reaching the front hall, and spying Corazon assisting her mother inside, Anabelle's heart missed a beat, the shocked girl nearly fainting, still completely oblivious as to what had occurred deep in Watson's Glen.

But when the knave winked a bright eye in her direction, her worried chest heaved a great sigh of relief and slowing, followed her elder sister into the parlour, anxious to understand what had befallen her parents. But even more so, to find out why Corazon was there.

May was all about the news, asking. "Mother, Father? What on earth has happened? Why are you both back so soon?"

The eldest Bolton daughter looked expectantly at her folks, as they sat themselves down on the nearest divan, their faces drawn and nervous, still white with shock from their close brush with death.

The minute they were seated, she dropped down upon the carpet directly in front of them, one hand on the hand rest, ready for the whole story. Bella selected a couch opposite, still gazing intently at Corazon, who remained standing next to the seat upon which her two parents now sat comfortably, all of them finally beginning to relax.

"My dear," the Duke began, patting May's hand, "we are home early, but only by the grace of providence. And all thanks to this young gentleman here," motioning to the grinning knave. Bella smiling at how her father now referred to Corazon as a gentleman.

"An incident occurred in the wood on the way to our appointment." stopping, he took out a handkerchief and wiped his forehead with it, before continuing. "Upon entering Watson's Glen earlier this afternoon, we encountered an obstruction in the roadway, requiring us to halt our progress to investigate. Subsequently, our coach was put upon by bandits. If not for the quick actions of our driver and this gentleman here, your Mother and I may have been assassinated!" he said it simply, but with true understanding of how close they had both come to death.

"Oh, my!" stated Melissa Anne, the whites of her knuckles showing as she gripped the arm of the couch in fear. Her mother, meanwhile, grabbed her husband's arm in support, laying her head on his shoulder. Normally, the Duke would have been embarrassed at his wife's actions, but today he lifted his hand to pat her lovingly on the shoulder.

"But who was it?" May asked intrigued.

"Apparently it was that same band of cutthroats that we had previously been warned about." he answered, wiping his forehead nervously one more time, his hand still shaking.

"What exactly happened, Father?" Bella asked, wishing for more detail, but looking up at Corazon, a look of wonder on her pretty face.

"My child, the criminals were about to attack our carriage and clearly with sinister intent, having already ordered our Carson to dismount. This fine gentleman (now it was fine gentleman) came out of nowhere to subdue the blasted miscreants. Carson assisted of course, but this man took down four of the five bandits by himself. Quite a show, I must say." then strangely he stopped, raising his head and yelling loudly toward the back of the room, "Where is that blasted Simon with our tea?"

"Oh, Mother, were you scared?" May was spellbound, not the least bit interested in tea.

"Of course, dear," her mother replied, "I was quite put out, the devils. How dare they attack us? But, of course, not as much as your Father. He kept going on about his appointment with the magistrate."

"Come now, darling, I did no such thing. I could see we were in trouble."

Then looking behind, as if almost noticing him for the first time, indicated for Corazon to sit. "My dear man, have a seat why don't you. You certainly deserve it."

Upon the invitation, with a polite nod of his head, Corazon took a seat next to Bella, the infatuated girl immediately moving over toward him almost unconsciously as he did so. Her parents, still overcoming their shock, didn't seem to notice her subtle shift in movement.

Then her father finally admitted he had been wrong, "So it appears my first impression of Sire Corazon, here was incorrect." bowing his head, ever so slightly toward him, he asked for forgiveness, "Therefore, I humbly apologise to you both." now looking quite intently across at the two youngsters, seated opposite him.

"To you Anabelle, for not believing when you told me this gentleman saved you from peril. And for you, dear Sire, for not only saving my daughter, but now, for saving my wife and I." he hesitated, still looking at the pair, "I cannot even fathom what I might do to repay you."

Corazon smiled mischievously, looking over at Bella, who had moved yet again and was now extremely close to him on the couch. So close, it was almost unseemly. "I am sure we can work something out, your grace."

"Yes, I am sure we can," he replied hesitatingly, not really understanding the knave's comment, or his look.

But then, however, the butler had returned with the tea, putting a sharp halt on the rather awkward conversation. Somehow, Simon had managed to get his coat on in the interim and now, dressed appropriately in his regular green and black, he appeared less flustered and more himself.

He took his time pouring the tea, the room now silent, the current subject matter for the Bolton family members and their guest alone. Once he had finished and had retired through the back entrance, the conversation was about to resume, when a loud banging began at the front door.

"Oh, who could that be, at this hour?" the Duke complained, sitting up and forcing his wife away from her comfortable spot on his shoulder.

There was the sound of shoes on the marble entry as Simon rushed to see who would be calling at this time of day, banging so rudely.

"Let me in!" barked the Chief Constable, his loud, deep voice, resonating around the entry hall as the door was opened, shortly after which Robertson burst into the front room, the flustered butler again following distantly in his wake. The policeman was wearing his full-dress uniform, but it did not appear as polished as usual, almost as if it had been applied, rather hastily.

He did not even give Simon a chance to make excuses for him, "There you are!" He stated warningly, his black gloved fist shaking and one good eye, glaring at Corazon. Then turning, with a brief nod of his head, as if an afterthought, stated quietly, "Good afternoon, your grace. This man is a criminal, and I have come to arrest him."

"How dare you burst into my house unannounced, Chief Constable!" the Duke stood, the hands on his frail arms shaking in anger, "And how dare you accuse my guest of wrongdoing." without letting the constable respond, he continued, "This gentleman, has just saved the life of my wife and myself. He is our guest and will not be going anywhere."

"Dear, Duke," Robertson voice now seething and severely condescending, "I am going to arrest this man, regardless what you want or say. Whether he is your guest or not!" pausing momentarily, he added, "He was seen entering Watson's Glen earlier today with malicious intent. I will see him hanged for it."

"Sire, it is you who should be hanged!"

This rather sharp exclamation from the Duke, surprised not only his daughters and wife, but Corazon as well.

"If this man had not, as you say, entered Watson's Glen when he did, I would not be here right now. This man is no menace, in fact, he is a blessing to us all." then he shook an arthritic finger at Robertson, his voice still angry, "And now, I will ask you to leave my house, this instant..., and never set foot in it again."

"My dear, Duke," Robertson said once more, this time more soothingly and with extreme self-importance "I am the law in this county and this man is a criminal. I will be taking him with me."

"Why, you insolent...." the Duke was going red.

"Your Grace!" Corazon cut him off, standing up. Unthinkingly, Anabelle, grabbed at his arm attempting to stop him, before consciously realizing what she was doing, and rather reluctantly letting go.

"It appears this gentleman and I have some business to attend to. Please do not trouble yourself. Let me see what I can do," and moving over to the Constable, he raised his arm, in apparent friendship. "Constable, I will gladly discuss this situation with you, outside, as gentlemen. Come."

In saying this, he brought his hand down forcibly on the policeman's right shoulder, patting him as a gesture of good will. The action, however, was received very differently. Robertson, cringing his teeth, immediately tilted sideways, dropping his arm away from Corazon's touch as if burned, grunting in pain.

"Just what I thought!" growled Corazon, angrily, "you, sorry excuse for a man, I ought to kill you here and now!"

Renewing his hold on his enemy, he purposely ground his hand deeper into the wounded flesh of the Constable's tender shoulder. Robertson screamed in agony, slashing out violently with his arm, knocking the wind from Corazon's lungs and forcing him rather heavily to the floor.

"What?" stated the Duke suspiciously, frozen in place, "I don't understand. You, our Chief Constable..., the leader of that marauding, murderous band? I don't believe it?"

Holding his already injured shoulder with his left hand, just like he had done in the forest, fresh blood now rising from the wound and dripping on the carpet, Robertson staggered back, yelling insanely. "Believe it, you old fool. And I did it all to get at him, that knave!" tilting his head toward the sprawled form of Corazon. All the while, easing himself backward into the hall, his secret now exposed. "I will see you all in Hell!" then turning fully, he ran from the house.

Chapter 16 – The Chase

As the Constable ran from the house, the old Duke stepped quickly across the room. Bending down, he held his hand out for Corazon to grab onto, "That wicked man must be stopped! Are you good enough to go after him?" he stated, helping the winded knave to his feet.

Corazon jumped up, shaking off the results of the blow, the air gradually returning to his lungs. "Certainly, your grace. It would be my pleasure," and with no further delay, he headed straight out of the room, right after the fleeing rogue policeman.

As he reached the gravel of the courtyard, he could see Robertson had already mounted his horse and was about to leave. Corazon ran over, diving at the animal, grabbing hard onto the saddle, preventing the horse from going anywhere. "Going somewhere, Constable?"

"Indeed, I am, knave!" Robertson shrieked.

Winding up with his tough leather boot, he kicked Corazon hard in the face. The vicious impact loosened the knave's grip, causing him to fall flat upon the stones.

"See you later, knave" and with a spray of rocks into his face, Robertson was off.

With no hesitation Corazon got up, blood now dripping from his surely broken nose. Running back into the house, his face smarting as much as his leg, he hollered, "Your, grace?" his voice echoing hauntingly in the entry.

"Yes, Corazon?" the Duke answered, as Corazon arrived back in the front room. Surprised the knave was still there, "Uh, weren't you going to go after him?"

"Absolutely, your grace, but may I ask first, if you have a weapon I might borrow?"

Looking around the room revealed nothing but pillows and teacups.

"This way!" was all the Duke said, running lopsidedly from the parlour.

Corazon followed, favouring his injured leg, his breath returning, wiping the blood from his sore nose. He was amazed how fast this old codger could be when he was on a mission and followed him into what appeared to be his personal study, stopping just inside the entryway.

The room was paneled in dark oak, all of the wood expertly carved, perfectly suited office for a regent. He saw the Duke reach up onto one wall, pulling down a ceremonial, family sword, from its mounting bracket.

"Here! Catch!" he stated, spinning then, quite expertly, throwing the blade towards the knave. Corazon caught it mid-flight, the hilts gold leaf glistening in the late afternoon sun as it landed in his outstretched hand.

"This should do your grace." he added smiling, then wincing, his nose smarting.

"Go get him, Corazon! For me, for us!"

"As you wish, your grace," then he was gone, running as best he could across the marble entry. As he passed the open door of the sitting room, Bella stood there just inside, beautiful as ever, despite the abject look of fear on her pretty features. The knave couldn't help it, detouring only briefly to brush his lips lightly against hers on his way out. She stretched forward as if wanting more.

"Later, my Sweet," he stated, "duty calls."

Bursting through the already open doors into the late afternoon heat, he may have heard her say the words 'I love you' but could not be sure. In the distance, he spied Robertson racing off on his stead, heading north, looking back to see if he was being followed.

Corazon, now frantically scanning the courtyard, spotted only the idle carriage and Carson, tenderly releasing the two fine horses from the huge vehicles harness. Rather awkwardly sprinting over, he yelled loudly to the surprized stable boy, "Carson, my lad, I will need to borrow Winter for a moment!"

"But, Sire, 'e 'as no saddle!" and it was true. The horse, now free from the hitch, had only a bit and a rein in his mouth.

"That's all fine Carson, I've ridden bareback before," and without giving the boy time to respond, he jumped up on Winter's back, grabbing the jockey's leather.

"Winter, my boy," he said patting his neck, "ready for a run?"

Neighing loudly, as if accepting his challenge, the stallion reared up on his hind legs. The surprizing action, almost toppling Corazon off on to the ground, before they had even gotten started.

But, despite the pain in his injured leg, by pressing his knees in forcefully against the animals hide, he managed to stay aloft, all the while murmuring his goodbyes to Carson. Then, at full gallop, they were away, gravel flying, following after the escaping Constable.

Carson couldn't believe what he had just witnessed, shaking his head and patting the remaining animal. That's when the Lady Bella and her sister also came running from the house. "Carson, we must have this horse." she stated as if it were just another Sunday ride.

"But M' Lady," he said, repeating himself, "the 'orse 'as no saddle."

"Well then you will take us to the stable and get one," she stated breathlessly, "and then we will follow that man."

"Very well, M' Lady," he stated shaking his head.

Dragging the remaining horse by the rein, the three of them headed around the back of the house and down the long path toward the stables.

As they passed the front door of the house, still hanging open, they heard their father yelling once again to the fragile butler.

"Simon, send for Sire Styles, immediately! Tell him it is urgent!"

But they were past, before they could hear any reply.

***

Once Corazon got used to his fragile seat and had Winter charging full speed in pursuit, he could already see that he was catching up to the Constable. Robertson might be the high man on the police force, but he was still only supplied with public money. So, while his horse was indeed swift, it was no match for Winter's speed and agility. In addition, the relative flat of the roadway made the difference between the two mounts extremely noticeable and the knave was certain that he would overtake the fleeing fugitive in minutes.

Looking behind him, Robertson could see that his nemesis was catching up and quickly. So, at the first chance, he turned off the gravel path and into the minor forest surrounding the Bolton property. There were many trails strung throughout the trees and selecting the next one that presented itself, he moved through the treeline and deeper into the wood, without skipping a beat. Corazon followed at his heels, having to roughly rein in Winter's lightning fast gate, in order to make the sharp turn into the bush.

"He's trying the even the stakes, Winter, my boy." Corazon said talking to his ride, "Just be careful in there, okay."

Clearly the horse did not understand plain English, but from the tone in his rider's voice could tell, it was time to be on guard.

The two horse and riders continued racing through the thin woodland, the afternoon sun creating tall, spindly shadows everywhere. As they moved, this generated a pattern of swiftly alternating light and dark, flashing by to play tricks with their vision. The noise of the frantic pursuit frightened the smaller wildlife, several birds alighting from a nearby trees, squawking angrily as the pair of adversaries made their way through. Corazon kept a diligent watch on the Constable riding ahead. On the lookout for when he might make his next move.

The slightly uneven footing on the forest path had truly evened the score, the two riders now progressing at about the same speed. The farther they travelled, the denser the wood became, allowing Robertson to disappear around the next corner. Corazon began pushing Winter slightly harder to keep his rival in sight. Unfortunately, no matter how hard he tried, he could not seem to manage it, the greater number of trees, thicker underbrush and rough ground making it impossible. The knave continued blindly, following along the path, expecting to spot Robertson again soon.

Corazon was not to be disappointed, because around the next bend, the crafty Robertson surprized him from the side. After having stopped on a dime, the Constable had lain in wait as the knave cleared the corner.

As their two steeds collided heavily, the Constables left arm at the ready, elbowed Corazon in the chest, almost dismounting him. The sudden disastrous movement also forced Winter quickly off the path and into the underbrush, where he caught his leg on a large bramble. Acting as a brake, the horse soon stumbled and fell. With nothing to stop him, the knave sailed over the neck of his collapsing steed, flying through the air, into the surrounding shrubbery.

But amongst the thick weeds was a large boulder and, while the various branches provided some shielding, Corazon landed headfirst into the mire, sliding towards the rock. With both arms extended for protection, his exposed head still managed to slam, quite hard, into the stone. The small bleed from his nose, that had already dried, was nothing compared to the cut that was now rather painfully opened in his head, as a result of the impact, the knave failing faint in the scattered bushes. Stupidly, Corazon attempted to get up right away, but seeing stars, knew it was useless, immediately passing out right where he had fallen.

Robertson drew in his mount and, coming to a stop much further ahead on the path, retraced his steps. Observing what had occurred, his adversary's horse stunned and out for the count and the considerable swath of blood now dripping from Corazon's head wound, he smiled villainously.

"I told you, I would see you in Hell, knave." he said out loud, laughing hysterically. "You only got what you deserved." and then with a loud "Hah!" he ordered on his horse, heading back to the trail and continuing down the path to freedom.

Within moments, he was around the next bend and gone.

***

Silence then returned to that part of the wood, the odd chirp of a small bird echoing in the valley. Then there was the sound of heavy breathing and rustling bushes, as Winter struggled to get up. Luckily the knot of groundwork that had made him fall, did not break any of his bones and after a lot of aggressive movement, rocking back and forth, he was finally able to free himself from the underbrush. This allowed him to get up on his feet and, gingerly stepping out of the weeds, trotted back onto the path. He whinnied loudly, as if calling for Corazon.

Slowly moving along the trail, his eyes scanned the shrubberies, sniffing and neighing softly. Eventually he found what he was looking for, the man laying silent and unmoving beside the large stone. The blood from his head wound was now partially dry, the flow from the wide gash finally beginning to clot. The horse bent his neck down, sniffing closer.

Drawing back his lips and extending a huge pink tongue from his snout, he licked the face of the knave, the sandpaper like surface leaving a red mark, the thick saliva coating his face. One more time, the concerned stallion attempted to wake his master, willing him to revive, hoping he would recover, to continue the fight. It appeared it was all in vain.

It was only when Winter decide to gently kick him instead that Corazon awakened, groaning loudly. Wiping the thick smelly goo from his face, he suddenly realized what it was and thanked the horse.

"Thanks Winter, for not giving up on me." he said before reaching up to affectionately pat his extended neck.

A throbbing headache made his first attempt to stand very unsuccessful. The extreme dizziness causing him to collapse immediately back to the ground. Groaning once again, he got slowly to his knees, now covered with mud from the small drainage ditch running along the side of the path. Slowly and carefully he got up on his feet again, his head aching furiously. The cut on his scalp had made a big bloody mess, but thankfully had stopped bleeding, which was a good sign. But the stars continued to sail around his vision and the ache in his neck and back were horrendous. On top of that, from the painful feel in his left arm, his wrist may have also been broken. But Corazon was determined. He had a job to do. One requiring him to continue the chase and stop that evil Constable once and for all.

"We can't forget this." he said to the horse, reaching down into the dirt for the broadsword and almost falling over. As he brought it slowly up, he could see that the attractive weapon was caked in mud, its gold hilt now black with dirt.

"Well, it doesn't have to be pretty to do the job." he mumbled, happier, his humour coming back to him.

Shaking his head to clear the fog, only made it hurt more. So instead, he turned it slowly from side to side to work out the kinks in his neck. Bending over gently, Corazon also stretched the muscles of his aching back. The short exercises proved fruitful, reducing the pressure on his spine and the searing pain with it.

Feeling a bit better, he attempted to remount Winter only to fail, miserably. When he failed a second time, Corazon stood till for a moment to get his breath back. With his current wrist, neck and back pain, combined with the lingering hurt of his leg injury, he realized he was a bit mess and would have to take things much slower. After a few minutes rest, very carefully, he tried again and on this third attempt, was finally atop his faithful stead once again. Pressing his knees in, he started Winter on a slow trot, heading down the path in the same direction, following the escaped Constable.

They had not traveled very far before Corazon realized where the track led. "This one goes down to the ravine doesn't it,

Winter," the horse nickering lightly in reply, as if agreeing. "If that's the case, I remember there's a short cut behind us, a little further back, that crosses the fields. If we're to catch him, that will be our only way."

Turning Winter around, he headed back up the trail, this time at a slightly faster pace, his vision finally clearing. The pain in his temples and body was still very intense, but at least he could function.

"Let's go, boy" and they trotted up the path into the underbrush.

***

*J*ust about the time Corazon's bearings were returning, Robertson, meanwhile, had nearly reached the end of the trail. Approaching the clearing of the trees, and presumably the open road, he noticed a good reason to slow right down. Reigning in his mount, he brought the horse to a veritable standstill.

The path ahead of him was a mire of murky water, mud and dirt. It was apparent that the natural drainage along the edge of the trail, rather than proceeding through to the ravine, had become blocked, causing a large pool to form, right in his path. The result was a deep, thick sloppy mess that required very careful, turtle like progress, the footing always in question. As he had no intention of his horse breaking a leg, he took the last half-kilometer at a crawl, inching along before at last immerging past the muddy obstacle.

The Constable had got the best of the ordeal, for while his horse's legs and body had become coated with filth, Robertson escaped relatively unaffected. Only his black boots bore the brunt of the grime, his marvelous cape only receiving a few light splashes.

As he exited the woodland, he appeared out onto the broad run along the ravine, the track he loved so much. His most favorite and treasured ride. Looking behind him one more time and seeing no one was following, he smiled widely in victory.

"I will head over to the next county to make my fortune," he said to himself, "right after I return home to clean out my strong box, of course!"

Laughing heartily, he spurred on his faithful horse and they were off. Racing along the track, rounding the precipice of the ravine, he felt alive and invigorated. His horse, well used to the trail, took it in stride, accelerating faster and faster. Robertson shouted with glee, the cool wind in his hair, fresh air in his lungs and, despite the excruciating pain in his shoulder, a bright smile on his face. The sounds of the forest cheering him on, the yell of a hunting falcon sounding high above.

Everything was perfect. Everything was finally going right for him.

Unfortunately, that's usually when things typically go wrong, particularly for the bad guy.

Chapter 17 – The Duel

Winter was a full gallop when Corazon broke out of the field and onto the gravel track surrounding the ravine. He looked quickly to the right, in the direction he was sure Robertson would be and when he did not see him there, he turned back left, toward the Bolton estate.

Completely unexpected by them both, Robertson had not yet made it past that point and, in looking the other way, Corazon completely missed the Constable coming towards him also at a full charge from the left side. The two horses collided with such force, that both men were physically thrown from their mounts. Grunting, the two antagonists flew through the air, before hitting the ground and rolling across the dirt, while their animals, also calling out in pain, collapsed into the field next to the trail.

Once again, for the third time that day, Corazon landed hard. With yet another impact, his head began to hurt even more. Luckily, he had managed to hold on to the sword, but this time he was certain, his left wrist had snapped. He was lucky, however, it was just his wrist, as his body had finally come to a halt with him laying half over the edge of the gorge, both his arms and upper chest supported only by air. Looking down the sheer wall, gave him goose bumps. In sight, were a few stray branches and brambles sprouting from the rock, but he really only noticed the very long drop down to the ravine's rocky bottom far below.

Struggling with his injured hand, he pushed back with his sword arm and, twisting his torso, eventually found himself lying face upward, looking almost casually, into the blue sky. "A far better view," he thought to himself, feeling entirely warn out, very itchy, and covered from head to toe in dirt and dust. "There has to be more to life than this!"

Robertson, had landed on the far side of the two horses, having been launched like a rocket out of his saddle, but fortunately, unlike Corazon, finding a stray bush in which to land. With a loud groan, he stood, turning around behind him to determine what the hell had happened. Seeing the two horses collapsed at the edge of the path and his rival, just turning away from almost sudden death, answered all his questions.

He did not know how the bastard Corazon had caught up with him but vowed that only one of them was going to leave there, alive.

Pulling his sword from its sheath, Robertson noticed that both his right leg and arm had been lacerated rather badly during his rough landing. In addition, the weight of his large weapon, dragged the arm down further, making it extremely painful on his damaged shoulder, fresh blood dripping onto the dirt. No matter, he mused, gabbing at the wound with his left hand, he would see this man dead if it was the last thing he did.

***

Far behind the two combatants, an extreme distance away but still on the main road, Carson and the Bolton girls capped the rise, now finally able to see the ravine trail and the two injured men far away. Anabelle, noticing immediately that Corazon was still prone on the ground with the Constable almost upon him, yelled with fear.

"Carson, hurry we must help him! Let's go!"

"As quick as we dare, M' Lady! This trail is dangerous. Please stay to the inside if you can! And remember, single file!"

The ladies spurred their horses, rushing as fast as they dared, up the trail towards the two enemies, heeding the warning of their stable boy, now following close behind. All of them keeping well inside and taking their time. Bella, with the most to lose, was faster, Melissa Anne, in remembering what had happened to her fiancé, ended up hanging back, taking it very slow.

"You go on ahead, Bella, I'll be there soon." May stated anxiously.

"Don't worry, May! You take as much time as you need."

Carson drew alongside May, "Will you be alright, M' Lady."

"Oh, don't worry about me, Carson, I'll be fine. I just want to take it slow, that's all. You go on ahead and help my sister," then, as an afterthought, "and Corazon."

"Very well, M' Lady," and he was off, soon catching up to the red head who was progressing along the dangerous precipice far too quickly for his liking.

Once together, Carson and Anabelle continued on their way, May continuing to lag even further behind, progressing at a much slower gait, very unsure of herself.

***

The two men were now poised for battle.

Corazon after having a slight rest, had slowly turned over, climbed onto his knees and then, with a distinct waver, gotten to his feet. While holding the Bolton family sword securely in his right hand, he moved well away from the edge of the deep crevasse and back onto the path. Rotating to face his rival, he planted his feet securely in the dusty soil, poised and ready. He continued to hold his weapon in only the one hand, his left one now useless, hanging limply by his side, burning with pain.

The knave risked a quick glance down at it. Noticing not only the excessive swelling, and odd angle of the appendage, but the deep blue-brown bruising at the wrist. "Yes, definitely broken," he thought to himself.

Robertson was not really in much better shape. With the shock of his fall, the pain of his prior injury and the new cuts he had incurred on his arm and leg, he could barely hold his sword up to fight. His clothes were a complete mess, his uniform, covered in mud and his wonderful cloak torn. To relieve himself of the weight, he shook it forcibly from his shoulders, discarding it on the pathway as he approached Corazon, who was now standing ready to receive him. Finally, within earshot he spoke, taunting his enemy.

"You should not have chased me, rogue," Robertson winced with pain, his deep voice wavering slightly in the building wind, the long afternoon coming to a close. "Your name is mud with me and always will be, despite your new protector."

When Corazon said nothing, Robertson continued, "But tell me, I always wondered why you did it? Why risk your reputation, jail, even perhaps your life, on a bunch of misfits and downtrodden whelps? Were they really worth helping? I know I would never have done it."

"You see, that is where you and I differ, Constable." Corazon also felt the chill as twilight approached but held his voice steady. "It was either me help them or let them all die. Laws, while necessary, are not always there to protect everyone. And sometimes, they help no one." he paused, shifting his feet, trying to gain some time, "But, because of your position, you are blind to it, Robertson. But regardless what you think or how you've been brought up, there is a difference between law and justice. Yes, the act of stealing in itself is wrong, seen as a crime in the eyes of the law. In your eyes as well, or shall I say..., eye."

"You dare mock me, scum."

Ignoring him, "And if what I did was purely that, then you and I would be in agreement, for it would be both wrong and foolish."

"So, you finally see the light. That won't stop me from killing you here and now."

Corazon did not stop, "But when laws provide for some and not for others, the boundaries change, the black and white quickly turn to grey. To steal from someone whom has everything in excess, because of the law, and then to give it to someone who has nothing, because of the same law, is not wrong. It is justice."

"The only justice you'll be receiving is the point at the end of my sword," Robertson replied.

"I am amazed at you, Robertson, I heard such great things about you, how you were a man of honour..., and man of the law. You would do nothing else but uphold the law. That's what made you dangerous." grinding his adversary to mush, he finished, "but now all you are is a common thief and murder. No better than the men you once despised." his head hurt, so he stopped speaking, "I will enjoy seeing you hang."

"Hang? You cretin, I have no intention of hanging." looking down at the weapon in his hand, "Once I run you though with this sword and dispose of your dead carcass over that cliff there," motioning with his head, "I will away to another place, to start over again." and he taunted back. "Unlike you, a poor vagabond, I have family money, and it will take me far. I have no need of a rich patron to provide for me."

"What makes you think I even need the Duke's patronage, Constable?" Corazon replied, adding, "and are you sure you can fight with that arm. It looks very painful."

"Better than you can fight with you head in the clouds. En guard!"

And saying this, he lunged, the two men coming together like a pair of titans, their blades clashing, the noise echoing across the chasm of the gorge.

Corazon's first swing pushed Robertson's blade sideways, allowing him to forcefully advance forward, making good use of the man's weak arm. But the Constable was not going to make it that easy, spinning his body around, to take the pressure off his shoulder, shoving his back hard into the knave, breaking his momentum. He then twisted in space, going down deep on one knee and pushing off, coming around for a fresh attack.

Corazon barely defended against it, the two rapiers smashing together again, the blades sliding up upon one another to the hilt, the fancy wrist guards deflecting the brunt of the force. The two staggered around together, their blades locked, and taking advantage of the momentary lapse in sword play, Robertson surveyed his adversary.

The knave was a mess. His clothes were full of mud and dirt, he had a broken nose, and a large cut on his scalp, the dried clot of brown blood, matting his fine hair. His forehead glistened with sweat and his breathing was short and uneven. Looking right into his eyes, he detected something wrong, almost as if the man was punch drunk, obvious remnants of his many falls that day. But the last thing he noticed was the horrid bruising around his left wrist, the arm hanging limp beside him, obviously broken and very painful, giving him an idea.

Corazon stared at his opponent, seeing his face patch had partially come loose, and catching a brief glimpse of the scar and damage done to the man's eye. From what he could see, it was a horrendous wound, the surrounding flesh all puckered and torn, the entire lid removed and the half-moon shape of a cloudy, off-white orb glancing back blindly from within.

The Constable's face was contorted with hatred, he too having a veil of perspiration coating his head, the dribbles of saltwater meandering down his face and cascading off his thick black hair, to drip on the ground. He was still favouring his shoulder, fresh blood visible and clearly, could not hold out much longer.

The two men acted together, Corazon spinning in place to release his weapon, Robertson, moving across their connected bodies. Once free of the knave's sword, he pulled down and right, towards his adversary's damaged left hand, forcing the handle of his weapon harshly into Corazon's injured wrist.

As the knave was already partially turning away, the violent impact was not nearly as bad as it could have been. Still it made him scream in agony, falling down on one knee in pain. Desperately, kicking out with his other leg, he fell completely to the ground, but the well-timed foot was enough to trip the Constable and he too fell backward, hard onto the ground in a cloud of dust.

It ended up doubly advantageous for Corazon, as it was Robertson's right foot he had displaced, making him fall right on his sword arm and his damaged shoulder.

Robertson himself yelled loudly on impact, the pain rippling through his entire body, stunning him almost senseless. For the briefest of moments, the two combatants lay on the ground, seething in anguish, unable or unwilling, to continue their fight. Their minds in turmoil, their bodies fighting back.

Suddenly there was the sound of horse's hooves as the young Bolton girl and Carson finally neared the battleground. Corazon looked up from where he lay, yelling, his voice wavering, "Come no further, I need you safe."

"But my love, you are injured!" the trill of fear in Bella's voice evident.

"Please, let me finish this."

For the arrival of the beautiful Anabelle, gave him renewed strength, the sight of the tear in her eye, gave him courage and the fact that she had called him my love, gave him the heart to finish this. With great agony, he pushed himself up, using the sword as a crutch.

The sound of Corazon's yell brought Robertson back to life and he rolled clumsily toward the knave, now also able to see the new arrivals. The sight of Bella on that horse sent him wild, but when she said she loved the heinous knave, he snapped.

The man was as good as dead, he thought, launching himself up off the dirt, slashing wildly with his blade and yelling, "Look you scum, your patron's daughter has come on a white horse to rescue you. Isn't that sweet. That is why your courting her isn't it? For her money?"

Their metal clashed again, the noise defining, several birds alighting from a nearby tree, only partially supported off the canyon wall.

At Robertson's taunt, Bella's face turned red, and a brief look of uncertainty crossed her features. But Corazon never saw this. He was too angry over the Constable's use of the word sweet. That's was what did him in. That word belonged to only Bella and him. On top of that, he could no longer tolerate the evil swine spouting hatred at her. Finally, forcing his hand.

He pressed the man and their swords continued to flash in the dying sun. Lunge after lunge, parry after parry, hit after hit, the two combatants were relentless, their pure hatred driving them onward. They were paying so much attention to their battle that they failed to notice both had moved well off the path. Unfortunately, in the wrong direction, as they were now on the gravel verge, approaching the edge of the ravine.

Their frantic footing knocked away some of the loose gravel and they spun, once again smashing swords, pushing against one another, each vying for supremacy.

"Not today, knave," Robertson raged, spittle flying from his mouth, "I will have your head."

"No, you won't, you've lost! You can barely hold your arm up," and the two turned again, moving ever closer to the edge, stones clattering down with each foot fall.

"You will be the one dying today, Corazon,"

Using the knave's name for the first time in their dual, Robertson had hit a nerve.

The use of his name just enraged him further, prompting Corazon to spin in place once again, pushing his back hard against his adversary and elbowing him in the chest, forcing him backward. Suddenly, the pressure relaxed and there was a yell. And Robertson disappeared over the edge.

"He's fallen!" yelled Bella, hard to tell if her exclamation was in pleasure or pain.

Indeed, he had. Robertson had vanished. Corazon dropped his sword and looked over the edge, dreading the worst. He had meant to bring the foul man to justice, not kill him. If it had been necessary of course, he would have, but he had felt that with the man's injury, he would have soon overpowered the insane policeman.

What he saw glancing over the verge, was not what he had expected. Robertson had not fallen. He had dropped his weapon, yes, but now hung helplessly from a stiff branch, rather unsteadily secured to the cliff face. And was now making an effort to reach back for the safety of the walkway.

"Here! Grab my hand!" Corazon yelled, dropping onto his chest and reaching out with his good right hand. The Constable held the branch with both hands, his left providing more support than the right, due to his injured shoulder. His position was precarious, for the roots of the lifesaving branch were beginning to loosen in the stone.

"Grab my hand!" Corazon repeated, this time Roberson did, pain wracking his features, his only hold now on the fragile lifeline with his right arm, while he reached upward for the knave's outstretched hand, with his left. The two warriors came together, grabbing on to one another, Corazon pulling with all his might. While he did so, Carson came up behind to help, and holding on to Corazon, allowed him to take more weight, the two of them dragging the battered Robertson up.

Releasing his injured arm from the branch, soon the constable had a hold of the plateau's edge, and with great effort, was heaved up onto safe ground. The two adversaries stared at one another briefly, their breathing heavy and sporadic, before the policeman spoke.

"Why? Why did you save me?"

Corazon remained silent, as if to let him finish.

After the questions, Robertson threw out a nasty observation, "Because, I would never have done the same for you!" and saying so, spat in Corazon's direction.

"I saved you for that very reason, Robertson. Because I am not like you and never will be." Corazon standing dutifully and wiping the man's spittle from his cheek.

Robertson screamed ferociously in anger, and before anyone realized it, he had grabbed the sword Corazon had dropped and lunged at the knave, murder in his eyes.

"Sire, look out!" Carson shouting a warning.

Just in time, Corazon jumped away, Anabelle screaming insanely, because he had jumped toward the ravine's edge, she thinking he was going over.

But Corazon was ready for the Constable's last-ditch effort, grabbing the trunk of the knurled tree that hung over the edge close by, and holding on to it with his good arm, spun around its base, narrowly avoiding the insane man's killing lunge.

Robertson fell forward, out into the open air.

Seeing what was about to occur, he tried rapidly to arrest his forward momentum. But without anything to support him and is upper body already off balance and over extended, once again, the policeman toppled over the edge.

Dropping the Bolton family sword in a vain effort to grab onto something, he reached out wildly, a look of stark fear on his face, a horrifying scream poised on his lips. But again, as if by magic, he did not fall.

Using his own bodies momentum, Corazon had continued his spiral around the tree and at the last second, released its small trunk, managing to grab onto the Constable's right hand with his own. Robertson fell, his free weight slamming his body hard against the rock face, dragging Corazon back heavily onto his chest, dust splattering in his face, loose gravel tumbling over the edge. On reflex, Carson dropped to the ground, grabbing the knave's legs, making sure his friend would not be dragged over the precipice.

Bella yelled in desperation, "Hold on to him, Carson!"

"That's just what I'm doing, M' Lady." the young man replied with a grimace.

Corazon looked over the edge, at the Constable hanging beneath him. Robertson's eyepatch had now completely disappeared, and the man stared angrily up at Corazon, with both his good and bad eyes.

The later now fully exposed, confirmed only a vacant disturbing void, with a cloudy yellow, sightless sphere, forever in blindness. The dead, crumpled flesh around the grisly opening all white and tattered, a viciously jagged, deep red scar running halfway up his perspiring forehead. The horrifying sight so forebodingly sinister, it made Corazon shudder to think if, indeed, it might be the work of the devil.

The Constable's one good eye, now thoroughly bloodshot, also looked up at him, displaying nothing but utter helplessness. It's only expression, pain and anguish.

The knave's right arm now extended completely over the jagged lip of the ravine; Robertson's right hand held perilously in his. With the tall man's mass upon it, Corazon could feel himself being forced ever harder against the sharp rock surface, the flesh on the underside of his arm, becoming scratched and broken.

The pain he was experiencing, bearing Robertson's full weight, was bad enough, but for the Constable, hanging below, it was shear agony. The man's injured right arm was now taking all the force, further ripping open the existing shoulder wound all the wider, tearing additional flesh, veins and musculature. Instigating a most horrific scream, that echoed frighteningly across the void.

This time there was no random tree branch to come to his rescue. Clawing uselessly at the sheer stone wall, Robertson, had nowhere to put his left hand, meaning nowhere to grip, no possibility of reprieve. He remained hanging by only his injured arm, flesh separating, bones loosening at the socket. The torturous pain, excruciating.

"Give me your other hand!" Corazon yelled.

"I can't," returned Robertson, grim faced, sweat pouring from his brow, trying frantically to bring his left arm up but failing.

After another few more seconds of futile struggle, he gave up, hanging limply, both men now each doing their best to get a better grip on the hold they had.

With fresh blood washing in gushes from his torn arm and the shoulder fully dislocated, the wounded appendage finally began to gradually separate from Robertson's body. The Constable looked up at the knave, white teeth grinding, his face firm, resolved.

"Let me go, knave."

As he said this, he opened his right hand, releasing his hold.

Corazon had no intention of letting this man go, no matter what he had done. He had to remain alive to face the music. But, unfortunately, he only had only caught a hold of Robertson's hand, not his arm. So, when the Constable let go, he was left with the full weight of the burden, the force becoming twice as strong.

All Corazon could think to do was hold on with his one good hand. His palm was sweaty from all the activity, and worse, the blasted policemen wore his black leather gloves, that now began to slip in his failing grip. Below him, Robertson continued to writhe in torment, as if willing his damaged arm to separate, resigned to his fate.

"Don't be a fool, Robertson! Grab on to me, you bastard, and we'll pull you up!" Corazon yelled back, frantically increasing the pressure of his grasp, disjointing the grievously wounded appendage further. Only succeeding in pulling the Constable's stretching glove, further off.

"I said I would see you in Hell, knave," Robertson croaked, the agony making it too difficult to speak, "Looks like I'll beat you there."

As he said this, he thrashed again. His glove finally came lose, Corazon's last vestiges of hold exhausted, and the man fell.

Surprisingly, Robertson didn't scream as he dropped. Almost as if the separation of the two men's hands, acted to release some of the pain. Corazon watched in morbid fascination as his nemesis, the man in black, plummeted downward, a brief sigh, of what may have been thanks, escaping his lips. Falling further, he tumbled, almost in slow motion, his body beginning to rotate, summersaulting on its way to doom.

Then, he was no more, the knave ultimately losing sight of him in the rapidly gathering darkness.

Reaching down, Carson, helped him up. Corazon, grabbing on solidly to his shoulder in support before quickly limping away from the dangerous edge of the chasm. Standing inelegantly upright, with the much-appreciated stable boy's support, he noticed he still clutched Robertson's black leather glove in his very sore right hand, now dangling over Carson shoulder.

"Perhaps I will keep this," Corazon contemplated, reflectively, his voice hoarse, "as a spoil of victory."

As the pair turned, heading back toward the path and further away from the ravine's perilous verge, Anabelle ran up, embracing him warmly, an anxious look on her flushed features. Pushing Carson away, she gently took the knave's weight upon her own shoulders, being very careful to watch out for his numerous wounds.

"You fool! You, handsome fool. What have you done?" she looked into his eyes, straining slightly, shifting her load.

Corazon groaned, a crooked smile forming, "I've done what I said I would do, my Sweet. I've rid this place of that bothersome policeman." then he chuckled, the action making him hurt all over, "Because you know what they always say, once a bad policeman, always a bad policeman!"

"You are terrible!" Bella stated, lightly kissing the side of his dusty, sweat stained face.

"Oh, my!" Corazon said, a bit surprized.

"What now?" Bella laughed.

"You will have to apologize to your father for me."

"And why is that?"

"Because, apparently," rotating his head slightly, "I've lost his wonderful sword at the bottom of the ravine." presenting another sly grin as they reacquired the path.

"It looks like you can do it yourself." chuckled Anabelle, pointing.

Looking up, they saw that May had finally arrived and alongside her were Styles and the Duke, who following shortly afterward, had ultimately caught up with her. The two men had escorted Melissa Anne the remainder of the way, she being quite pleased with herself, in getting to ride next to Styles. But now dismounting, May was even more elated, as the junior constable took her arm, holding her steady, no longer due to fear, but because of a possible swoon.

Her father initially did not look pleased at their intimate contact, but eventually acquiesced, after a solid answer to his question.

"Corazon, so glad to see you are alright," not even noticing it was his younger daughter holding the man upright, "so the Chief Constable is gone?"

"Yes, your grace," Corazon motioning with his head to the ravine, getting a renewed headache because of it, "he will not be bothering us again." adding, "He fell. By his own accord, your grace."

"Indeed," this coming from Carson. "I saw it all your worship, twice, Sire Corazon tried to save him, each time the Constable refuting his help. He actually let go, in the end."

"Twice, you say?"

"Yes, M' Lord," Corazon answered.

"Well then. It looks like we'll be needing a new Chief Constable, won't we." Glancing backward at the young man holding up his eldest. "Styles?"

"Yes, your lordship." the thin man stated, standing up straight, and to May's obvious displeasure, dropping her arm.

"Any chance you might be interested in the role?" the Duke asked, smiling deviously, "It will give you certain privileges, of course." nodding towards Melissa Anne.

"Oh yes, your grace, why certainly, your lordship." Styles, agreeing to the promotion twice, looking astounded with delight, "I would be honored to assume the role."

"That's settled then." confirmed the Duke, smiling even more. "And young man, you had better take my daughter's arm again, before she faints."

With this indirect blessing, May reached over, and grabbing Styles arm, kissed him lovingly on the cheek. The man turned ten shades red, as the Duke, now leaving them to it, turned back to Corazon.

"Well, my fine friend, from the shape you're in, it looks like you could use some medical attention. I see my youngest has taken up the role of nurse maid. It appears to suit her."

Next, he looked to his stable hand, "Carson it's time we all headed back to the house before it really gets dark. Let's make haste!"

"Certainly, your grace!"

As the Duke, and his tack man, moved away to deal with the horses, and May and Styles dropped into muted conversation, Bella helped Corazon over to Winter, who had recovered from his second fall, snickering lightly, "Can you ride, my love?"

"I think so, with your help. But my left arm is no good. I will have to ride single handed."

"That won't be any trouble. I'll hold on tight to you the entire way," Anabelle stretched up, kissing him warmly on the lips, receiving a mouthful of grit in the bargain.

As they climbed aboard, Bella commented, "Well, that's something."

"And what's that, my Sweet?" Corazon's voice asked, still tired and weak,

"My Father will just have to put up with both of his daughters loving vagabonds." laughing, "Wonder what Mother will make of all this?"

Anabelle held tight to Corazon, as they waited for the others to climb carefully onto their own horses, Carson using a rope to pull the two extra mounts.

Then, without further delay, they all returned to the manor house. But with the sun finally completing its fall in the west, they went the field route, staying as far away from the dreaded ravine as possible.

Carson and the Duke were the only ones riding alone. For each of the couples rode together, one behind the other on the same horse, the women holding very tightly to their hero's, their smiling faces lying affectionately on the shoulders of their chosen vagabond.

Chapter 17 – The Wedding

It was several weeks later, on the eve of Melissa Anne and Styles' wedding day. A large reception had been organized at the Bolton manor, and it seemed like every resident of the village was in attendance.

As usual, the bride to be, looked very attractive in her costume selection that evening, her delightfully decadent, golden beige gown, elegantly equipped with the requisite ruffle around her breast. The groom, Styles, stood very tall in his black dress uniform, his new, long lined cape, settling just below the knees. Standing next to his fiancé, the happy couple welcomed their guests proudly, giving a warm and personal greeting to each and every one.

Anabelle, however, sat off to the side, pining away. She rested on her knees in one of the many couches, with her arms crossed along its back and her pretty face in her hands, looking expectantly out the mansion's front window, down the ever-darkening, tree lined drive. It was beautiful evening and the sun had just set, leaving the sky a spectacular bright orange, with an even more radiant, dark pink glow beneath.

Her mother, noticing Bella's melancholy, and knowing the exact reason for it, drew close in consolation, tenderly touching her youngest daughter arm.

"He may not come dear. You know men like him; they always have important things to do." she went on, while Anabelle continued watching the approaching shadows, "Remember, it was several days before he could even walk again. I am sure he is still convalescing over at the Robertson estate."

"Yes, Mother, I'm sure your right." Bella continued to stare outside as she spoke, her voice a very soft, flat monotone. At her mother's mention of the old Constable's house, she added, "It was very nice of Father to donate that nasty man's property for use as a local hospital, wasn't it?"

"Yes, it was at that." the Duchess returned. Then speaking of Corazon once more, she offered, "You've been there several times and you've seen his condition. I'm sure he is just fine."

"Indeed, I have Mother, and it is a splendid place. I'm certain Sire Corazon is well taken care of."

"That's it dear, think on the bright side." and patting her arm once again, the Duchess left the girl to brood, heading off to entertain her numerous guests.

Bella, changed position, reclining rather sadly on the comfortable divan, still looking out into the night. She was dressed in a blood red frock, with pink trim, her signature whale bone corset safely tucked away beneath its many layers. Breathing evenly, her chest rising steadily, she sat there thinking about all that had happened. Thinking about herself and about her Corazon.

Upon their return to Eastborough Hall, that evening of the confrontation, they had immediately sent for the doctor. The portly man arrived shortly before supper, expertly stitching up Corazon's various wounds and setting the knave's hand and arm in a splint, before placing it in a sling.

But it was not just the physical wounds that required mending. The stressful battle and the multiple falls, particularly the sharp impact with the boulder, had resulted in several contusions on Corazon's brain, requiring that he remain on bed rest for many days.

Initially, thinking it was likely a brain bleed, the doctor was not certain he would even survive. So, the Duke had provided a room for Corazon in the house, and every day Bella waited on him, taking care of her Knave of Hearts. The doctor also visited daily, checking on his condition, often shaking his head with uncertainty and leaving the house with a sad expression.

For weeks, Corazon remained immobile with a high fever. His perspiring body would thrash and groan, often yanking the sheets from around his wounded form. When many had given up, Bella remained vigilant, attending to his needs, wiping his brow, even changing his dressings. Spending every waking moment taking care of him, and willing him, with all her heart, to get well again.

Ultimately, her unceasing ministrations proved fruitful and, several weeks after the fateful day, his condition began to improve. With his foggy head finally clearing, Corazon started eating again, and then subsequently each day, the doctor greeted him with a smile. Informing the Bolton family that their saviour was finally, truly on the mend and would eventually recover, but not to forget that he still had a long way to go.

With this very satisfying report, and with the new village hospital opening up, to the tragic dismay of his daughter, the Duke arranged for the knave to be moved there for his extended convalescence. Bella was heartbroken, but no matter how much she pleaded, she could not change her father's mind.

When the day arrived for Corazon's departure, Carson requested that he be the one to transport him, making sure all was in order throughout the journey. Anabelle, travelled alongside the invalid, holding his hand, keeping him company, not wanting to let go. She vividly remembered her tears as she left him in the hospital bed, sleeping soundly.

But Anabelle, further recalled with great sadness that, after that day, she had rarely been able to see her beloved Corazon. Perhaps, only once a week, if she was lucky, the Duke now keeping a much closer eye on her and her movements. Just the thought of their separation, tore at her heart constantly, fresh tears erupting on her cheeks, daily.

She had kept herself busy, however, by helping her sister with her wedding plans. Arranging the food, the flowers and all of the other small things that go into a big wedding. The one thing her Corazon had done to help, during that happy time, was to provide the name of an old seamstress in town. Bella having ended up as her go between, purchasing all of the fabric and organising all of the gown's fittings.

Anabelle smiled, wiping her face, remembering the seamstress as a lively, happy old woman. Her house was a bit shabby yes, but clearly the Bolton family patronage had brought renewed prosperity to her lifelong business. And the old dear had the nicest looking sewing machine Bella had ever seen. The continuous visits had kept her occupied, providing her at least some measure of joy.

And the result proved Melissa Anne's wedding dress to be something most spectacular. The tight bodice, the full skirt, the lace, the silk and the ruffles, all combining into a perfect gown, well suited to her big sister. It even had the essential fabric addition near the neckline. Bella laughed to herself every time she thought about it.

Just then, out of the corner of her eye she spied a sparkle off in the distance, the sharp image suddenly fetching Bella away from her various remembrances. Initially, she thought it might have only been a reflection of candlelight off the window. But as it continued to waver, getting closer, clearly it had to be something else. So, rising up rather excitedly off her seat and placing her warm hands on the cool glass, she continued to stare, squinting eagerly out into the darkness.

Eventually, her heart skipped a beat, for she could finally make out the shadowy figure of a man on horseback, heading up the lengthy drive. As all of the invited guests had already long since arrived, it was surprising that there would be anyone else coming in so late, but the approaching horseman appeared determined. Visibly, drawing up the gravel path in front of the house with a purpose.

When Anabelle ultimately noticed the subtle details of the rider and his left arm firmly strapped up in a sling, she frantically jumped off her perch before the front window, stumbling briefly, before charging into the reception hall.

"Bella, dear!" her mother called, slightly taken aback by her youngest's sudden burst of energy.

But Anabelle ignored her, making her way swiftly through the milling village elite, dodging back and forth, in an effort to get through the overly crowded room. Finally, running through the grand foyer, before stopping, gasping for breath, at the front door, just as Simon opened it and the figure of Corazon stepped inside, his hair all windswept, his face rosy with the cold.

"Why, welcome and good evening, Sire Corazon." Simon greeted him pompously, "So good to see you again."

"It is good to be back, Simon," but his greeting was muted, for Corazon had already turned his head, glancing behind the butler to stare at the beautiful young woman who had run out so elatedly to meet him. Taking in her pretty face, her luxurious auburn hair and her stunning figure.

"I missed you, my Sweet" he said, expertly side-stepping Simon and walking up to Bella, placing his cold right hand on her cheek and pushing her disheveled hair back behind her ear. His touch making her shiver.

"The nurses at the hospital, while obviously concerned for my wellbeing, were not nearly as dedicated as yourself."

"Shut up you fool and kiss me!"

Taking her in his good arm, he bent down to kiss her. Bella's was a very warm, moist kiss. Corazon's lips, however, were still quite chilly from the ride in and so they had to linger for a while to heat up. The couple remained entwined that way for a very long time, way past any proper allowance for a decent greeting. Simon, now thoroughly embarrassed, after closing the door, left them there on their own, toddling off to find something else to do.

When they finally pulled apart, both were completely breathless, Bella more so, having just run the gauntlet to meet him at the door.

"It's very nice of you to come, Sire Corazon." she stated, her manners returning.

"Well, I could not miss it. After all, your sister is marrying a vagabond tomorrow and I must wish her well."

"You fool!" lightly punching his shoulder, "Now that Father has promoted him, Chief Constable Styles is considered upper class and everything. He will soon be provided with a plot of land, a small house and barn at the back of our estate, so that he and my sister can live up to their station. Also," she chuckled, "where Father can keep an eye on them." taking his arm and leading him up the hall toward the reception room.

"It really is good to see you again." Bella smiling up at him as she leaned over, putting her head tenderly against his shoulder.

"Corazon, my boy!" their intimate moment now broken by the sound of the Duke's voice, as he welcomed them in, "Good to see you up and about!"

"It's good to be up and about, your grace. I missed this place. Missed everyone." saying this as he looked down at Bella.

"Well, come on in and take a load off. Have a drink! We're celebrating of course!"

The Duke himself, obviously already having enjoyed a healthy share of the drink that was on offer.

Arm in arm, Corazon and Anabelle entered the room to be welcomed by her sister May and Styles.

"So good to see you, Sire Corazon," they said in unison, "we were not sure you would make it."

"Neither was I, but I just had to come. My sincerest best wishes to you both. You make a fine couple."

"And so, do you," May sated outwardly, looking at Bella on Corazon's arm, "tell us, when are you two getting married?"

The awkward question silenced the knave, and it was Bella who came to the rescue, "Melissa Anne dear, Corazon and I haven't even discussed that yet. Give us some time. You and Styles have been courting forever, so you're already long overdue."

And then everyone laughed, breaking the ice, releasing the tension and putting things back on an even keel.

The rest of the evening went very smoothly, the family members obviously enjoying themselves. But because of his injuries and fainting tiredness, Corazon left early, promising, if possible, to return the next day for the ceremony.

Kissing Bella lightly at the door he said, "Tomorrow, then, my Sweet."

"Yes, tomorrow, it is." then hesitating, she asked, "Corazon?"

"Yes, my Sweet, what is it?"

"Don't you wish it was you and I getting married tomorrow?" she probed rather expectantly, her voice breathless.

"My Sweet, not now. But I assure you, we will have our own tomorrow. And soon."

***

But tomorrow never came. Or at least the tomorrow Bella was wishing for. Her Corazon never showed up for the following day's grand event, his absence never fully explained.

But, even without his presence, the occasion was a massive success, the Duke announcing the gift of the land and home as part of the festivities. Styles was flabbergasted with the generous offering, blubbering his awkward words of thanks before the huge assembly, yet still looking dashing in his dress uniform.

Melissa Anne was over the moon with delight with the entire affair. And she looked gorgeous in her spectacular gown and jewels, her hair tied up dramatically in a coif above her head, the pinky white flesh of her neck and back showing above the low neckline of her magnificent dress.

They had even invited the ancient seamstress to attend. The charismatic old woman, smiling with pride at her creation, enjoying herself immensely and making a few more important contacts in the process.

It was a beautiful day, everyone appreciating the festivities, food, wine and dancing to the full. One of the best parts of the exciting day was when young Carson arrived to show off his own new dress uniform as an assistant constable. Styles had been so impressed with the young man's actions that day at the ravine, he had invited him to join the force. And, with the Duke's blessing, he had heartily agreed.

It was a great and blessed day and at the end of the affair, the bride and groom headed off in the Bolton's best carriage, to spend their wedding night at the lavish village inn.

The wedding's only attendee that did not enjoy herself, was Bella Bolton. While she completed her role as maid of honor very well, smiling constantly throughout the service, all the guests thinking she looked almost as beautiful as the bride, in fact, she had spent the entire day completely miserable. For, when it was certain that the knave was not going to appear, she turned inward to herself, becoming quite sad and withdrawn.

While her sister was celebrating in her marriage bed that evening, no doubt having the time of her life, Bella went to bed at Eastborough Hall with salty tears in her eyes, not knowing what she had done, what she could do.

Wondering what had happened and where on earth her handsome knave, Corazon, was.

Chapter 18 – All's Well that Ends Well

The weeks after the wedding passed very slowly in the house of Bolton. May continued to occupy most of her free time in the mansion, despite having a perfectly good coach house down the lane. The only time she stayed there was in the evening, after supper, when her husband demanded it. There was, however, a very good reason for her to be spending the majority of her days in the main house while her husband was away, fighting crime. Her sister, Anabelle.

After Corazon's no show at the wedding, his strange absence continued, the reason for his disappearance a complete, unexplained, mystery.

For the day after the wedding, Bella and her father had ventured over to the Robertson estate hospital, hoping to check on the knave's condition. But he was not there. And when they inquired, they were told he had vanished the day before, saying he was off to plan a wedding. They must have got the message wrong, for he would more likely have said, off to a wedding, but as he had not even shown up at the affair, both Anabelle and the Duke were at a loss as to where he might have gone. They had regrettably, retuned to Eastborough Hall the same afternoon, completely perplexed, the Duke to his duties and Bella to her room.

Ever since that afternoon, Anabelle had been sad, depressed and uncommunicative. Her mother had tried everything, including the foolish suggestion that her daughter consider the fine-looking young man who had just inherited a large estate down the lane. This only served to make matters worse, for after her rather thoughtless suggestion, Bella refused to talk to her mother, retreating to her room, permanently.

With her efforts to no avail, the Duchess resorted to the recruitment of her older sister to try to bring Anabelle out of her permanent melancholy. Melissa Anne had agreed, spending the last few weeks trying to bring up Bella's spirits, telling her stories, and relating their many fond, childish memories. It was the stories of her new husband's antics in the bedroom, and May embarrassment of them, that really started her laughing again.

The therapy initially worked. Their sisterly comradery resulting in Anabelle agreeing to spend her mornings in the sitting room with the rest of the family and to attend the occasional dinner. It was a start, but there was still a long way to go. There really seemed nothing that would completely draw her out, leaving May perplexed and in need of help.

One night as they sat in bed, Melissa Anne and her new husband were talking about her sister's condition.

"Bella used to be such a happy girl," Styles observed, playing with May's hair.

"Well, you know dear, I think the only way we are going to see that Anabelle again, is to ensure the return of than Corazon fellow." lovingly, she turned to her husband, touching his chin, "Say, can you, or some of your men, do some investigating into his disappearance, perhaps find out where he went?" her gently stated request, not really a request at all.

"I might be able to try, my dear, but it will take some doing. The man's been gone a long time. The trail has been cold for months." Styles making the excuse but knowing he'd be doing it anyway.

"Please, my pet, do it for me," saying it with such a face and pleasantly demure voice, that he could not resist.

"Fine, Melissa darling, I will try. I will have young Carson begin work on it, first thing tomorrow."

"Oh, thank you, my love. I always knew I married the right man." May said, cuddling up to her husband affectionately.

***

Several more weeks passed and the investigations into Corazon's disappearance continued. After some searching and many questions, it was established that he had not only left the village and the county, but the country as well. So, Carson had been sent abroad to continue the search.

Meanwhile, May did her best to get her sister well again. With some effort, she managed to get her out of the house, the two now spending up to an hour each afternoon, under the sun on the estates wide grass lawn. These picnics appeared to be working, with Anabelle smiling periodically.

This was a far cry from her typical day that for her would consist of sleeping and more sleeping. But even with May's small successes, most evenings, on returning home, Anabelle would regress, once again retreating to the comfort and safety of her room, missing dinner with the family. The entire process then beginning anew again, the following day.

May was at her wits end with worry. No one had heard anything from Carson in almost a week and Styles had taken to spending a lot of time at the precinct library, studying the problem. There seemed no end in sight to the issue, none of them any closer to solving their various concerns.

One afternoon, as Bella slept, Melissa Anne entered the front lounge at Eastborough Hall, dying for a cup of tea. Her father sat in his favorite chair and seeing his eldest daughter enter, called her over to sit with him.

"So, my dear, how is our poor Anabelle? Is there any improvement?" asking with true concern in his voice.

"Oh, Father I don't know what to do. Every time we find something that makes her happy, it works for a while, only to soon find out, that for some other reason, she has once again regressed." May's expression falling as she looked away out the window, pacing like a caged animal.

There was silence in the room for a moment. Only the tick of the clock, and the far-off sounds of several tradesmen working outside, to break the quiet.

To disrupt the awkwardness, the Duke stated the obvious, "It's that darn boy, Corazon, isn't it?"

"You know it is, Father!" May said, scolding him, "If only you had let them get married, when they had the chance! I just think back to the days the man lay here, in this house, on his death bed. When Bella was so attentive. If you had permitted it then, things would be so much different!"

Melissa Anne, stopped her pacing, turned and gave her father a sharp look, her hands on her hips, tapping her leg.

"Sit my dear, sit. Please. All that movement of yours is giving me a headache."

Rather reluctantly, May took a seat opposite her father, clearly flustered and wanting to move. She jammed her hands between her knees to stop them shaking.

"My dear, let me explain something to you. Something that you should already know very well. We are Boltons and I am the Duke. You and Anabelle are my daughters. The two of you, therefore, must marry in accordance with your station. You, yourself were very lucky as it was. For it was only after I had promoted your husband, that he became eligible. Do you understand?"

"But what of all the good things Corazon did for us, Father. For the people of Eastborough?" defending him, almost as strongly as her sister would have done.

"Regardless what the young man did for us..., or the people." the Duke suddenly became very contemplative, "I too remember he saved your Mother and I's lives that day..."

"See, what did I tell you!"

"Yes, but please, let me finish."

Huffing, May quieted, allowing her father to continue, "As I was saying, regardless of what he has done, there is no denying the man is a vagabond. A man with no station, no family. I hate to say it, but that evil rogue Robertson had more pedigree than our young Corazon."

"But Father, Anabelle is madly in love with him. That must count for something!" May was adamant, her voice loud.

"Indeed, it does and would fully, if she was the daughter of a merchant, or seamstress." he politely patted his daughter's leg, "but, Melissa Anne, dear, she is not. She is a daughter of the Duke of Eastborough and must, despite all that, marry within her class."

There was a swish of skirts and third voice joined the conversation.

"Then I wish I was the daughter of a merchant, and not yours!"

Unbeknownst to the two of them, Anabelle had come downstairs, also searching for some tea. She was still dressed in her nightgown, a full-length, dark blue silk shift wrapped around her. Despite the costume, she still appeared quite striking, her beautiful auburn hair tied loosely atop her head. But young Bella retained deep grey bags under her bright green eyes, betraying her ongoing sadness. Even with the long face, and general sloppiness of her attire, she still looked pretty, her youthful radiance not yet drowned out of her fully.

After hearing voices, she had entered the room quietly, listening in on most of their conversation.

"Bella dear, why it's good to see you up and about!" the Duke stated, trying in vain to change the subject.

"Or perhaps be the daughter of that lovely seamstress woman," Anabelle continued not listening to her father. "She was a caring sort. Perhaps if I asked her, she would adopt me?"

"Don't be silly, Bella dear," May offered, standing up and helping her sister to a seat, "come in, come in, we were just talking about you."

"Yes, I know." Bella responded, rather belligerently. "But you weren't just talking about me, but of Corazon as well. "Where is he, Father? Where could he be? Why won't he return to me?"

"My dear, we do not know where he is." looking very sadly at his youngest daughter, "Your sister has had Styles out looking for many weeks, thinking his reappearance might wake you from your melancholy." then adding rather stupidly, "but even if he does come back, you must get on with your life. You have duties, responsibilities and you cannot possibly complete those married to a vagabond!"

"Oh Father, you just don't understand." Bella began weeping, the tears blackening the bags under her big eyes, "Don't you know anything about love? Don't you know that you must marry for love! Not money, position or prestige! But love!"

"My dear, I'm afraid you're living in a fantasy world. Look at me, I got married, and I never loved your Mother."

"What!" exclaimed the two girls together, shocked.

"Hold on, no!" the Duke became flustered, having to justify himself. "What I meant to say, is that when we did get married, we did not love one another. Hell," and he covered his mouth at the swearword, "we barely knew one another, your Mother being from another country. But the two of us learned to love and remain so now. The two of us have been married these almost 35 years."

"We realize that, Father, but times have changed." this from May, defending her sister, knowing what it was like for her when Styles was out of reach. "The world is a different place from what it was 35 years ago."

The Duke became flustered, his voice rising, "I simply do not care. My daughter cannot marry a vagabond! No matter how good hearted, dashing, handsome or talented he is!"

"Did someone mention me?" a new voice emanated from the entry of the room.

The three Boltons looked up, as one, to see Simon holding open the door, for the new arrival. He was a very well-dressed, rugged looking, young man. Over his muscular chest, he wore a fancy, navy blue tunic and dark red jacket, each trimmed in gold, and carried an expensive looking short sword in a black leather sheath on his left thigh. He had a large satchel strapped over one shoulder and deep plum tinted hose enclosed his strong muscular legs. Knee-high, black leather riding boots, equipped with silver spurs, completed his marvelous outfit.

The gentleman, for he was clearly a man of wealth and means, had a wide face, possessing chiselled features and a square jaw, his long, dark hair, tied back conservatively, low on his head.

But it was his large, bright blue eyes that gave him away and upon seeing the face of her Corazon, Anabelle jumped up from her chair, running over. In seconds, all the months of sadness were wiped away from her pretty face.

"Oh, my Corazon, where have you been!" despite the company, she jumped wildly into his arms, the knave lifting her high into the air, spinning her around, before planting a warm, arduous kiss on her tepid lips. After retuning her gently to the ground, further demonstrating his injured wrist had completely healed, he answered, simply, "I have been away, my Sweet. But have now returned."

***

"My, my, Sire Corazon," the Duke commented, rising rapidly to meet the young man, "It appears you have finally resorted to wearing your spoils. It does rather suit you though."

"Father!" gasped May,

"How dare you, Father!" Bella cautioned, "Corazon is here for me!"

While she was speaking, and the two women looked at their father in shock at his rudeness, Styles entered the room, followed closely by Carson. The pair had bright pink faces and had clearly been outside riding, both their chests heaving, each one rather breathless.

"See, I told you he would get here first," Carson commented.

"Indeed, my boy, you were correct. He did get here first."

May, passing Bella and Corazon, still standing near the entryway, ran over to her husband, eagerly kissing him on the cheek, "Darling, you're back!"

"Yes, my love," and after his wife's rather enthusiastic greeting, going even redder, due to the mixed company, "and I was hoping to be here first, before our friend had arrived."

"Too late, my good man," Corazon replied in earnest, "my horse is just no match for yours, I'm afraid."

"Well, Sire" continued Styles shaking his hand, "I am glad to see you made it here safe and sound.

"Well, now that Corazon is back," Bella announced, "I would like you all to know that we are going to get married."

Everyone stood still, shocked at the pronouncement, her father's expression the worst, but not stunned to silence.

"But my dear, we have already discussed this. It cannot be allowed." he continued, gazing at May and her husband, and motioning to Bella's brother in law with a wrinkled hand, "Your sister's choice was bad enough." then he considered, saying politely, "No offence, Styles."

"None taken, your grace" still red with embarrassment, absorbing the veiled insult with great dignity.

"You cannot marry some..., vagabond." this time pointing to Corazon, standing there in all of his finery.

"But, your grace," Styles interjected, politely as possible, "That is the news I wished to covey. The reason why Carson and I have been travelling so hard to get here. And why we wanted to arrive, before young Corazon here."

"Yes, then what is it?" asked the Duke impatiently, "Out with it boy!"

"Well, your worship, the news is... he is not a vagabond at all," The news stunning the Duke and his daughters, equally.

"Carson's only just returned and told me today. It turns out, young Corazon here is Spanish royalty."

"Is this true, Corazon? What my son in law says about you?" the Duke asked.

Bella looked up at her knave, gabbing his arm and wishing with all her heart for a positive response.

Corazon was silent throughout the entire exchange, "Well," answering quietly, but truthfully, "it appears young Styles is far more adept at his position than his predecessor, ever was."

Bella held her breath, clinging as much to hope, as she did to her would be fiancé.

"But he is correct..., I am the son of the Spanish King."

May almost fell over faint, while a great smile burst upon the freckled face of little her sister.

There was a hushed silence in the room at the knave's pronouncement, nobody moved, except Styles, attempting to support his swooning wife. The Duke stood there, flabbergasted.

Corazon continued, "You all know me as Sire Corazon, but my real name is Sabastian Francisco. And in truth, I am a prince of the Spanish court."

Bella spoke up, still holding tightly to his arm, "But why use Corazon then?"

"Because my dear, I obviously could not use my real name. And *corazon* means heart, in Spanish." smiling down at her, "And you remember, you always referred to me as your Knave of Hearts.

"Oh, Corazon!" she blushed, "I mean, Sabastian." Bella paused, then broke down, her questions coming fast and furious, "But I must know why? Why did you run away, I have missed you so! It's been unbearable."

"And for that, I sincerely apologize, my Sweet."

Then he told his story, "When I was last here, you remember it was for the party on the eve of Melissa Anne's wedding." smiling towards her, May returned a sly grin, fanning herself, "Anyway, I arrived late, but in time for most of the festivities. I left a bit early, with the excuse that I was not feeling well."

"Yes, I remember, we had such a good time." Bella stated looking right into his eyes.

"We certainly did, my Sweet. I shan't forget it." patting her affectionately as he continued, "As it was, in reality, I felt almost perfect, except for my arm of course. That was still rather swollen and still had some serious healing to do. So, I left, not because I was ill, but because I felt extremely sad."

"Sad? But it was the most wonderful evening." Bella hyped.

"Yes, that's true, but for all of you. I saw firsthand how much the importance of family was for you all, and how the presence of a true family bond, and the love that came with it, was so good for the soul. It got me thinking back to my own family and how I missed them all..., despite their rather grievous limitations." he stopped for a moment, swallowing some tea to moisten his throat.

"I also reconfirmed that night, with a renewed longing, that you, Anabelle, were the woman I wanted to be with for the rest of my life. But sadly, I was also aware, from the developing situation with your sister and her fiancé, that your father, as proved today, would not accept me as I was."

"But that day when you left, why didn't you come to May's wedding on your way home?" Bella wondered, out loud, "When Father and I arrived at the hospital to find you gone, they said you had left to go to a wedding. Why is it that you never arrived?"

"My dear, what I said when I left was, 'I was off to plan a wedding...,' yours and mine, and I left that very day to reconcile with my family, so that I might put everything in order to make that happen. That's why I missed May and Styles' wonderful day. And I sincerely apologise to them both for it."

"Oh, that's fine, Corazon," Styles quipped, jokingly, "you didn't miss much."

Melissa Anne elbowed her husband hard in the kidneys, causing him to double over. "It's okay, Corazon..., apologies, I mean, Prince Sabastian," she returned, bowing her head slightly, "you had more important things on your mind."

Chuckling, at the married couple, the Prince continued, "So it was clear to me then, that it was time to return home, to go back to the world of my youth and reclaim my title, so that I would be able to return here, today. To collect you." staring lovingly at Bella as he said it, "Knowing your father would now have no choice, but to accept me."

Sabastian then looked up at the Duke, the old man still shell-shocked from the surprise reveal, asking, "So, your grace, based on what you have heard, I will ask you now." and very respectfully, lifting Bella's hand in his, requested, "May I have the hand of your daughter, Anabelle?"

The Duke retuned his look, with wide eyes, "Well, son, it is I who should be doing the apologies today." looking fairly sheepish, he continued, "It seems, regardless that my entire family saw the good in you, and despite all our adventures together and what you have done for our community, I was still uncertain."

He hesitated, everyone waiting on bated breath, "but realizing now who you are and where you come from, who am I to say no. Welcome to the family, my boy. I am so glad to have you back!"

With that, the room burst out in happiness, Bella kissing her prince, Styles kissing May. Afterwards there were handshakes all round, everyone getting into the act, even Simon getting patted on the back, in thanks.

"Oh, and what's this? What have I missed?"

It was the Duchess, entering the room from the rear, now seeing everyone enjoying themselves.

"Mother, Corazon..., I mean, Sabastian and I are to be married." Anabelle reported, blushing brightly, tears of joy in her eyes, all hint of the dark bags now gone.

"Married? Well, my darling, it's about time. What took you so long?" and with this candid observation, the entire group broke out in peals of laughter, wishes of congratulations encircling the room more.

Then Susan arrived bringing in fresh tea, and the happy group sat down to enjoy some refreshment, the couples on seats together. Even young Carson was allowed to join in.

As things calmed down a bit, Bella realized she was still dressed in her nightgown, and getting up to leave, made her excuses. But Sabastian grabbed her arm, and rising, stood beside her, taking Bella in his arms, kissing her passionately.

The Knave of Hearts

When they came up for air, "You have no need to change on my account," he stated amorously, "I happen to like you just the way you are."

"Oh, Sabastian, I cannot sit and have tea with a Prince of Spain, in my nightdress." Bella blushed at him.

"Why ever not, you appear well dressed enough for me." he said teasingly, "When we are married, you might be considered slightly overdressed for morning tea."

Turning deep red, Anabelle replied, "but that my good man, is for later. This is now." playfully flipping his nose with one of her fingers.

Then giving him a quick peck on the cheek, she ran from the room, leaving him alone on the couch. At the entryway, she turned around briefly saying to the assembly, "And don't let him go anywhere!"

Making them all laugh heartily once again.

Once the room had quieted down, May took the opportunity to ask a burning question, "Corazon..., Oh, I am so, sorry, Prince Sabastian. You said that you were planning the wedding, what exactly did you have in mind.

"Well, Melissa Anne, I intend for us to be married at court, in Spain. My Father insisted on it, as part of a bargain for letting me back into the fold, as it were. You are all invited to come of course, and the King will be footing the bill and providing everything you require for the duration."

"That is marvelous," the Duchess stated, "I have always wanted to go to Spain."

"And so, you shall your grace, and you will be able to say as long as you wish." Sabastian stated with pride.

"But Prince Sabastian," the Duke asked, "does that mean you and Bella will be living there?"

"Absolutely not, your grace, we will live here, of course. After all, there is a community that needs our help. I will, every now and again, return to my birthplace occasionally for visits. Perhaps during the winter season. But for now, this will be our home."

Saying this, young Bella finally returned, her polite entry, promoting a wide smile across her new fiancé's face.

For immediately Sabastian recognized the beautiful form fitting, pink and white gown, as the same one he had presented to her that day they first met in the cave. She had cleaned and pressed it, the trim now almost snow-white, the pink as rosy as May's cheeks. Anabelle had quickly done her hair up in a proper bun, but a few stray stands hung down, lightly encircling her head. With the bright morning sunlight streaming through the windows, they glowed like a halo around her pretty face.

Rising in his chair to meet her, and bowing gallantly, kissing her hand, Sabastian offered, "I approve of your choice, M' Lady. I am now extremely pleased you elected to change."

"Why thank you, your highness," Bella replied, curtsying, now bursting with happiness, "I am so glad you approve."

Kissing him lightly on the cheek, they sat closely together, holding hands.

After a small break, drinking tea, May asked another question, "You previously spoke of helping the community, your highness. Your previous occupation, strange as it was, included assisting the poor of this county..., using the most unconventional means. With you and my sister getting married, you can't possibly be thinking of returning to your old ways, now, can you?"

"No, my dear sister," May turned bright pink as he said this, very much liking the thought of having this handsome prince as her brother in law. "Of course not. That is why I have arranged with my Father, the King, for a fund to be set up. One that Bella and I might distribute, providing a continuous source of possible income for those in need." and he smiled, "that was one of the parts of the bargain, I previously spoke of. One that I demanded."

"Bargain, what bargain? Bella was intrigued.

"Oh, just the one that says you're to be married at court, in Spain, my dear," her father answered, smiling.

"Oh, Sabastian is that true? We are to be married in Spain?"

"Well, my Sweet, after all, I did say I was heading home to prepare for our wedding."

And they kissed again, and this time it was warm and wet and lingering.

THE END?

Epilogue

The man awoke in a deep sweat, his head split, pain wracking his body, aches and soreness in places unknown and unseen. His head felt heavy, his body listless, what was left of his mind in a complete fog, as if he had been sleeping for days, no, weeks, perhaps even for months. All his memories and thought processes halted, frozen, no longer functioning, as if his brain had been completely shut down for an unknown period and only just reawakened.

He was resting comfortably on a pillow, strapped to a cot, its soft mattress filled with straw, the frame made of rough-hewn wood. The fabric straps, while loosely fitted, held him securely in place and, just for a moment, he struggled. But with each small movement, he felt the pain in his extremities becoming much worse, so for the moment, held off, deciding instead to use his highly blurred vision to review the situation.

His right arm was strapped tightly against his chest, immobilized and inflamed. While he could see it, he could not feel it, almost as if it were dead. Both of his legs were also firmly restrained, hung with more straps, at a sharp angle from some form of iron ring secured in the ceiling of the chamber. Thankfully, those he could feel, but with the agony being so strong, he almost wished he couldn't. His back was immobilized on a stiff board of some kind of wood, that lay atop the bed, but his neck was free, supported only by the soft pillow.

Clearly, he was inside a private house, the very plain, plaster walled room also containing a dresser drawer, side table and chair. Dark pink, flowery patterned curtains hung over the windows, keeping the sunlight at bay. Definitely not a village hospital, he thought.

Then he noticed something shiny out of the corner of his eye. And stretching his neck until it hurt, he looked across the room. In the far corner, opposite the bed, just within view, there was a long sword, leaning against the wall, balanced precisely on its tip, as if floating. It was of a very ornate design, unique in every sense of the word, it's sparkling golden hilt glinting, as if it were somehow calling to him. It presented an almost hypnotic effect, the man turning away, having to close his eyes to break the spell.

Laying back he took a deep breath, regretting the action, the pain surging along his spine as he did so. Taking smaller, even breaths, he relaxed, enduring the pain.

Soon, there was a sound outside the room and with a distinct creak, the chamber's only door opened, a hag shuffling her way inside.

She was a grizzled old woman, with pink wrinkled skin and matted grey hair, but retaining an air of supreme importance, and deservedly so. Dressed plainly in a grey jumper and dark grey hose, she grasped a handmade knitted black shawl tightly over her thin shoulders. But despite this rather unassuming couture, she had a jeweled ring on every finger and numerous, large gold chains hanging loosely around her neck.

The woman wandered over to the dressing table, retrieving a small goblet of liquid before returning to the bedside. Without asking, she grabbed his chin with a cold, stiff hand, forcing her patient to drink the foul-tasting concoction. Gaging as it went down, the man complied, not having any way, to push it aside.

"So, you're fully up are ye?" her rhetorical question was asked with a low wispy voice that retained a bad crackle, as if the woman had an ongoing lung disorder. "'Tis nice to see ye finally awake." and she chuckled, her laugh, slightly disturbing. "I've been taken care of ye fer long past a 'alf year. I'm surprized ye lasted. Ye were one tired and broken, gentleman."

"Where am I?" the invalid asked, the only question he could think of, his voice strained, high pitched. It hurt him to speak. In fact, everything hurt.

"Why, ye's 'ere in me 'ouse, in the midst of da glen." clearly not telling him anything at all.

"Why have you bound me up like this?" he asked her.

"Ye fool! Ya would'a fall ta bits without it. Yer right arm was nearly off when I found ye, as it was!" she laughed again, the hairs rising on his neck, "Why are ye bound indeed? Hah!" with that the woman began fussing with some of his bindings.

"But who are you?" the broken man choked, continuing his questions, desperately wanting an answer that made some sense.

Standing up tall, which was hard for her as she was so short, she said, "Tis I, Landa Steel. And I's a witch. A very smart and wise witch. And a good thing I's is, for wit'out me, ye'd be singin' with da angles!"

"More like laughing with the devil," the man stated, somehow knowingly.

"Yer prob'bly right, good Sire." and she cackled again, her laugh once more grinding through him, making him shiver, "Come ta think of it, ye do strike me as da devil's type..., seein' as you've only got da one eye!"

And Robertson stared with his one good eye at the strange woman, his memory completely fogged, not understanding, but knowing he was definitely on the mend, and that, by some miracle, this old hag, this witch, had saved him.

"Thanks for all you've done. I will be sure to repay you when I can." he promised.

"I'm sure ye will, Sire, I'm sure ye will." the witch crowed, smiling wickedly, "But I'm also sure, you'll 'ave someone else ter pay back first, before dat."

And laughing again, making his skin crawl, she left him there, wondering who he was and what on earth had happened to him.

Other Books by P. J. Hatton

The Time Chronicles

The adventures of Ryan Scott, his time machine and his marvelous future experiences can be found in the four books of the Time Chronicles series:

The adventure begins with:

The Kanusan Legacy

Book 2 – An Artificial Utopia

Book 3 – Repeating Mistakes

Book 4 – A Future Hollywood

And coming soon, a new and different kind of medieval adventure

The Queens of Pendragon

Printed in Great Britain
by Amazon